S0-ASN-844

The Maiden, the Matron, and the Crone are the three aspects of a woman's journey through life. She is considered to be the trinity of life itself: past, present, and future, and her importance has existed in the storytelling of many cultures throughout the ages.

Each story in this book is a living pearl of wisdom, and I guarantee that when you finish this heartfelt collection you will never feel the same about unicorns, bag ladies, cleavage, or yourself, again. The Maiden, the Matron, and the Crone have something to contribute to everyone.

Enjoy and share.

Maiden, Matron, Crone

LOGAN-HOCKING
COUNTY DISTRICT LIBRARY
230 E. MAIN STREET
LOGAN, OHIO 43138

Maiden, Matron, Crone

edited by
Martin H. Greenberg and
Kerrie Hughes

DAW BOOKS, INC.
DONALD A. WOLLHEIM, FOUNDER
375 Hudson Street, New York, NY 10014
ELIZABETH R. WOLLHEIM
SHEILA E. GILBERT
PUBLISHERS
www.dawbooks.com

Copyright © 2005 by Kerrie Hughes and Tekno Books.

All Rights Reserved.

DAW Book Collectors No. 1329.

DAW Books is distributed by Penguin Group (USA) Inc.

All characters in this book are fictitious.
Any resemblance to persons living or dead is coincidental.

If you purchase this book without a cover you should be
aware that this book may have been stolen property and
reported as "unsold and destroyed" to the publisher. In such
case neither the author nor the publisher has received any
payment for this "stripped book."

The scanning, uploading and distribution of this book via the
Internet or any other means without the permission of the
publisher is illegal, and punishable by law. Please purchase
only authorized electronic editions, and do not participate in
or encourage the electronic piracy of copyrighted materials.
Your support of the author's rights is appreciated.

First printing, May 2005
1   2   3   4   5   6   7   8   9

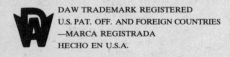

DAW TRADEMARK REGISTERED
U.S. PAT. OFF. AND FOREIGN COUNTRIES
—MARCA REGISTRADA
HECHO EN U.S.A.

PRINTED IN THE U.S.A.

ACKNOWLEDGMENTS

Introduction copyright © 2005 by Kerrie Hughes.

"A Lingering Scent of Bacon," copyright © 2005 by Brenda Cooper.

"Choice of Ending," copyright © 2005 by Tanya Huff.

"Strikes of the Heart," copyright © 2005 by Nina Kiriki Hoffman.

"Misery and Woe," copyright © 2005 by Jean Rabe.

"In Sight," copyright © 2005 by Charles de Lint.

"The Gift," copyright © 2005 by Jody Lynn Nye.

"Bearing Life," copyright © 2005 by Devon Monk.

"Advice from a Young Witch to an Old Priestess," copyright © 2005 by Rosemary Edghill.

"The Three Gems of the Fianna," copyright © 2005 by Fiona Patton.

"The Things She Handed Down," copyright © 2005 by Russell Davis.

"Seeking Gold," copyright © 2005 by Jane Lindskold.

"Opening Her Door," copyright © 2005 by Alexander B. Potter.

"The Unicorn Hunt," copyright © 2005 by Michelle West.

CONTENTS

INTRODUCTION
by Kerrie Hughes

THE MAIDEN, the Matron, and the Crone are the three aspects of a woman's journey through life. She is considered to be the trinity of life itself: past, present, and future, and her importance has existed in the storytelling of many cultures throughout the ages.

The ancient Celts connected her to the moon cycle as the waxing, full, and waning moons, and associated her with birth, life, and death/rebirth. The Vikings assigned the runes Teiwaz, Fehu, and Isa to each aspect of her cycle in much the same way. Romans told her tale with the three goddesses of time and fate, the Parcae. The Greeks named them the three daughters of the night or the Morai. Later, in England, they become the Wyrd sisters who weave the web of the world and foretell events around the cauldron of life. There are many more tales too numerous to list here and many more original stories were probably lost through the assimilation of conquered peoples. Often the remaining stories are dismissed because of their connection to pagan ideologies or rewritten to accommodate the ruling classes and monotheistic sensibilities.

I have studied the mythology of the triple goddess for more than twenty years and feel our modern society would benefit from a healthy dose of female strength and wisdom. All around me, I see women who are lost to themselves because they have no guidance beyond television and patriarchal cultural mores. Popular culture teaches our daughters that they are only sexy when they are desired by men and more likable when they are weak and vulnerable. We learn that mothers at their best are the servants of the household or are interfering teachers of neurotic habits who only want to control the lives of those they care for. Our image of the elderly woman is of an old lady too addled to listen the way of the worship of youth and better off ignored. These prevailing attitudes are perpetrated by men and women, young and old, so one cannot be blamed without giving credit to the other.

I am a woman who wants to communicate that feminism is not a dirty word and self-esteem is beautiful. Society does not need to fear the female who chooses to follow a path that is contrary to today's media presentation of an ideal woman: generally speaking, the eternal Maiden who has 2.5 children by a husband and disappears from sight when the wrinkles appear. A woman can be a Maiden for as long as she chooses and skip the child-bearing aspect of Matron without giving up the caring aspect she is associated with. A Maiden could also enter the Matron aspect early and devote all of her attention to one brood and the broods of the generation to come, with or without male companionship. Perhaps she prefers Crone companionship, or maybe she is actually a he who desires the same freedom that women have to choose these paths. Crones in particular are an overlooked aspect of the trinity because American society has no place for an old woman beyond babysitting and we are now a nation that has thousands of elderly women displaced by divorce or economic constraints and afraid to do anything other than await death as painlessly as possible.

It is for these reasons that I am delighted that DAW, in particular Sheila Gilbert and Betsy Wollheim, has given me the opportunity to invite thirteen creative and fascinating writers to dance with the Maiden, the Matron, and the Crone. These authors are from various walks of life and in different stages of their careers, they are varied in their religious upbringing and sexual preferences, and I thank them all for agreeing to write about their own encounters and share their often personal visions of the trinity. It is heartening to read about strong Maidens, incredible Matrons, and guiding Crones.

From Tanya Huff we get a story of defiance in the face of fate. Fionna Patton gives us a trial of wills, and Brenda Cooper provides marvelous advice and hope for the next generation. Michelle West makes us look at the world around us with a new view, albeit a disturbing one. Nina Kiriki Hoffman shares a story of generational challenges and transformation. And Jean Rabe shows us that wisdom is in the eye of the beholder. Of particular interest is Jane Lindskold's story, which is really the second part of a trio of short stories that begins with the upcoming *In The Shadow of Evil*, an anthology edited by John Helfers and Martin H. Greenberg, and continues in the forthcoming *Women of War*, an anthology edited by Alexander B. Potter and Martin H. Greenberg. So if you are enamored of her tale in here, please look for these other collections for more stories of Andrasta.

I also want to thank Russell Davis and Alex Potter for sharing their insights on writing and editing. They have been very encouraging to a Matron of words and art. I also want to thank Marty and Roz Greenberg for the generosity they have shown me and the opportunities they share with everyone who has a story to tale. Finally, I want to thank my husband John Helfers, who has given me more than can be expressed in mere words.

Each story in this book is a pearl of wisdom, and I guarantee that when you finish this heartfelt collection you will never feel the same about unicorns, bag ladies, cleavage, or yourself again. The Maiden, the Matron, and the Crone have something to contribute to everyone.

Enjoy and share.

A LINGERING SCENT OF BACON
by Brenda Cooper

Brenda Cooper's collaborative fiction with Larry Niven has appeared in *Analog* and *Isaac Asimov's Science Fiction Magazine*. She has published solo fiction and poetry in *Analog*, *Strange Horizons*, and *The Salal Review*, and short nonfiction at futurist.com. She lives in Bellevue, Washington, with her partner, Toni, Toni's daughter, Katie, a border collie, two gerbils, and a hamster. By day, she works as the City of Kirkland's CIO, and gets to apply her interests in science and technology and the future to day-to-day computer operations and strategic planning. She can sometimes be found speaking about the future, and suggesting that science fiction books make great reading. The rest of the time, she's writing, reading, exercising, or hanging around with her family.

ELISE STUMBLED out of the truck at the fork in the highway, slammed the door, and watched it drive away. Good riddance. The old man had asked her to take her pants off. She'd refused, and at the next fork in the road, this one, she'd told the old geezer, "Hey, since you're going east, I'm going north."

He'd blinked at her in surprise, as if every sixteen-year-old girl going down the highway ought to let any old man have his eyeful. But he'd pulled over and let her out. He wasn't strong enough to hurt her.

Still, she shivered, and the hairs on the back of her neck stood up. It was early, too—maybe 9:00 AM. Most weirdos came out at night. Hitchhiking had taught her the world was full of two kinds of people: those who wanted to use her and those who wanted to help her. In their own way. No one just wanted to give her a ride. She shouldered her bedroll: a striped blanket rolled around two pairs of clean underwear, a pair of jeans, a shirt, and three books, tied together with an old belt.

The road was empty. It didn't really matter which way she went, so she might as well honor her own word and go north. Besides, late summer blackberries lined the road in that direction, some as big as her thumb. Elise hitched her bedroll over her shoulder and ate berries until her fingers were purple and sticky and her stomach no longer felt like an empty metal bowl—just half-empty. She squinted up the road. She was in southern Oregon, and someplace up the road was Bellham. Keith, a fellow runaway she'd met in Mount Shasta City, told her Bellham was cool. Maybe she'd go there.

A faded yellow truck passed her, but Elise kept her thumb in her pocket. Not after the last one. She'd walk a while. The morning was warming, and this part of road ran through forested hills just beginning to turn the yellows of early fall. Later, she'd have to hitch again; Bellham was too far to walk. Just not yet.

The sun melted the mist up off the damp road, so it looked spooky and magical even in full morning light. Off to her right, a small stream gurgled, buried somewhere in the cascade of tall, spiky berry bushes. It would be nice to find a nest off the road for a nap, but the wall of berries was better for browsing on than walking through. A hawk screeched, really close, and Elise looked up for the bird.

It called again. She stopped, smelling butter and bacon. A twist of smoke rose behind the berries. Just a little, barely enough to see against the light blue sky. She noticed a tunnel in the bushes where someone had used a machete, or at least something sharp, and hacked through the woody stickers. The hawk's screech came from the same direction as the smoke and the smell of bacon. Elise stopped and stared a moment, and a shiver ran down her back. Then she shrugged. Why not? She was fast. She'd run away if she didn't like what she found. There was no bacon on the empty road.

Elise hunched over her bedroll and crab-walked through the four-foot-high tunnel. Thorns pulled her long hair and snagged her sleeves and the frayed bottom of her jeans. Mud sucked at her shoes as she crossed a thin stream. The butter and bacon smell tickled her stomach. She walked so long her back ached before the tunnel opened up to a grassy spot, about twelve feet around, surrounded by berries on three sides and a dense stand of alder, fir, and cedar on the far side. The thick vegetation made the light seem like early dusk.

In the center of the little clearing, a tall, older woman, (maybe thirty), sat tending a small fire. Her blonde hair hung in a long braid and turquoise earrings shaped like long raindrops—or teardrops—dangled nearly to her shoulders. She wore a denim shirt over jeans and moccasins.

Elise stepped out of the tunnel and stood all the way up, blinking at the woman. "Hello," she said. "I smelled your breakfast."

The woman waved Elise toward her. "You're hungry." When Elise hesitated, the woman said, "Come on, I won't bite."

Facing the woman, Elise sat on the damp grass, hunched over her bedroll. She looked over her shoulder to make sure she had a clear path back to the tunnel. Only there was no tunnel—just a wall of berries. She pointed toward it. "Didn't I—"

"Berries grow fast." The woman's voice was laughter and the tinkling of water, the sound of stars at night in the desert.

Elise felt soothed by the woman's tone, even though her own inner voice said that it really was weird the berry tunnel had closed, and she should be scared. "But—"

The woman shook her head and handed Elise a greasy paper plate with three pieces of bacon on it. "No point in talking about it. It won't make sense. I knew you'd come today."

Elise's hunger had fled with the loss of her escape route. "You made the hawk sounds."

In answer, the woman screeched softly, and a hawk answered from the tree above her. "Some of them. Relax. I'm Lee."

Lee was Elise's middle name; she could remember this woman's name. She'd learned to find out which kind of person she was dealing with early. "Did you want me to come here? Me specifically? Why?"

"You are making dangerous choices."

The helper kind. Well, take help where you can get it. But don't let them change you. Elise picked up a piece of bacon and ate half of it before answering. She watched Lee eat her own breakfast, trying to understand her situation. "What difference do my choices make to you, anyway?"

"That old man, he wasn't really dangerous, except to your spirit." Lee's eyes were bright with conviction. "But you barely got away from Small Tommy."

Small Tommy was a trucker who'd tried to rape her in the back of his Kenworth; she'd escaped by biting his thumb to the bone. No one but she and Small Tommy knew what she did, though, how she'd tasted blood and bit harder, teeth scraping bone, and jumped out of the truck, leaving her poetry book behind in her mad scramble to get free. No one knew. It made her mad Lee knew she was stupid enough to get into that situation, to leave her book. And besides, Lee couldn't know; how could she know? Elise narrowed her eyes and said, "I met a lot of people who helped me, too."

Lee's voice was casual as she said, "He's killed three other hitchhikers."

Elise swallowed hard, pulled her knees in to her chest. "Hey, how do you know these things? How do you know about the old man?"

Lee shook her head, and handed Elise a water bottle from her pack. "If you don't settle soon, you will die. That's why you called me."

She must be dreaming. This was all too weird. She drank the water anyway. It tasted cool and sweet. "I called you? Who was cooking bacon?"

Lee looked at her curiously. "Who likes bacon?"

"Doesn't everyone? Why do you care?"

"About you? Don't worry, it's selfish."

Had she gotten that hard? Lost so much trust in people? Her head was spinning. "I'm sorry, Lee," Elise mumbled. "I appreciate the breakfast." Her voice rose. "But I don't like disappearing paths. And you know too much." She felt like she'd fallen down a rabbit hole.

Lee smiled. "Look, you don't have much more time. The path you're on will kill you, spirit and body. Choices you make will determine which dies first, but you must jump the path completely to live."

"I'm not going home." To what? Bruises from her mom's latest boyfriend, beatings and touches her mom wouldn't even acknowledge? Her mom, drunk on the couch, calling her a liar with that slur in her voice? "I'm not going home," she repeated.

"It's time for you to make your home."

"No."

Disappointment flashed across Lee's eyes, then it

was gone, followed by determination. "Perhaps I didn't make myself clear. Make a home. Of your own. The road is no home. You're prey. Is that what you want?"

Elise blinked. "I like traveling."

"There are other choices." Lee stood up. She was tall, almost six feet. She looked at Elise. "Go on now—you've got decisions to make."

Elise turned around. There was no tunnel. Instead, a clear path led to the road, berries trimmed neatly back. She turned back to ask Lee about it, and Lee was gone. The fire was gone. But Elise held a piece of bacon in her right hand. She stared at the empty clearing for a long time, then ate the bacon and walked down the path, shaking her head, feeling floaty and a little like she was dreaming.

Back on the road, she started shaking. Too weird. She couldn't stay there. She didn't want to risk another ride yet either, so she started walking fast, almost jogging. A semi rumbled by, then a truck full of young men. A hawk called above her, but she didn't look for it, or for tunnels or paths.

She slowed, breathing hard, and walked uphill, along the side of the road, sweating as the sun climbed toward midday. By noon, she was tired and her legs felt heavy and slow. She started watching for cars that looked safe. An older white sedan with one crumpled fender struggled up the hill, and Elise stuck her thumb out wide.

The car pulled over, and Elise leaned in the open passenger side window. "Are you going to Bellham?" she asked.

The driver was an old woman, wearing a camouflage-green fisherman's hat. The hat shaded her eyes from this angle, but she had a wide smile and felt friendly enough. Her voice was slow and warm. "Nearly. Town just before, Killdeer. You can walk from there if you want." The driver raked a pile of papers off the passenger seat, making room. "Get in."

"Okay. Thanks." Elise climbed in and set her bedroll on the floor under her feet, within easy reach. She looked over at the woman and a shock of recognition thrummed through her, although she couldn't say why. She leaned over and extended a hand. "I'm Elise."

The woman patted the top of her hand instead of taking it, then planted both of her hands on the steering wheel and started the old car laboriously up the last of the hill.

"Granddaughter," the woman's voice seemed to fill the car with its even, slow tones. "Thank you for trusting me to take you. We were afraid you'd take more risks."

Elise's stomach went hollow and her voice shook. "We?" She swallowed. "I don't like this. Please let me out."

The woman pulled the car slowly over into a gravel turnout and turned to look at Elise. "I didn't mean to frighten you."

Elise could see the woman's eyes completely for the first time, and they looked like Lee's eyes, with the edges crumpled down like dried apricot skin. Old eyes. A deeper recognition dawned in her. "You look like my grandmother. I met you? When I was little, maybe seven?" Another shock, colder and harder, drove up her spine. "But . . . Mom said you died."

"Might as well ask about tunnels by the road."

Elise looked around. The door was unlocked. She could get out if she wanted to. She picked up her bedroll, keeping it close, but didn't move to open the door. When she glanced back toward the woman, she noticed a brown leather lacing hanging from the rearview mirror. A turquoise teardrop earring dangled on it. "And Lee? You know Lee?"

The woman smiled. "Lee? Yes. You've met her? That's a good sign."

"I don't understand any of this."

"Think of me as a guardian spirit—a helpful ancestor. Will you answer a question?"

Elise looked around again. Tall trees stood around the turnout, mostly cedar. Closer in to the car, vine maples just beginning to yellow at the tips of the leaves. She bit her lip, checking for pain. This was no dream. "All right."

"Where are you going?"

"Bellham."

"No, where will your choices lead you? You've been traveling for six months now, and you've nearly died twice. Small Tommy and the time you got sick alone in the Arizona desert."

"I'm not going home. I don't give a damn if I ever see my mother again." Elise heard the anger in her voice. Her mom was this woman's daughter! Maybe. She swallowed. "I couldn't stay home anymore."

"Neither could your mom. She was curious and wild and brave, just like you. Did she tell you she left the day she turned sixteen? She went with a man—not your dad—and followed his blues band for two years, but it was the same no-direction decision. Keep running, and you'll be like all the parts of her that never grew up."

Elise chewed on her tongue softly, weighing the woman's words. She'd never heard about the blues singer, never heard her mom listen to the blues. She had no idea who her dad really was—it wasn't something she thought about anymore. There had been a succession of boyfriends, as far back as Elise could remember. Nevertheless, she didn't think of her mom as not-grown-up. She thought of her as stupid.

"Cat got your tongue?" her grandmother asked.

"No. I do." Elise laughed softly. Then a tear slid

down her cheek, surprising her. "I didn't think any-body cared."

"I watched your mom throw herself away, and I did nothing."

She didn't know how to feel about this woman, about getting teased into a strange tunnel that was really a path and into a white car with a weird old woman who might be her grandmother and might be someone—something—else. But she went down the tunnel, and she stuck out her thumb. She shivered. "How did you find me?"

"You dreamed me here. You still haven't killed yourself, even though you're trying hard. I thought I'd better respond."

Elise shook her head, confused. "But what about Lee? Who is Lee?"

"I don't think you are ready for me to tell you that."

So she dreamed her own grandmother to keep se-crets from herself? "Look, I'm confused. I get it that I can't just wander around forever, asking to get in trouble. Is that what you want me to stop?"

"Is that what you want to stop?"

Elise swept a second tear off her cheek and sat up straighter. "Yes, I want to stop. Somewhere. But the world isn't making that easy."

"Well, to start with, you have to decide not to let the world stop you. It's no harder than deciding to leave home."

"I don't even have any ID. I lost my purse a week after I left."

"Oh—that?" Elise's grandmother reached over be-hind Elise's seat and pulled out a battered black leather purse. "I'm afraid your money was gone when I found this, but your learner's permit and your school ID are in here. You really should keep your purse cleaner." She handed the purse to Elise.

Elise's hands shook as she opened the flap. Sure enough. Her wallet, an old journal, a pack of matches, and some damp blobs that must have been pieces of paper. Her green comb with two teeth missing. The purse itself was stiff and water-stained, and its metal rivets were rusted almost through.

"How?"

"You left it at a rest stop. You really should be more careful."

"So you've been following me?"

"No. I got the purse for you day before yesterday. Whoever took your cash left the purse under a bush."

"Thank you." Elise sat back in her chair. "I guess we can keep going now."

"All right." The woman pulled the car back out onto the highway.

"What's your name? When I met you, I only heard grandmother."

The woman smiled. "So Karen at least taught you to be polite. I'm Gisele."

"Oh. Gisele. I'm sure I never heard that."

They were silent for a few miles. Elise had no idea what to say, what to ask. It was like she'd left the real world someplace back along the road, and she hadn't found her way back yet. She turned the purse over and over in her hands, rubbing at the water stains, trying to soften the leather. Before, she would have thrown away anything in such sad shape. Her mom wasn't rich, but never so poor they had to make do with broken old things. "She is okay at making money, Mom is, just not so good at living."

After a while Gisele said, "I'm not surprised. She was smart enough. Karen always loved new things, like a raccoon in a trash dump, entranced with paste-jewelry baubles. I told her not to be so concerned with such things, and I'll tell you the same." Her voice grew louder, almost rasping. "Family matters. People matter—that's what you should focus on. Loving stuff is the worst—" She broke off, her knuckles whitened on the steering wheel, and she sighed deeply. "I'm sorry, Elise. I promised myself not to lecture you. I have one chance to help you, and this is it." She sighed softly. "Karen always hated my lectures. Maybe that's part of why she left. I'm smarter than that now."

Elise realized she'd half thought Gisele was an angel, not a real person. She suddenly didn't want to lose this old woman who knew her, and she wanted to see Lee again, too. "Lee disappeared before we had a decent conversation."

Gisele kept staring straight ahead at the road, but her hands had relaxed again. "The world is stranger, and kinder, than you know. Crueler, too. I can't explain how this happened except I came because you need me, and I know I won't be here long. Your need was very strong to call me."

"But what about Lee?"

"That's a harder question. Look, we'll be going our separate ways soon, so can I tell you something, give you something?"

Elise looked around, but she couldn't see anything that looked like a town, and she didn't remember any signs recently. But they were driving up and down small forested hills, and she guessed a town could be anywhere. "Okay."

"First, look in the glove box."

Elise pulled it open. A manual for the car, a stone, a flashlight, and an envelope. "In the envelope?"

"Oh sure. I almost forgot that. There's some money there. Put that in your purse. But put the stone in your pocket." Gisele smiled. "I already know you forget your purse sometimes."

Elise folded up the envelope and stuck it in her purse. It didn't seem polite to look in it. She took the stone out and held it up. The rock was smaller than her fist, flat, as thick as three quarters glued together. It was slate gray with narrow white crystal bands running through it. The outside was smooth, like a river rock. Three wavy lines had been carved into one side, and filled in with something that turned them black.

"Why do you want me to have the stone?"

"When you get to Bellham, I want you to give the stone to Kate in the used bookstore. She'll recognize it. Can you do that?"

"I'd like to know why."

"I'm not sure I know why. But I know that's the right answer."

"Thank you." She wasn't ready to promise anything, not to anyone. But the rock, the money, her purse; they were cool. Scary.

They pulled up over a rise and passed a sign that read, "Killdeer, 1 Mile."

Elise swallowed. She wanted back into a world she understood, and she wanted to stay with Gisele. The conflicting desires left her feeling hollow, unable to act.

Gisele pulled the car over at a fork in the road, where a single-lane road turned off for god-knows-where. "All right. This is my stop. Bellham is just two miles up the road, at least the outskirts of it." The old woman tipped up her hat and peered at the sun. "You can make it before dark if you go now."

"I'd rather stay with you." Elise put her hand on the door handle. "Will I see you again?"

"Not for a long time."

Well. Elise had expected her to say "no." But why did she have to go at all? She stepped out and watched Gisele pull her hat down close over her eyes, and, squinting into the sun, drive slowly away up a side street. Intense loneliness washed over Elise as soon as the car left her sight.

She pulled the envelope out of her purse. Three

twenty-dollar bills. No note, nothing personal, just an envelope with three bills. She shook her head. Did being crazy feel like this? But the bills were still in her hand. She shoved them in her pocket and looked around. Killdeer was about six houses. No store, nothing. Only three of the houses had cars parked out front, and there wasn't anyone moving around. A few mailboxes by the side of the road didn't seem to go with the houses, so maybe there were more houses in the trees. She glanced up the road toward Bellham, then back the way she'd come. She wanted to go back, see if the path was still there, see if there was some way to prove she'd met these women. She shouldered her bedroll and started walking up the long hill leading out of Killdeer.

By the time Elise crested the hill, she was tired and ready to believe Lee and Gisele were a dream. Her legs hurt all over again, and her mouth was dry and cottony. A tan truck with a rifle rack in the window (no rifles) pulled up, and a red-bearded man in a flannel shirt smiled at her and asked "Hey, do you want a ride?"

She licked her lips, feeling her dry mouth and her empty belly, her sore aching feet. A fast ride to Bellham would be great. Then she thought of Gisele, and Lee, and shook her head. She could make it two miles. "No, no thanks."

The driver looked at her quizzically. "You sure?"

He looked safe. Elise reached for the handle, then tugged her hand back. "No, I like walking."

"Suit yourself." The truck pulled away, tires crunching on gravel.

As she walked, shadows grew across the road, and it seemed to take forever to find the outside of town; a gas station and a little store. Bright blue paint surrounded dirty windows and the store inside looked cramped and smelled dusty. Canned goods and snacks and drinks filled dented white metal shelves. Elise broke one of her twenties to buy a bottle of water and some peanut M&M's. She stood just outside the store and watched the road for a long time, feeling crazy and off-center.

She went back in and bought another bottle of water, carrying it to town with her. Most stores were closed, and she was too tired to look for the bookstore. She found a town park by the river and clambered along the overgrown bank until she found a clear spot under a cedar tree. She rolled up in her blanket, and used the last light to read two chapters of a mystery book. When the light faded the words to ants, she watched the stars, listening to the sway of branches above her head and the sound of little animal feet in the thicket around her until she drifted to sleep.

When she woke, light was just turning the branches above her from black silhouette to gray, to green. She lay shivering, trying to ignore a root digging into her shoulder blade, fingering the rock and the money in her pocket. She should just move on through. Go on. That was what she'd do. She wasn't supposed to let people change her. She liked traveling, she liked new places, and she'd made friends on the road: Keith in Mount Shasta, Paulie and Donna in Monterrey, Indian John in San Francisco. She'd go on.

Elise used the park bathroom, brushed her hair, put on her clean underwear, and started walking. She caught herself looking for the white car. She passed a bead store and a hardware store, both still closed. She smelled coffee, and quickened her pace, passing a real estate office and a dentist and then coming face to face with the source of the coffee smell, and a sign that said, "Kate's Used Books and New Baked Goods." Damn. The first place with food was the one she didn't know if she wanted to find.

Elise felt dizzy standing outside it, but her empty

belly was stronger than the strange feeling washing over her. She went in, immediately relaxing in the warmth. Books lined three walls, and stairs led up to more books and a few tables. The shelves and furnishings were all wood, mostly rough-hewn, and the tables were simply cut-up logs. Here and there, display cases of cards and jewelry and small sculptures interrupted the flow of books. The whole place smelled of wood and coffee and warm bread.

A tall, thin woman with long gray hair looked up and waved at Elise. "Coffee?"

Elise smiled. "You bet." She walked up to the case, warm smells pulling her stomach like a magnet. "Is that a blueberry scone?"

"Marionberry." The woman set the scone on a napkin and filled a big ceramic mug with coffee. Her summer-sky colored eyes were welcoming and slightly curious. "Cream's over there." She pointed at the end.

"How much?" Elise reached into her pocket for the change from yesterday's water. Her hand brushed the rock.

"Can you pay?"

Elise nodded, fingering the rock, her skin prickling. The previous day was unreal, and she wanted to go on, not stop, but what if Gisele and Lee were right? "Are you Kate?"

The woman smiled. "Yes. This is my store. That'll be two dollars."

Elise brought her hand out with both the money and the rock. Nothing to do but ask. She was already down the rabbit hole. Her voice sounded squeaky in her ears. "I . . . I found this rock. Does it mean anything to you?"

Kate smiled and took the stone, turning it over in her hands. Then she handed the stone back to Elise, took the two dollars, and said, "Go on, eat. I'll join you after I take the muffins out of the oven."

Elise had nearly finished her coffee and was halfway through the crumbly warm scone when Kate joined her at the table. "So, what's your name?"

"Elise."

"Well, Elise, I'm glad you found your way here. Glad you came in. Some people don't." Kate looked at Elise as if she were sizing her up, her eyes flicking across Elise's outfit and bedroll, and her lips pursed softly.

"You mean more people get these rocks? What does it mean?"

"The symbol—the three wavy lines—stands for water, for the feminine, for the three faces of the goddess. Some people say that when you are given something with this symbol, it means you're ready to face yourself, to find out who you are, to connect with your emotions."

"What if I don't want to?"

"Well, the stone was a gift, right? Someone told you to bring it to me?"

Elise hesitated. This was as strange as the two women from the previous day. "Yes."

Kate sipped her own coffee. "Gifts freely given mean you are free to choose what to do with them. You did not have to come here." Kate glanced at Elise's bedroll. "You're traveling, right?"

Elise nodded.

"Away from something, or to something?"

"Away from someone."

"All right. My teacher told me that when all your movement is away from things, you're a target. People can see that in you. I can see it in you. People who mean you harm can see it, too."

Elise bristled. "I've got myself out of a lot of bad situations."

"And will your luck ever run out?"

Elise shifted in her chair. She wasn't going to answer that.

"Well," Kate said, "I know the answer anyway. If

you tempt fate long enough, you lose. You came in here, and you looked for me, and someone suggested that you do that, right?"

"But I don't know why."

Kate shrugged, looking unconcerned. "You'll figure it out. Three or four people a year find their way here, and most of them stay for a while, and then they're strong enough to move on. Would you like to stay and help me here?"

Elise looked around at the piles of books to read, breathed in the smell of coffee and scones. She liked the smell, the warmth, the way the light fell in through the windows and lit dust motes in the air. Except she wasn't used to walls anymore. "You want me to work here?"

"You can stay a few months before you need to move on. I'll help you with that, too, if you want. You'll earn a wage, but I'll save half of it for you until you're ready to go."

"But I still don't understand how I got here."

"You acted, you left whatever was making you uncomfortable, and then you asked yourself for help. That's the only way people get here."

"I didn't help myself. Two women helped me."

Kate smiled. "An old one, and one about my age?"

"Old, and younger than you. I think. How did you know?"

"That's the symbol on the stone. Maiden, mother, crone."

"So I'm the maiden?"

Kate looked at her and laughed warmly. "Not in the usual sense, no. At least I'd guess not. I think you're in that awkward transition between phases. But really, each is all three."

A customer came in the door, and Kate stood up. "Why don't you look around? I'll show you in a minute."

Elise took her empty plate and cup and set them by the register. She looked in the nearest case, and saw a number of little carved figures, all wood or ivory, all looking like the symbols from a totem pole. The next case held jewelry. There were beaded earrings and wooden barrettes and some silver and turquoise in the back. Elise bent down to look at the silver.

The customer took her bag, and called "Good-bye" to Kate.

Elise gasped. "Where did you get these?" She pointed at the case.

Kate came over and stood next to her. "Which ones?"

"The long teardrop earrings in the back. I swear I saw them yesterday, on the woman I met." They were Lee's earrings. They had to be. Or twins.

Kate smiled. "No. They're new. One of our local jewelers brought them in just last week. He said it had been years since he's had good enough turquoise to make any so big."

"But . . ."

Kate smiled an odd little smile at her, and Elise shook her head, still confused. But her belly was full and she wasn't shivering. She glanced at the earrings, then at the door. She could pick up her bedroll and walk right out. She could.

Elise turned toward Kate, who watched her silently.

What was over the next ridges? What rivers, what woods, what people? Her hand roamed to the strap of her purse, hanging lightly over her shoulder. She heard the star-and-honey voices of Lee and Gisele in her head, and a faint scent of bacon wafted over from the kitchen. "Are you cooking bacon?" she asked Kate.

Kate shook her head. "No, but I'd be happy to."

Elise smiled and blurted out, "Can I have the job?"

Kate nodded. "But you do have to work."

"Where do I start?"

Kate cocked her head and laughed. "With a shower."

Elise grinned as she followed Kate up the stairs.

CHOICE OF ENDING
by Tanya Huff

Tanya Huff lives and writes in rural Ontario with her partner, six cats, and an unintentional Chihuahua. After sixteen fantasies, she's written two space operas, *Valor's Choice* and *The Better Part of Valor*, and is currently working on a series of novels spun off from her Henry Fitzroy vampire series. In her spare time she gardens and complains about the weather.

W HEN THE PHONE began to ring, several people within the morning rush heading for the Spadina subway station literally jumped. The incessant 24/7 warble of cell phones from pockets and purses hadn't prepared them for the strident and insistent ring of old technology. A couple of the older commuters actually moved to pick up—their responses set in a childhood before call answer when such a ring demanded immediate attention. One after another, they changed their minds upon actually reaching the booth. Perhaps it was the prevalent scent of urine, or a perfectly valid fear of catching something virulent from the grimy receiver, or the sudden certain knowledge that the call couldn't possibly be for them.

And the phone rang on.

"All right, all right, I'm coming. Don't get your damned panties in a twist!" An elderly woman dressed in several layers of grimy clothing pushed a heavily loaded shopping cart along the crowed sidewalk, scattering pedestrians like pigeons. Although collisions seemed unavoidable, no collisions occurred. A heavily perfumed young woman did snap one heel off a pair of expensive shoes after making an observation about street people and personal hygiene and asylums, but that was probably a coincidence.

Possibly a coincidence.

Actually, not likely to be coincidence at all.

The shopping cart finally parked by the booth, a gnarled hand, with gnawed fingernails surprisingly clean, picked up the receiver.

The ringing stopped.

The sudden silence turned heads.

"What?"

And the city dweller's innate ability to ignore the poor, the crazy, and most rules of common courtesy turned heads away again.

The voice on the other end of the phone was pleasantly modulated, genderless, and just a little smug. "Mrs. Ruth, this is your third and final warning. The power is about to pass. Please see that your affairs are in order."

Mrs. Ruth—the eldest avatar of the Triple Goddess, She who was age and wisdom and kept council during the dark of the moon—slammed the receiver back down onto the phone, coughed for a while, spat a large gob of greenish-yellow phlegm onto the stained concrete, and snarled, "Bite me."

She'd known for months now that her time was ending. It was, after all, what she did. What she was. She knew things. She knew the name of every pigeon who'd lost its home when the university tore down Varsity Stadium. She knew the hidden places and the small lives that lived in them. She knew the pattern of the larger lives that filled the city with joy and laughter and fear and pain. She knew that something was going to happen only she could prevent and she bloody well wasn't going anywhere until it did and she had.

"They can come and get me if they want me to go that badly!" she told a passing driver as she crossed Bloor Street against the lights, deftly moving her cart through the places the cars weren't. The driver *may* have questioned how he could hear her, given that his windows were up, his air conditioning was turned on, and he was singing along with a Justin Timberlake CD his daughter had left in the car, but she didn't stop to find out if he had. Another day she would have; questions were her stock in trade. Today, she didn't have time.

The trouble with knowing things was that not everything known was pleasant. There had always been dark places in the pattern; she acknowledged them, kept an eye on them, and if asked for her help, assisted in removing them.

Asked for her help. That was the sticking point.

"I can't just go fixing things willy-nilly," she pointed out to a young man jogging past.

Without really knowing why, he slowed and asked, "Why not?"

"Well, what will you learn from that?" Mrs. Ruth responded. "That I can fix things?" She blew a moist raspberry. "You have to learn to fix things yourself. I'm just a tool in the great toolbox of life."

"But what if you can't fix that . . . thing on your own? What if you've tried and it stays unfixed?"

"Ah, then you have to learn just who to ask for help. Your parents have been married for what, twenty-nine years?"

"Yeah, but . . ."

"You think that maybe they know a thing or two about staying together?"

"My parents have always said they won't interfere in my life."

"Uh-huh."

"So I should ask them . . ."

"Ask them what they had to do to make their relationship work." Which was, quite possibly, the most direct answer she'd given in thirty years.

"But . . ."

Not that it seemed to matter. "Just ask them, bubba."

He frowned at her then and reached into his belt pouch. "Power bar?"

"Sure."

And off he jogged, feeling good about himself because of a little effortless charity. He'd already forgotten the conversation, but that didn't matter; the things he'd needed to know he already knew and now they were lying along the surface of his thoughts where they'd do him some good.

Mrs. Ruth snorted as she watched him jog away. Time was, she could have spun her answers out for blocks, switching between allegory and insult at will. No one appreciated words of wisdom that seemed to arrive too easily. Trouble with common sense was folks had stopped appreciating anything considered *common*. Granted, they'd stopped some time between coming out of the trees and walking erect, but it still pissed her off.

Time was . . .

Time wasn't. That was the problem.

The wheel of life turned. Sometimes, it ran over a few hearts on the way. As a rule, her job was to remind folk that there wasn't a damned thing they could do about it.

"Why did this happen to me?"

"Because."

"It's not fair!"

"No, it isn't."

"How can I stop this?"

"You can't."

But she could. It was within her power to change

the pattern—if she could just hang onto that power long enough. She was *not* having her end and this particular bit of darkness coincide.

"I'm not denying that it's time," she muttered at her reflection, keeping pace in the windows of parked cars. "There are days I feel more tired than wise."

Her reflection snorted. "Then let go."

"No. I can't let it happen again."

"You can't stop it from happening again, you old fool."

Mrs. Ruth sighed and raised a hand to rub at watering eyes. That was true enough where *it* referred to the general rather than the specific. But she could stop this particular *it* from happening and she was going to.

With only one hand guiding it, the shopping cart twisted sideways and slammed into the side of a royal blue sedan. The car alarm screamed out a protest.

"Oh, shut up!"

The alarm emitted one final, somewhat sulky, *bleep* then fell silent.

Shaking her head, Mrs. Ruth dug into the depth of the cart, shoving aside old newspapers with headlines that stated the obvious about the city being on edge, her entire wardrobe except for the blue socks which she'd left hanging on the bushes by the church, and eighteen faded grocery bags filled with empty cookie boxes and Tabasco sauce. Down near the top half of the 1989 Yellow Pages, she found a coupon for complimentary body work at Del's Garage on Davenport Road at Ossington. Del had played high school football with the owner of the car and was about to be in desperate need of a good lawyer. The owner of the car had married a very good lawyer.

"There." She shoved it under the windshield wipers. "Two for one. Don't say I never did nothing for you. And stop staring at me!"

Her reflection suddenly became very interested in

getting a bit of secret sauce off the sleeve of her shapeless black sweater.

Frowning slightly, Mrs. Ruth laid her palm against the warm curve of glass and wondered when her joints had grown so prominent, her fingers so thin. She remembered her hands fat and dimpled. "You look old," she said softly.

Under the crown of her messy gray braid, the lines on her reflection's face rearranged themselves into a sad smile. "So do you."

"You look older!"

"Do not!"

"Do, too!"

"Excuse me, are you all right?"

Mrs. Ruth turned toward the young woman standing more than a careful arm's length away—compassion's distance in the city. "When he asks you how you did it, tell him it's a secret. Trust me; things'll go a lot better if he never knows."

Or had that already happened? Past and future threads had become twisted together.

And why was she speaking Korean when the girl was clearly Vietnamese?

"No! Not now!" Her hands closed around the bar of her shopping cart and she closed her eyes to better see the fraying threads of her power and draw them back to her. Through force of will she rewove the connections. Breathing heavily—a moment later or ten, she had no idea—she opened her eyes to see the young woman still standing there but clearly ready to run. "I'm fine," she told her through clenched teeth. "Really, I'm fine."

With no choice but to believe, the girl nodded and walked quickly away.

On the corner of College and Spadina, a phone began to ring.

"I will repeat this only one more time," Mrs. Ruth growled in its general direction. "Bite. Me. And in our second official language: *Mange. Moi.*"

People moved out of her way as she hobbled toward the Eaton's Center. Most of her scowl came from the pain of a cracked tooth caused by all the clenching.

In nice weather, he ate lunch on a bench outside the north end of the Center where he watched small children roll past in strollers or dangling from the hands of hurrying adults. These children were too young, but he enjoyed speculating on how they would grow. This one would suddenly be all legs, awkward and graceful simultaneously, like a colt. That one would be husky well into his teens when suddenly his height would catch up with his weight. Her hair would darken. His dimples would be lost. After his sandwich, his apple, and his diet cola, he'd go back into the store and later, when school was out, he'd help the parents of older children buy expensive clothing, clothing the child would grow out of or grow tired of long before they'd gotten their money's worth from the piece. The store had a customer appreciation program—every five hundred dollars spent entered the child's name in a draw for the latest high-tech wonder. Names and ages and addresses were collected in a secure database. Where secure meant accessible only by store staff.

She knew all this when she lowered herself down beside him on the bench and arranged the layers of her stained black skirts over her aching legs. "I won't let it happen, bubba."

Knowing what he knew, hiding what he hid, he should have asked, "Let what happen?" and that question would have given her a part of him. Every question she drew out after that would have given her a little more. It was how conversations worked and conversations could be directed. Direct the conversation, direct the person having it.

But he said only, "All right."

White noise. Nothing given.

"Everyone has limits. I've reached mine."

He said, "Okay." Then he folded his sandwich bag and slid it into his pocket.

Her presence used to be enough to make them open up. Today, holding on to her power by will alone, not even leading statements were enough. Should she release enough power to draw him to her, she'd lose it all before she had time to deal with what he was.

He stepped on his empty diet cola can, compressing it neatly. Then he scooped it up and stood.

Mrs. Ruth stood as well.

He smiled.

His smile said, as clearly as if he'd spoken aloud, *"You can't stop me."*

A subconscious statement he had no idea he was making.

"Oh, right! You're a big man facing down an old lady! I ought to run over your toes until you can't walk!" He looked startled by her volume, admittedly impressive for a woman her age. More startled still when she grabbed his sleeve. "How'd you like a little Tabasco sauce where the sun don't shine!"

"Okay, that's enough." The police constable's large hand closed around her wrist and gently moved her hand back to her side. Fine. Let the law handle it. Except she couldn't just tell him what she knew, he had to ask.

She glared up at him. "Never eat anything with mayo out of a Dumpster—all kinds of evil things hiding in that bland whiteness."

She was hoping for: "What the hell are you talking about?"

Or even: "Say what?"

But all she got was: "Words to live by, I'm sure. Now move along and stop bothering people."

Over her years on the street she'd met most of Toronto's finest—a great many of them even were—but this big young man with the bright blue eyes, she didn't know. "Move along? Move along? Listen bubba, I owned these streets while you were still hanging off your mother's tit!"

"Hey!" A big finger waved good-naturedly at her. "Leave my mother out of this."

"Your mother . . ." No, better not go there. "I can't leave yet. I have something to do."

When the bright blue eyes narrowed, Mrs. Ruth realized she'd been speaking Hungarian. She hadn't spoken Hungarian since she was nine. The power was unraveling again. By the time she wove things back into a semblance of normalcy, the cop was gone, *he* was gone, she was sitting alone on the bench, and the sun was low in the sky.

"Shit!"

She had no time to find a Hero and the other Aspects were too far away even if they'd agree to help. Which they wouldn't. The Goddess was a part of what kept this world balanced between the light and the dark. She was the fulcrum on which the balance depended. Should the balance shift in either direction, her aspects would come together to right it, but this . . . evil was nothing unusual. Not dark enough to tip the scales and with light enough in the world to balance it.

"Business as per bloody usual."

And all very well if only the big picture got considered. One thing the years had taught her—her, not the Goddess—was that the big picture didn't mean bupkas to those caught by the particulars.

Getting a good grip on her shopping cart, Mrs. Ruth

heaved herself up onto her feet. She could still see to
the point where the dark pattern intersected with her
life although she no longer had strength enough to see
further. Fine. If she followed the weft to that place,
she'd have one more chance.

"The Gods help those who help themselves."

Laughing made her cough. But hell, without a sense
of humor she might as well already be dead so, laughing and coughing, she slowly pushed her cart north on
Yonge Street. She couldn't move quickly, but neither
could she be stopped.

"After all," she told two young women swaying past
on too-high heels, "I am inevitable."

The elder of the two paled. The younger merely
sniffed and tossed pale curls.

That made her laugh harder.

Cough harder.

Phones rang as she passed, handing off booth to
booth, south to north like an electronic relay.

At Yonge and Irwin, a middle-aged woman held her
chirping cell phone up under frosted curls, frowned,
and swept a puzzled gaze over the others also waiting
for traffic to clear. When Mrs. Ruth pushed between
an elderly Asian man and a girl with a silver teardrop
tattooed on one cheek, her eyes cleared. She took a
step forward as the cart bounced off the curb—boxes
rattling, newspapers rustling—and held out her phone.

"It's for you."

Mrs. Ruth snorted. "Take a message."

"They say it's important."

"Do they? What makes their important more important than mine?" When the woman began to frown
again, she rolled her eyes. "Hand it over."

The phone lay ludicrously small on her palm. She
folded her fingers carefully around it and lifted what
she hoped was the right end to her mouth. "She has
to pay for this call, you inconsiderate bastards." Then

she handed the bit of metal and plastic back and said, "Hang up."

"But . . ."

"Do it."

She used as little power as she could, but it was enough diverted she lost another thread or two or three . . . Breathing heavily, she tightened her grasp on those remaining.

At Bloor Street she crossed to the north side and turned west, moving more slowly now, her feet and legs beginning to swell, the taste of old pennies in the back of her throat.

"Could be worse," she found the breath to mutter as she approached Bay. "Could be out in the suburbs."

"Could be raining," rasped a voice from under a sewer grate.

She nodded down at bright eyes. "Could be."

From behind the glass that held them in the museum, the stone temple guardians watched her pass. Fortunately, the traffic between them was still heavy enough, in spite of the deepening night, that she could ignore their concern.

By the time she reached Spadina, more and more of her weight was on the cart. When the phone at the station began to ring, she shot a look toward it so redolent with threat that it hiccupped once and fell silent.

"Right back where . . . I started from." Panting she wrestled the cart off the curb, sneered at a street car, and defied gravity to climb the curb on the other side. "Should've just spent the day . . . sitting in the . . . sun."

By the time she turned north on Brunswick, the streets were nearly empty, the rush of people when restaurants and bars closed down already dissipated. How had it taken her so long to walk three short blocks? Had she stopped? She couldn't remember stopping.

Couldn't remember . . .

Remember . . .

"Oh, no, you don't!" Snarling, she yanked the power back. "When. I. Choose."

Overhead, small black shapes that weren't squirrels ran along the wires and in and out of the dappled darkness thrown by the canopies of ancient trees.

"Elderly trees," she snorted. "Nothing ancient in this part of the world but me."

"You're upsetting the balance."

She stared down at the little man in the red cap perched on the edge of her cart, twisting the cap off one of the bottles of Tabasco sauce. "Not so much it can't be set right the moment I'm gone. Trust me . . ." Her brief bark of laughter held no mirth. ". . . I know things."

"You're supposed to be gone now," he pointed out, and took a long drink.

"So?"

That clearly wasn't the answer he'd been expecting. "So . . . you're not."

"And they say Hobs aren't the smartest littles in the deck."

"Who says?"

"You know." She thought she could risk taking one hand off the cart handle long enough to gesture. She was wrong. The cart moved one way. She moved the other.

"You're bleeding." The Hob squatted beside her and wrinkled his nose.

"No shit." Left knee. Right palm. Concrete was much tougher than old skin stretched translucent thin over bone. She wouldn't have made it back to her feet without the Hob's help. Like most of the littles, he was a lot stronger than he appeared and he propped her up until she could get both sets of fingers locked around the shopping cart handle once again. "Thanks."

He shrugged. "It seems important to you."

She didn't see him leave, but it was often that way with the gray folk who moved between the dark and light. She missed his company, however brief it had been, and found herself standing at the corner of Brunswick and Wells wondering why she was there.

The night swam in and out of focus.

Halfway down the block, a door closed quietly.

Her thread . . .

His thread . . .

Mrs. Ruth staggered forward, clutching the pattern so tightly she began to lose her grip on the power. She could feel her will spread out over the day, stretched taut behind her from the first phone call to this moment.

This moment. The moment her part of the pattern crossed his.

A shadow reached the sidewalk in the middle of the block, a still form draped over one shoulder. The shadow, the still form, and her. No one else on the street. No one peering down out of a darkened window. A light on in the next block—too far.

This was the reason she'd stayed.

The world roared in her ears as she reached him. Roared, and as she clutched desperately at the fraying edges, departed.

He turned. Looked at her over the flannel-covered curve of the child he carried.

It took a certain kind of man to break silently into a house, to walk silently through darkened halls to the room of a sleeping child, and to carry that child away, drugged to sleep more deeply still. The kind of man who knew how to weigh risk.

She was falling. Moments passing between one heart-beat and the next. Her power had passed. She was no risk to him.

He smiled.

His smile said, as clearly as if he'd spoken aloud, *"You can't stop me."*

It was funny how she could see his smile when she could see so little else.

Then he turned to carry the child to his car.

The power has passed. The voice on the phone, no longer held at bay.

"What part of 'bite me' do you not understand?" As the sidewalk rose up to slap against her, curiously yielding, Mrs. Ruth threw out an arm and with all she had left, with the last strength of one dying old woman who was no more and no less than that, she shoved the cart.

Few things hurt worse than the bar across the front of a heavily laden shopping cart suddenly slamming down just above the heel. He stumbled, tripped, fell forward. The child slid off his shoulder. His head slammed into the car he'd parked behind, bone impacting with impact resistant door.

The car alarm shrieked.

Up and down the street, cars joined in the chorus. "Thief! Thief! Thief!"

Their vocabulary was a little limited, she thought muzzily, but their hearts were in the right place.

Lights came on.

Light.

Go into the light.

"In a minute." Mrs. Ruth brushed off the front of her black sweater, pleased to feel familiar substantial curves under her hand, and watched with broad satisfaction as doors opened and one after another the child's neighbors emerged to check on their cars.

Cars had alarms, children didn't. She frowned. Should

have done something about that when she still had the time.

He stood. A little dazed, he shoved the shopping cart out of his way. Designed to barely remain upright at the best of times, the cart toppled sideways and crashed into the concrete, spilling black cloth, empty boxes, and bottles of Tabasco sauce. One bottle bounced and broke as it hit the pavement a second time directly in front of the child's face. The fumes cut through the drug and she cried.

He started to run then, but he didn't get far. The city was on edge, it said so in the papers. These particular representatives of the city were more than happy to take out their fear on so obvious a target.

The Crone is wisdom. Knowledge. She advises. She teaches. She is not permitted to interfere.

"She didn't. I did. The power passed before I acted. I merely used that power to get to the right place at the right time. No rules against that."

You knew that would happen.

Not exactly a question. Mrs. Ruth answered it anyway. "Nope, I'd had it. Reached my limit. I had every intention of blasting the son of a bitch right out of his Italian loafers. Fortunately for the balance of power, I died."

The silence that followed filled with the sound of approaching sirens.

But the cart . . .

"Carts are tricksy things, bubba. Fall over if you so much as look at them wrong."

And the Tabasco sauce?

"What? There's rules against condiments now?"

You are a very irritating person.

"Thank you." She frowned as her body was lifted onto a stretcher. "I really let myself go there at the end."

Does it matter?

"I suppose not. I never was a vain woman."

You were cranky, surly, irritable, self-righteous, annoying, and generally bad-tempered.

"But not vain."

The child remained wrapped in her mother's arms as the paramedics examined her. The drugs had kept her from being frightened and now she looked sleepy and confused. Her mother looked terrified enough for both of them.

"They'll hold her especially tightly now, cherish each moment. When she gets older, she'll find their concern suffocating, but she'll come through her teenage rebellions okay because the one thing she'll never doubt will be her family's love. She'll have a good life, if not a great one, and the threads of that life will weave in and about a thousand other lives that never would have known her if not for tonight."

The power has passed. You can't know all that.

Mrs. Ruth snorted. "You really are an idiot, aren't you?" She pulled a pair of sunglasses from the pocket of her voluminous skirt and put them on. "All right, I'm ready. Life goes on."

But you knew it would.

"Not the point, bubba." She turned at the edge of the light for one last look. It wasn't, if she said so herself, a bad ending.

STRIKES OF THE HEART
by Nina Kiriki Hoffman

Nina Kiriki Hoffman has sold more than two hundred stories, five adult novels, three short-story collections, and a number of juvenile and media tie-in books. Her works have been finalists for the Nebula, the World Fantasy, and the Endeavor awards. Her 1993 novel, *The Thread That Binds The Bones*, won a Horror Writers Association Bram Stoker Award. Her fantasy novels include *The Silent Strength of Stones*, *A Stir of Bones*, *A Red Heart of Memories*, *Past the Size of Dreaming*, and *A Fistful of Sky*.

I HAD BEEN a plantwife seven years when I noticed my grandmother's first stumbles. My grandmother's mind wandered now, and her magics followed.

Omara, my grandmother, the king's wizard and herbalist, was the mother of my heart. Laran, the mother of my body, was a warrior in the castle guards, often off on missions on behalf of the king, and rarely warm to me when she was home. She had never wanted a child. She had never named my father for me either; perhaps she did not know which bed-friend of hers he was. Sometimes my mother gave me careless kindnesses, but more often she was unhappy to see me.

She called me Kishi, the line between sea and shore. Perhaps that was how she saw me, a place where two worlds fought, a barrier between her carefree life before and her life after I arrived.

When I was young and stupid enough to still seek her, I saw how she gambled and drank with the others, how the mother I sometimes knew as kind disappeared as the evening progressed and the drinks and games grew deeper. Someone else wore the face of my mother then, and this new person did not like me.

If I approached Mother in the midmorning, while she was still sorry for her excesses of the previous night but before she started drinking again, I could sometimes wile promises from her, such as permission to go with the guards to the forest when they went scouting for griffin spawn or dragon larva. When I went with the guards, I could go deeper into the forest than I could alone, and find plants my grandmother had not yet taught me.

Gran never went off on campaigns the way my mother did. She trained me in herb craft and stayed with me my whole childhood. We shared a room between the stillroom and the kitchen.

Gran taught me the doctrine of the signatures, how a plant would always show you what uses it had if you looked carefully enough. Even an unfamiliar plant would reveal itself, if you could see the aura around it.

Many of Gran's magics were small and benign—you'd miss them if you didn't know where to look. An herb under a guest's pillow to keep dark dreams away; a sweet leaf halfway down the wick of a candle to quiet strife; butter mixed with cinders to settle a sour stomach. Gran's magics were the magics of smoothing lives.

Gran had other magics inside her, ones she did not unleash in these untroubled times. There were tales among the guards of the days long before my birth, when Gran was young and her hair was wild and red, flame that streamed out around her as she strode battlefields in her long black robe. I heard more than once how, when we were attacked by the nation to our north, Gran burned smokes and cast spells that laid whole regiments low: boils, flux, blinding headaches, rashes, the leaching of strength from muscles, magics that left battlefields choked with collapsed soldiers. Kinder than killing, some said, but the guards did not think magic made honorable battle tactics, even though it disabled soldiers, put the burden of caring for the fallen on the enemy, and eventually won our king the war.

Everyone was still afraid of Gran, though she hadn't cast such spells in years.

She taught me everything good I ever knew, except the lore I learned from my plant husband. When I was fifteen, I had a strange courtship with the Old Man in the Ground, wild cucumber. Gran and I came across the Old Man in one of our forays in the forest. Before I could stoop to study him, Gran dragged me back. In his signature, I saw the throbbing red of passion, but when Gran looked, she said she saw the dark purple of poison.

"Stay away from this one, Kishi," Gran told me. "There's no good in it."

But the red called to me. I was young and gawky then. None of the castle boys paid me any attention. I watched human auras as well as I could, but they were never as clear to me as plant auras. I knew passionate things happened in people all around me, and Gran talked to me about the ways of men and women, but nothing called to me as clearly as the signature of the Old Man.

Gran had never been wrong about a plant's signature before. Still, I woke in the middle of a moon night, and there was a scent on the air that drew me out of the castle, through the village, past the edges of where humans lived. Old Man in the Ground waited for me in the darkness. I searched out his signature from among the others. It glowed green and red in the darkness, promise and passion. I went to him and surrendered myself, and he accepted me.

What he planted inside me made me a more gifted

herbalist than Gran could ever be. He strengthened
my vision and gave me the power to hear plant voices,
and even speak with those plants that lived swiftly
enough to hear me. He taught me to see even more
plant potentials; in our union, we learned how we
could act on each other. I learned healing on a level
below words.

My plant husband also made me unfit for a human
husband, an outcome Gran had foreseen and feared.

Eventually Gran accepted my decision to be a plantwife, though it continued to trouble her. She loved the
king, the queen, the three princes, and all the life of
the castle. She wanted me to be her legacy to them.
She had spent her life in service to this land, and she
sensed that with the powers my husband had given
me, I could go anywhere plants grew and find a life
that would satisfy me. The ties of duty and love that
bound her to King Eleks and the country did not grip
me so hard. I was too odd to make friends easily,
though I did count Maple, the cook, a friend, and
Kian, the youngest of the three princes. Gran feared
my solitary nature would make it easier for me to
leave, robbing King Eleks and the country of my skills.
I was the only apprentice Gran had.

She did her best to weave me into the tapestry of
castle life. She linked me to others by work; she put
me in charge of all the foods we got from the wild. I
worked with Maple on menus and did much of the
shopping for fruits and vegetables, once Maple trusted
me to pick the best at the market. I led young men
to the forest. They carried home whatever fruit, roots,
seeds, herbs, and lichens I picked. I showed carpenters
trees ready for harvest, and found downed wood for
the woodcutters. At the castle, I held morning medical
consultations with the ill, diagnosed ailments, mixed
herbal remedies, and dispensed cures.

Everyone I worked with thought me odd, but they

respected me. I suspected that none of them thought I was human; I didn't feel as though I were.

When I was seventeen, Gran wiled Prince Kian into desiring me. Gran thought that if Kian gave me a child, something my plant husband could not do, it would lock me to the life of the castle. There was no hope of a recognized union between me and the prince, for his future lay in political liaisons. Had I a child of his, though, I would be more valued.

My plant husband gave me the power to undo Gran's wile by changing my scent into one that disgusted the prince. He never consummated his attraction to me. Later, when Kian knew what had come over him, we spoke to each other and straightened out the tangle. We returned to being the friends we had been before, when we explored the forest together.

I thought no more about Kian's brief lust for me until Gran's troubles came, five years later.

At first, only small things told of Gran's confusion. One washday, all the white laundry turned pink. Protection spells around the castle broke down and let in biting insects, and each bucket lowered into the well brought up frogs. One morning nothing the fireboy did could start a fire in the kitchen's stoves and hearths.

People complained to Gran about the troubles, which came thicker as time passed; sometimes Gran remembered the problems long enough to correct them. When she didn't, people came to me.

At first I didn't build connections between the problems in my mind; I just figured out how to fix them. If they required wizarding only Gran could do, I reminded her to work on the solutions until she did, but I was surprised how many problems I could solve myself in consultation with my plant husband, who knew warding ways that did not work like straight magic. Insects could be repelled with scent; dyes could be altered, fixed, or washed out with a combination of crushed leaves and moon-silvered water; as for the frogs, they could be summoned out of a well with a certain scent, and set loose elsewhere. I spoke to dead wood and it woke to fire.

More and more small things claimed my attention every day. As I solved problems, I saw how much Gran had done in her full power to make life easier for everyone around her, and how much she was losing now.

On Seed Blessing Day in early spring, I woke before the sun. The force flowers I kept in pots on the stone windowsill, the ones that bloomed in response to my urgings instead of the seasons, had not yet opened for the day; their leaves were spread to the light, though, and the air smelled of sage and mint and lemon balm. Gran lay asleep in her bed, her face softened with dreams. I dressed quietly so I would not wake her. She needed more rest than she used to.

Today I would make enough mulled cider to serve everyone in the castle and the village. I had been collecting spices for months.

It was the day of the spring moon, when people brought their seeds to the temple for blessing. The king would walk the fields, giving each plot of earth a drink and a prayer for a fruitful season.

In the dark, cavernous kitchen, the fireboy was already at work. He had blown the embers on the big hearth awake, and fed them wood. The smoke was fragrant, whispering of wood dry and dead. As I came in, the fireboy stepped outside, headed to the wood shed to bring in the day's supply.

In the weak new flames of the morning fire, the bunches of dried herbs hanging from the rafters cast flickering shadows across the low ceiling. I lit the lamps and plucked leaves from various herb bundles for the morning tea, crushed those that needed crushing, roused the sharp, smoke-edged scents of Rise and Wake and Pay Attention. I stitched the leaves loosely into a linen bag and got out the big pot.

I went out in the cool morning to haul water for tea. The fireboy, his arms full of wood, halted when he saw me. He was large, taller than I was, and not clean. He was a new boy in the kitchen, probably in his late teens, got from the workhouse in the village after the previous fireboy had moved to the stables to take care of the horses. He slept among the ashes of the open hearth, near the source of his power. Black ash smeared his nose and chin, and his ginger hair was greasy with much rubbing to make it lie flat.

He stared at me as I walked past, then dropped his armful of logs and grasped my arm. My first thought was that something was on fire, and he was dragging me out of the way of disaster. I turned, and saw that the danger was his regard. The dark centers of his eyes flared wide. His grip tightened. He jerked the pot out of my hand and dropped it, then pulled me up against his sooty self. What a smell of smoke, grease, and stale sweat; I choked on it. He dragged me into the wood shed, then threw me down on the chilly floor among the scattered bark and slivers and shoved my skirts up above my waist. I cried out as he fumbled for the ties at his crotch.

My grandmother was powerful in battle; she knew how to fight. I had grown up in peaceful times. It had never occurred to me that I would need to know how to defend myself.

The wedding ring my husband had given me unwound from around my wrist, a live green band of vine that most times lay quiet as a tattoo against my skin. It twisted through the air between us and closed around the fireboy's throat. The fireboy did not respond right away, so busy was he readying himself to mount me. But after too long without air, he choked and fell forward on top of me. I lay panting and shuddering under his weight, trapped by fear and shock. My wedding ring dropped from the fireboy's throat and twined around my arm again, and from that, I took strength.

I shoved the fireboy off and scrambled to my feet, adjusted my skirts. I felt the pulse at his neck. His heart still beat. The small herb-harvesting knife at my belt came into my hand, and I thought how easy it would be to slit his throat, here in the wood shed where few people went.

Instead, I ran out through the castle gates, away from the gray stone walls that cradled the workings of government and all the servants who served those workings. I ran through the wattle-and-daub-and-thatched-roof village, past cultivated fields and fenced pastures, and on to the wilderness. I left the road and plunged into the woods, wending between sleepy plant auras and the deep greens of tree signatures. It was dark and cold under the trees, but I was warm in my run. I slowed, though; instead of trampling underbrush I pushed past ferns and young trees and bushes. They knew me and made room for my passage. The scent of waking forest calmed me, helped my heart slow.

I went to the clearing my husband had claimed, where his vines covered the ground, with their large, hand-shaped leaves, their thick, succulent vines, and the tendrils that spiraled from the stems at the leaves' bases to clasp anything that ventured near and stood still long enough. I waded in where the vines coiled thickest, and they rose to wrap around me. The hairs on the stems that pricked and stung others caressed me. The bitter scent of my husband's green soul surrounded me. My husband embraced and supported me. Tendrils wrapped around my arms and legs and belly and neck, wove over my face. Presently I calmed and told my husband what had happened.

The leaves in the clearing grew agitated. Some of the vines reached out to climb nearby trees. I felt my husband's anger, and I gloried in it.

He fed me the fruit he grew only for me.

He examined me, and found that there had been an alteration in my signature, an added fragrance that was not my own. He told me it cried out to male humans that I was ready to bear children and they should mate with me. It was similar to the fragrance Gran had set on me to attract the prince five years earlier, though less specific.

My husband studied the fragrance and disabled it.

Later, I rose from his embrace. He left more of his marks on me: scratches from our encounter, but also twists of tendrils around my arms and legs, waist and neck, augmenting my wedding band.

By this time the sun had risen, and I was two hours late for my morning duties.

Why had Gran laid a magic on me that would make the fireboy desire me?

The village was awake when I walked back. Vendors were already selling special festival cakes and apple ale. People wore ribbons and gathered for games.

The farmers had set up market in the village square, as they did twice a week, with canopies stretched above spaces where they would sell vegetables, fruits, and whatever they made at home. One or two greeted me, but many others ducked their heads when they saw me. Some knew I was a plantwife. Most were afraid of me. It didn't stop them from seeking me out when they needed healing or blessings. All sold their wares to me, though few met my eyes.

"Kishi?" said Marcola. She was a textile vendor. I sold her skins from some of the roots I collected, and lichens I harvested on the slopes of Higara Mountain. She used them for dyes. She had never feared me.

"Marcola. Do you need anything this season?"

"More of those little nuts that have no name. They make a butter brown that goes well in hunter pants. I'll take as many of those as you can get me."

"That's not so easy." I needed a warrior escort to get to the place where I had found the nuts. It was a day's ride, too close to our northern border for me to wander alone.

Every time I asked the guards to go with me somewhere, my mother made it plain that she resented my asking anything.

Marcola shrugged. "When you can. What happened to you, Kishi? Those green lines on your arms."

I glanced at my arms. The tendrils of my husband wove like lace up and down them, as though I wore an undershirt of green spiderweb. "It's my armor." I thought I was giving her a fanciful answer, but then recognized the truth in my words.

Marcola frowned. "Did something happen? Are we expecting an attack?"

"Not the country. Just me."

She touched my hand. "Are you all right?"

I turned my hand so that my palm was up, and she closed her hand around it. "I think I will be," I whispered, surprised by her care. No one at home ever asked these questions. Gran used to, but since I became a plantwife, she had put distance between us.

"Take care." Marcola released me.

"Thank you."

I went home. I hesitated at the kitchen door. What if the fireboy were there?

I slipped in. Cook was busy preparing breakfast for the royal family and the festival guests. She frowned at me. Someone else had made the morning tea, not even using the teabag I had prepared earlier, which still lay among herbs at my cutting board. I dipped up a mug and drank. It had very little flavor. I made a fresh pot.

The fireboy was not there.

I apologized to Maple for being late.

"Angry I should be," she said. "You gone, the fireboy run off. I had to lay my own stove fires, and it's been so long since I did it, I've almost lost the knack. How am I supposed to run a kitchen on a festival day without you?" She handed me a knit bag of tiny onions, armed me with a knife, and aimed me toward my cutting board. I dropped into the rhythm of helping with the meal preparation, made the morning blessings, then went to the treatment room, where the sick waited.

The fireboy was one of those waiting. He did not meet my gaze, but stared at the rush-matted floor. He kept his hand on his throat until I came to him after all my other patients had left, then let it drop so I saw the red stresses around his neck.

"Do you remember what you did?" I asked him.

He nodded, his gaze dropping.

"Are you sorry?"

He nodded. His brow furrowed in confusion. He waved his hands. He opened his mouth, but no sound came out. My husband had hurt his voice.

"You couldn't help it," I said.

He nodded vigorously.

"I understand." The terror and anger I had felt when he threw me down flickered through me, but I let it seep away. If Gran had put a spell on me, how could this boy resist? He had no magic to fight it. "You won't do it again?"

He shook his head, covered his eyes with his hand.

I got out a healing ointment and massaged it into his neck, spoke words to wake its power. I finished and turned away. He touched my hand, and I glanced at him. He traced a finger up my arm, across the green loops and swirls of my husband's embrace, then met my gaze, a question in his eyes.

I willed the tendrils to rise up and wrap around his hand. He stood, trembling. I willed them back to my arm. "They won't hurt you unless you hurt me," I said.

He nodded. He touched his throat, mouthed "Thanks," and left.

Not until I was helping Cook and her workers prepare lunch did Gran come into the kitchen, and then she was sleepy and smiling. "What's the matter, Kishi? What happened to your arms? More of your—" she would not call my husband my husband; still she resisted my marriage, "—wildcrafting work?"

I glanced at Cook, then tugged Gran back to our room. "You laid an attract spell on me, Gran. Why did you do that?"

"I didn't. I wouldn't. What are you talking about?"

"Gran! The fireboy attacked me this morning because of a spell you put on me! You made me into something he wanted without thought! He hurt me. Why? Am I being punished?"

"I wouldn't do that." She studied me with narrowed eyes. "There is no touch of such a spell on you, Kishi. Why are you telling me an untrue thing?"

I didn't know what to say. My husband was sensitive to all the flows of energies, natural and otherwise, and he had recognized the signature of Gran's spell. He had taken the taint off, but why wouldn't Gran remember she had put a spell on me? "Gran—"

"What were all those cauldrons doing on the hearth in the kitchen? Why are you making such a lot of spiced cider, Kishi?" Gran asked.

"It's Seed Blessing Day," I said.

"How could it—surely that's not for another month?"

"It's today, Gran. Look where the sun falls on the floor."

She glanced down, then up at me, her face confused.

I didn't want to see her confusion. "I have to address the mulling spices, Gran."

"What should *I* do?" Gran said.

A cold finger of fear touched my heart. Gran had never asked me that question before.

"Shouldn't you speak with King Eleks?" I couldn't remember a day when she didn't wake and consult with the king at breakfast about what they would do. But breakfast was long past.

"The king!" Gran turned and left the room.

The king would already be in the fields, pouring a blessing every fifty steps, from a jug of liquor I had made of strength and fertility from last year's fruits, mixed with tincture of wild plants that would help excite this year's crops into growing strong and wild and well.

Would Gran know to find King Eleks in the fields? I should have mentioned it. I had told her it was Seed Blessing Day, and she knew it was late morning; where else would she look for him?

How long would she remember what I had told her? She had trouble remembering all sorts of things. She did not always know if it were washday or market day or even a day on the lunar calendar when we harvested herbs. I had to tell her things more than once, sometimes more than five times.

Lunch would bring everyone back to the castle. If Gran didn't find the king in the fields, she would find him then.

A knock sounded at the open door. "Kishi?" Cook said.

"I'm sorry." Cook was in the midst of meal preparation, and I had left her. I followed Maple back to the kitchen. As she sliced a fragrant roast, I laid a blessing on it.

When the servants had taken the food to the great hall, Cook led me to the dark pantry and had me bless the new provisions that had arrived by wagon that morning, then gave me a length of festival red ribbon as thanks. "I hope you're all right," she said. "You are never gone when I need you. What happened this morning?"

"Gran put a spell on me," I muttered. I felt I shouldn't tell anyone about Gran's weaknesses, but Cook depended on me, and I had failed her.

"You, too?"

"What? What did she do to you?"

"You know those lemon tarts she loves? Two days ago I made two hundred of them. Supper was late because I couldn't stop making tarts. My apprentice made the meal. Is there some charm you can give me that will protect me from Omara's magic?"

"I wish there was," I said, "but I'm not sure I can protect myself from her yet." I took Cook's hand and pressed my wrist to hers, asked my green armor if it could protect Cook. It didn't move. I sighed. "I'll study this. I've never needed protection from Gran before."

By the time we returned to the kitchen, the dishes from the first course had come back, and the other two courses were waiting in their serving dishes. It was time for those of the house staff who were not serving to make their meal. We gathered around the servants' table and Cook gave us each dishes, then set communal bread and stew in the center. I said the blessing and everyone grabbed food. I sat between Cook and her apprentice. Gran's chair, between me and Cook, went empty.

I would have to find Gran.

Before we had finished with lunch, my mother came in. She wore her padded practice tunic, which was cut here and there from missteps in swordplay and knifework. The side lacings were undone. She clutched her stomach. Her hair had come loose of the greased braid in which she normally locked it. "Kishi," she moaned.

Everyone looked at me. I rose, nodded to Cook, and went to my mother. I led her to my room, settled her on my bed, and sat facing her. "What happened?"

"When I woke this morning and dressed for practice, my commander came into the room I share with the other women. He ordered them out, then took me. He did not ask. He threw me down and covered me. Owain, whom I have trusted with my life in battle! Only it was not he who did it. He was not home in his eyes. After he finished, my sword partner came and took me. Peter, my friend and right arm for eighteen years! I pleaded with him, but he was not inside himself either. He was like a sleeping person, except he countered every force I used to fight him. They are the only ones in my battalion stronger than I am. Nothing I did stopped them. How could they do that to me, the two men I respect most in the world? Afterward they were confused and ashamed, and then they forgot, though the whole battalion heard me cry out and fight. None came to help me. Now I am useless. No one will trust me in battle. Why did this happen to me? Have I displeased some god?"

I took her hands in mine. My husband's green lace reached across to wind around Mother's wrists. "Kishi!" she cried.

"It's all right, Mother. It is just my husband looking to see what happened to you." The tendrils took my mother's taste and measure, and told me what I feared: Gran had put an attract spell on her, the same one she had used on me. "Gran did this," I whispered.

My husband tested another thing, tasted my mother's blood, found that her body had already initiated the change.

Should I tell my mother she was pregnant? So early on, we could stop it without endangering her. I could concoct an arbortifacient with herbs I already had. I did not imagine she would want to keep the child.

The lace released my mother and wrapped itself around my arms. I squeezed my mother's hands and let go.

"Gran did this?" Mother repeated. "I know I've always been a disappointment to her, but why punish me so? I gave her you."

Mother had always been a disappointment to Gran? What did that mean? Mother was one of the king's best warriors. Perhaps that was a skill Gran didn't value.

"Mother, did you ever see Gran in battle?"

"Oh, yes. She was magnificent. She saved our country from invasion three times in my memory, Kishi, and several other times according to history. She put fear into our enemies. That's why the borders have been untroubled for so long. No other king has a mage with Omara's powers." Mother sat back. "But she hasn't done anything dangerous in years. Are you saying her spelling me has something to do with battle?"

"No." I hugged myself. "It is not an outward battle. Her mind is wandering, but she retains her powers."

"She did this to me without even knowing?"

"Sometimes she knows." I took my mother's hand. "She did a like thing to me this morning, but my husband protected me."

"Oh, Kishi." She gripped my hand harder than was comfortable.

"Mother, you are with child."

"At my age?"

"So says my husband. I think Gran did this to us because she wants more children of our line."

Mother stroked my hair. "Poor Omara," she murmured, then laughed, a harsh sound. "I gave her you, the perfect daughter, and you decided to end our line instead of having the children you were supposed to have. No wonder she's crazy."

Mother's words hurt like a blade to my belly. When had it ever been my job to have a child? Always, according to Gran. Never, according to my husband. My mother had not pressed me one way or another, but then, she had never shown any sign of caring what became of me. She was kind to me in a rough way; it was as though we were people of different stations who bumped into each other once in a while at the well and exchanged words about the weather.

Now Mother blamed Gran's ailment on me?

Mother turned away. "A child," she said. "By one of two strong men. I cannot return to my chosen work in this house. I'll need to leave this country and apprentice myself somewhere no one will know I was forced. I cannot abide the thought of staying in a place where everyone knows such a shameful thing about me."

"Doesn't the shame lie with the men who did this?"

"No." She pressed her hands to her belly. "The shame lies in being overcome. I can still be respected as a warrior if someone defeats me in battle, as long as I can defeat others; but this woman thing, to have someone force their way inside me, that is shameful. There is truly a baby started inside? How can you know this so soon?"

"It is one of my gifts."

She shook her head. "You have always been strange."

I hesitated, then said, "Mother, do you want to rid yourself of this child?"

She closed her eyes and sat silent for a moment. "I'll think about it. Thank you for the offer, in any case."

Just then Gran came into the room. Mother shrank from her.

"Laran! What are you doing here?" Gran asked.

"Omara, what did you do to me? Do you hate me so?" Mother said.

"What?" Gran, bewildered, looked at me.

"You laid the same spell on her you laid on me."

"Kishi, I did not spell you."

"You did. You spelled me and you spelled Mother. You made us hosts to men against our wills."

Gran pressed her hand to her forehead, then held out two fingers of her left hand and made the gesture for revealing the unseen. Red lines of a spell wrapped Mother round, and her stomach glowed orange. The lines bore the unmistakable signature of Gran's magic working, a certain shiver in the weft. Mother stared down at herself, then looked to me, startled. The red and orange faded, leaving my mother a pale ghost in her practice tunic.

"Oh!" Gran cried. She struck her chest with her fist. "Oh, I—" She sank onto her bed and covered her face with her hands.

"Kishi," she whispered presently. "I didn't do that to Laran."

I knew she had seen her own signature. Still, I asked, "Who did?"

"The other who lives in my head."

"Mother," said my mother.

"Half the time, I'm not awake," Gran whispered. "Someone else is, and she does things while I sleep. I wake in places I don't remember. People look at me with fear in their faces. They say I've done things I never did. Even the king fears me now. Kishi—"

I sat beside her. My grandmother, my guide all my life. The wisest person I knew. The only other time I had seen her afraid was when she learned I had lain with my plant husband. Then she thought I had been poisoned. In some ways, perhaps, I had.

"Kishi," Gran whispered. "It's time for you to stop me."

Everything inside me halted. The ice of a lost moment edged my fingers and toes.

"I'm awake now, but when I'm not—who else can stop me?"

"Will you let me stop you?" I asked, so afraid I had difficulty shaping words.

"If you do it now. The other Omara—"

Husband, I thought. *Help me.*

I took my grandmother's hands, and the green lace of my husband unknitted from my arms and wove a bridge to my grandmother. He wove around her body and sent tips under her surface to where her blood moved. She shuddered in his embrace. Our best calmers and soothers flowed into her.

Gran cried, "What are you doing to me?" She shivered, but did not pull away.

"Will soothing you stop your other self?"

"I don't know." Her eyes drooped shut.

Half the self my husband had gifted me with wound around Gran. It snapped its ties to the rest of him, which stayed with me. I felt afraid. My husband and I worked well together, but when he did things on his own, I didn't always like them. Who would I prefer to have in control? Wild Gran, who tortured my mother and me for reasons we didn't understand, or my husband, who did not think like a human?

I eased Gran back onto her bed, lifted her feet, folded her hands on her chest, then glanced at Mother.

She wiped her face. "I never thought this would happen," she said. "She was supposed to be strong forever."

A knock sounded. King Eleks stood on the threshold. He stared at Gran. "Kishi?" he murmured.

I went to the door, and he led me down the hall into the stillroom.

"What is it?" I asked.

"She came while I was blessing the last field," he said, "and there in front of all my people and the priestesses, Omara, my good right hand, defender of the kingdom, upholder of justice, exemplar of wisdom, and master of magery, laid a lust spell on me. It was only by grace that I was wearing the charm she made me last year to ward off spells. The charm protected me, mostly, but I had a difficult time keeping myself together until I finished the ceremony, and after that I was fortunate that the queen was waiting in our quarters. Kishi, I value Omara above many, but this is not the first time she has done something contrary to the country's best interests. What can you tell me?" he asked.

"Age." All my fear spoke, and still my voice came out a whisper. I did not want to believe that anything could harm my grandmother. An enemy had finally found her, and it came from within.

"As I feared. Is there nothing you can do to stop it?"

"I've put her to sleep for now. I don't whether there's anything I can do to halt what age is doing to her."

"If you cannot halt the process, can you do something to halt her? Omara has been my greatest treasure, the one who has made my rule fair and good. She has given us freedom from war and strength in peace. I owe her everything. But I also owe it to her not to lose everything she has gained for me because she is ill."

"I'm doing what I can."

He took a deep breath. "Kishi, with Omara impaired, I need another wizard."

"Majesty."

"Omara has been training you to be her assistant and replacement, though you have not come to court when she helped me with judgment."

I looked away from him. Ever since I chose my husband, Gran had left me more and more alone. I had been picking up the slack in all the domestic duties she used to do around the castle. But what of judgment? What of battle? I was not qualified for either of those things, not the way Gran had been.

"I'll help however I can, Majesty, but I am not my grandmother's equal."

"Omara has no equal. That's why we have been so prosperous these latter years. None of our neighbors has such a puissant wizard; they all fear Omara, and leave our borders alone. I hesitate to advertise for a new wizard; that will let the other rulers know we're vulnerable. Do you know any in the wizard community who would suit?"

I shook my head. Gran had taken me to wizard gatherings, but my skills were odd compared to most, and I had never made friends easily.

"I shall write to some trusted friends," he said. "Meanwhile, we must contrive. Sit at my right hand during judgment tomorrow."

"Majesty?"

"I need you." He left.

I went back to our rooms. Gran slept, her breathing soft and slow. Mother rose. "What did he want?"

"He wants a wizard, and may settle for me until he gets one."

"Kishi, you *are* a wizard."

I shook my head and herded my mother from the room.

She came with me as far as the kitchen, then paused with a hand on my sleeve. "I can't go back to the barracks."

"You can stay with me and Gran."

She thought, then shook her head. "I'll go to the temple and talk to the priestesses. They'll help me think about what to do next."

The rest of the day was given over to the festivities of Seed Blessing Day. I served a lot of cider, blessed many meals, laid hands on women's stomachs and men's groins and recited charms for fertility. It gave me a strange pang to prepare others for an experience I never expected to have myself. I knew my charms were potent. Already there were babies born to those I had blessed last year and the year before.

Gran slept through everything. I went to our rooms between ceremonies and looked in on her. She always lay in the same position.

After the evening feast, when all had gathered, servants, guests, and the royal family, in the great hall for Seed Blessing Day music and storytelling, King Eleks sought me out again. "See the castle seamstress tonight. Tell her to make you three white robes, the first by tomorrow. I need you to look like a wizard."

"But, Majesty—"

"This will help, Kishi," he said. "When Omara sees you, she'll be reassured. Perhaps she won't lay any more spells on us." He left.

Prince Kian, his arms circled by green ribbons, approached me. "What did father want?"

"He wants me to act as his wizard." I could leave. Tonight, before the king tied me here with bonds of duty and obligation like my husband's green lace. He was wiling me into place as surely as Gran could have.

Why did I want to leave? Here I had a place to sleep, food to eat, and the respect of the household. The king wanted to give me greater status, whether I was worthy of it or not. What more did I want?

"Good," said Kian.

"I'm not a wizard."

"Of course you are. Name one other person in the kingdom with your ability with plants. You're not the same sort of wizard your grandmother is, but you are a wizard."

I looked for his signature, and saw a faint flicker of blue and green around him. I didn't understand what these colors meant in people. In plants they meant health. They were clear colors, so they might mean he wasn't lying to me, but I wasn't sure.

Maybe I was a sort of wizard. No one else in the kingdom was a plantwife, or my husband would have told me, the way he sometimes passed on rumors of blight or fire or the fertilizer of blood shed in distant battlefields.

Kian touched my shoulder. The lace of my husband shifted on my upper arm, restless at the touch of another. "Think about it," Kian said. "Not many pay attention to you, but I know some of what you can do. You are a wizard, and you have strengths. Father can use your help." He gripped my shoulder and released me.

I sighed, and went to find the seamstress. I gave her the king's instructions about sewing me robes. She had drunk much cider and was the worse for it, but she grumbled and took my measure.

At the end of the day, I went back to the room I shared with Gran. Damp spring air came in the window and filled the room with coolness and the scents of young plants and moist earth, over the wall in the fields beyond. Cats prowled the courtyard, yowling spring songs. The moon sent silver light through the window. It rested like gilt across Gran's face. She had not stirred since I had put her to sleep that afternoon.

I went to Gran's side and took her hand. "Let her wake," I told the green lace on Gran's arms. She frowned, stirred, and woke.

"Kishi?"

I wondered which Gran had awakened. "Gran."

"Why am I lying down, and why is it so late?" She turned to stare at the moon.

"Do you remember what you said before?"

"What I said before? When?"

"How there are two of you?"

"Two of me? You are not making sense, heart's daughter."

So this was the one who wasn't aware of the other. This was the one who cast hurtful spells. Or was it?

"Do you remember what you did to Mother?" I asked Gran.

"What I did—" She lifted her arms, stared at the lines of my husband's lace, dark in the silver light. Her eyes widened. "Kishi, what is this?"

Was this a third Gran, who couldn't remember any of her earlier selves?

"You set spells on me, on Mother, on Cook, on King Eleks. Perhaps others I don't know about. Spells that hurt us. My husband is protecting you from yourself."

"Take it off this instant, or I shall force it from me."

"Gran! Be the wise judge I know you are. Think. I am not one to attack you without reason."

"You're jealous of my position. You've always wanted my power. You want to unseat me and steal my place."

"Gran!" My stomach turned over, and there was a sour taste in my mouth.

"You're a serpent's child who has crept into my heart and waits to bite it."

"I'm not!"

"You have plotted my downfall ever since you met the Old Man in the Ground. Take these green lines off now or I will kill them, and poison the one who gave them to you." She raised her hands, and her fingers took spellcasting form.

"Gran!"

"Kishi, take this off me, *now*."

I held my hand out toward her, called to the tendrils wrapped around Gran's arms. They did not respond. Instead, tendril tips dived under her skin and pumped sleep into her. She screamed, a terrifying noise of rage and fear, the cry of a hunting hawk and a hunted animal. She collapsed on the bed.

A storm of weeping shook me. I lay on the cold stone floor and let sorrow cradle me. I knew how Gran had planned to use her hands. The spells that came from those finger positions spread hurt and harm. I had never seen Gran take such positions with an aim to using them; she had only ever shown them to me to teach me what to be wary of if an enemy ever aimed spells at me.

Presently warmth seeped through me, nudged aside my despair. My husband had shifted the sea inside me, stilled the wild waves and weather. *It is time,* he said.

Time for what?

Time to make her fears come true.

Something pulled at my left arm. I opened my eyes and looked. In the moonlight, a dark rope of twisted strands led from my hand up over the edge of the bed to my grandmother. It tightened, pulling me toward her.

Up, Wife. It is time. A forest giant has fallen. Lightning has struck her, and she is no longer capable of good growth. Use what she has to nurture the next generation.

I can't do this.

You can and you must. You know who she used to be. It is what her well self would want.

I scrambled to my feet and sat on the edge of Gran's bed. My husband pulled my hand into Gran's, bound our hands together with a net of vine, my fingers interwoven with Gran's.

"Isn't there anything we can do to heal her?"

Look.

I saw/felt a vision of an ailing forest. The stream ran only in trickles, and many of the trees were dead or dying. Some of them had been struck by lightning, others eaten by insects or disease. A few trees still stood tall; light still fell on them and nourished them. Elsewhere the sky was dark and gloomy, though no rain fell.

She is like a wounded tree, that sees its death ahead and spends all its last energy putting out seed. These were the spells she cast on you and your mother and the king. She craves children to carry her life on past her end.

Under the surface of Gran's soil, a tide of something not water flexed and flowed. I tasted it with the senses of who I was in the vision, something with roots and leaves and body, something that was all mouths of different kinds. The tide tasted of strange intoxicants. It geysered up one of the fire-twisted trees and shot out the top, flew to another part of the forest and struck a living tree, withered and wilted it. I heard a scream.

The magic has grown stronger than her control of it, said my husband. *Take it, Wife. You have the strength to contain it. I can help. It only hurts her now.*

Where had the tide come from? How could I take it?

My husband had shaped me as a tree in this landscape. I put down myriad roots, and Gran's magic flowed into me through them.

I tasted blood, grit, iron, bitter orange, decay, sour apple, vanilla, all riding on a stream of power rich and strange and frightening. I grew drunk as it invaded me. It flowed through me, opening walls and shifting rivers. At first I was stupid under its flood, and let it go where it willed, but then my husband spoke to me. *Control it, Wife. Cage it. Put it where you can use it, and don't let it change the parts of you you want to preserve. Watch and confine and direct it.*

I wasn't sure I knew how to do what he said. He held me in his embrace and helped me choose. *Hold it here,* he said, and showed me how to store the power in leaves and fruit and trunk, how to tame the tide, turn it from flood into potential.

More and more and more came. At first I felt overwhelmed. Then I learned to let the process of storing it click from thought into habit.

Don't take it all. Leave enough to sustain her, my husband said, much later.

I stopped pulling in power and glanced at the landscape of my grandmother's mind.

It looked cold and haunted now, the dark twisted shapes of dead trees everywhere, and yet, nearby, I saw a clearing. Seven healthy trees grew there, and the meadow was watered by the little power that still flowed. Flowers starred the grass.

I could not walk to the meadow in the shape I wore now, a thick-trunked tree heavy laden with fruit and rustling with lively leaves, but I could send a root to it. I tasted the undersurface of the clearing. Clean, strong like the smell of fresh, worm-aired earth, a comfort that reminded me of Gran as I had first known her, warm arms that hugged me when I cried, soft voice that eased my fears.

Go down, said my husband. I sent my roots below the soil of Gran's clearing. The power here tasted clear and sweet. I did not pull it into me, but pushed down deeper.

Far below, I reached bedrock. My rootlets stubbed themselves against a wall, moved over it through the soil until they found an opening into Otherwhere.

Build, said my husband.

I didn't understand him, but my muscles responded. The opening was too wide, and let through too much power. Some of it stained as it passed into the dirt of my grandmother's mind, darkened and flowed out to the places I had pulled it from before. I reached with my roots and grasped stones around me, built them into a rim that blocked the flow, shut it down to a small stream, just enough to nourish, not enough to storm through her mind and drown it again. I used some of the power I had gotten from her to strengthen the wall. I spelled it strong enough to abide, and restrain the influx of power.

Afterward, my husband and I pulled up my new roots; I thinned my tree self and flowed along my husband's vines back into myself.

Fitting all I had taken from Gran into myself was a job I would not have been able to do alone. My husband helped me sort and store and reshape. He showed me how to claim new territory, space invisible and unattainable to my solo self. I had not known my own forest could grow in so many directions.

I found the river of my own power, the conduit to a different Otherwhere, and traced its flows, making sure they were open and clean, not blocked or filtered through fragile or dark places.

Another long, strange process. During it, I felt myself turn into someone new and terrifying.

I knew that I was my own forest, a host to my husband, even here, in the heart of the castle. I could leave, and carry everything with me. I could stay and be complete.

Only when we had finished our sorting and exploration did I notice someone shaking my shoulder.

"Kishi! Kishi! Wake up!"

I opened my eyes. How strange to be human-shaped again. How limiting. How different.

Stored inside me, great heaps of power fruit, blankets of bud, flower, seed, stem, and leaf. Some of the new leaves were the red of blood, some the purple of poison, but most the varying greens of hope and promise. The forest inside me had grown in many directions.

How had Gran ever lived a quiet life, with all of this power rustling inside her?

What was I going to do with it?

"What have you done?" cried Cook. Hers were the hands that gripped my shoulders.

I lay beside Gran on the bed, my fingers still meshed with hers.

Gran sighed. Her free hand rose, and she rubbed her eyes.

I lifted my free hand and rubbed my eyes, too. "Maple?" My voice tasted rusty.

"Kishi!" said Cook.

"What's wrong?"

"You two have been lying here twined together with green vines for three days now! What on Helnia's Hearth have you been doing?"

I worked my hand loose of Gran's. My fingers were stiff. Three days for me to go through my grandmother's mind and steal her power. I shook my head and pushed myself up.

"We've been trying and trying to wake you," Cook said. "The kitchen is in chaos. I never realized how many things you do to keep it in order. The king has been going mad as well. He hasn't held judgment since Seed Blessing Day. Are you truly awake now?"

My mouth tasted acrid. My stomach clenched like a fist. "I need porridge."

Cook hugged me, pressed my face against her floury front.

"Can't breathe," I told her eventually.

She released me. "We thought we had lost you."

"No," I said. "I have done a terrible thing."

"A terrible thing, Kishi?"

"I took away her wizard powers," I whispered.

Cook's brow furrowed. She glanced at Gran.

Gran sat up. She smiled at me and Cook. "Good morning."

"Lady Omara," Cook said. "How are you?"

Gran's stomach growled.

"Porridge for both of you, and pray Helnia I don't burn it. Kishi, do you do something to stop me from burning things? Never in all my born days have I burned so many things as these three days you've been asleep." Cook tugged me to my feet. "Bathe and put on other clothes, Kishi, my lady. You stink as though you'd been working in the sun." She bustled out.

I went to our wardrobe. Hanging beside Gran's white robes of peacetime wizard office were three new white robes, with longer hems, to fit my taller form. The seamstress had done the king's bidding. I hesitated, then lifted down one of the old and one of the new robes.

I led Gran toward the bathhouse.

Gran gazed around as though she had never seen the hall, the yard, the bathhouse before. She wore a smile that did not change, and her eyes were bright and shallow.

Powdery light came into the tub room from five long, narrow windows just under the roof. Between slants of light lay shadow. The water woman poured hot and cold water into a large tub and left us. Steam rose from the surface, blocks of it in the air where light touched it, invisible in the darkness.

I led Gran to the clothes hooks, hung our robes up beside the towels in one patch of light. "Take off your clothes, Gran."

She dropped her robe as though she had no modesty and stood before me, her aging flesh decorated with a loose green spiral of my husband's tendrils.

The Gran I used to know would not have abided my husband's touch.

I removed my tunic and skirts more slowly.

My husband's embrace of me was much more intense than the shadow self he had left on Gran; I wore a webwork of vines. Gran touched a junction of six lines that lay over my breastbone.

"Pretty," she said.

I felt the water with my hand, then stirred to mix the hot and cold. I tugged Gran into the water with me, and she sat, smiling, and let me wash her. I had never helped her wash before, though I remembered being a small child, the gentle roughness of the rag as she had scrubbed and soaped me, the pleasure as she poured warm rinse water over me. I stopped in mid-wash to hug Gran, and her arms met around me. Almost I could pretend she was her old self.

Afterward, she needed help with the fastenings of her robe.

The inside of my wizard's robe felt soft against my skin.

Gran took my hand. I looked at both of us, gowned in wizard white, and shivered.

I left our other clothes behind, with the dirt of the bathwater. A different me had come out of the water, and a different Gran. I did not know either of us yet.

We went outside.

My mother waited by the bathhouse door, arms crossed over her chest, hands buried in her armpits. Her hair was trained back into its greased braid again, not a strand out of place; her face was pale, her shoulders hunched. She wore a heavy, quilted dress, clay red, with black ties lacing the sleeves and knitting the front together. The skirt was narrow, but so long I only saw the tips of her soft shoes below the hem. I could not remember the last time I had seen my mother in a dress.

I pulled Gran to a stop.

"Laran," Gran said. She smiled.

"Omara." My mother stared at the ground. She glanced up. "Kishi."

"Mother? How can I help you?"

Her arms loosened. Her hands dropped to grip her stomach. "I've seen the priestesses. I've consulted the oracle. Signs say I should stay here, stay the way I am. While I was at temple, Owain came to me. He spoke to the others in my battalion, discovered what he had done to me. He apologized. Everyone knows now it was a battle spell gone awry—" Mother glanced at Gran.

Gran looked confused. Mother turned to me.

"I don't know what she remembers," I said.

"Do you remember spelling me, Omara?"

Gran touched her forehead with the tips of her fingers. "I didn't sleep so well last night," she said. "Or, which night was it? I sat up after Kishi went to sleep, and my mind kept racing around and around. I knew there were things I'd left undone. It came to me that I could solve everything with a few spells. I sent them out to do good work, and then I could sleep."

"You're not going to do that again, are you?" Mother asked.

Gran frowned, pressed her forehead. "Nothing's here anymore."

Mother glanced at me. I nodded. She sighed, returned my nod. "Owain and I have talked. He said he will care for me as he would any warrior wounded in battle, that I will have time to heal, and then I can come back to work. If I bear the child, will you take it when it's born?"

"Oh, yes," I whispered, and then knew that in spite of my strange marriage, I, too, had had mother dreams. I stroked the green band at my wrist. My husband coiled a tendril around my fingers, released me. "Yes, Mother. Please."

"I'll see how the pregnancy treats me. If it's too much trouble, I may come to you for help in ending it."

"I know herbal cures to ease pain in pregnancy. Come to me if you need any kind of comfort."

She stepped forward, pressed a kiss to my forehead,

then turned and left. Gran stared after her, brow furrowed.

"Come on, Gran." I took her hand. We went to the kitchen.

At the servants' table, Cook gave us porridge. As we ate, the king came to the kitchen. He knelt before Gran, his head bowed.

"Get up, Eleks," Gran said. "You look silly."

He raised his eyes to me. I felt a strange regard from him, something that stroked across the stolen powers in me. I realized he had his own measure of wizardry, one that looked deeper than normal people could.

He rose. "Please come to court, Lady Omara, Lady Kishi. We have many matters to sort out today."

"I haven't finished my porridge," Gran said.

He flushed and glanced at our bowls. "I beg your pardon." He stood and waited while we finished eating, then led us to the courtroom.

Two seats sat to the right of the king's throne where only Gran's had been before. The king seated me beside him, and then helped Gran to the second seat. She gazed out over the court with an unthinking smile.

I looked at the courtroom from the dais, a perspective I had never had before. The doors to the outer room stood open. A crowd pressed tight in the outer room, fidgeting, restless. The first three sets of petitioners waited in the courtroom, flanked by guards in case arguments grew heated, and advocates to help them state their cases.

"Let us hear the first matter," said the king.

The bailiff led two men forward, both claiming the same pig, one because it was born from his sow, and the other because it had fed from his garden.

When we had heard the arguments on both sides, the king turned to me.

This was not a dispute that required wizardry to resolve. I understood it was a test.

One of the new trees in my inner forest dropped a fruit into my mouth. I bit it. The taste of it murmured to the king: "Let them sell the pig. One fifth of the price goes to the man who provided the seed, and four fifths to the man who provided the fruit that built its body."

The voice that came from my mouth was Gran's, the words couched in my husband's idiom, the judgment mine. I closed my eyes, contemplating my internal mix. A touch on the back of my hand came from the king, who turned and spoke my judgment in a voice that could be heard by everyone in the room.

A touch on my other hand came from Gran. Her hand rested on mine, light and cool, without gripping, but without censure.

I opened my eyes and looked at my new future.

MISERY AND WOE
by Jean Rabe

Jean Rabe is the author of more than a dozen fantasy novels, and three dozen fantasy, science fiction, and military short stories. Her latest novels include *The Finest Creation* and *Lake of Death*. She is an avid, but lousy, gardener; a goldfish fancier who loves to sit by her pond in the summer; and a movie-goer . . . if the movie in question "blows up real good!" Visit her Web site at www.sff.net/people/jeanr.

WILLUM TRIED his best to look around the kitchen, glancing first at a pot dangling over the fire and simmering with something sweet, next at a cluttered shelf midway up a smooth earthen wall.

The shelf was brimming with stones and feathers. There were also a few unlit tapers on it, along with some odd-looking objects he didn't take time to register. He knew that the shelf served as the witch's altar to some goddess she'd mentioned on his first visit, and whose name he'd subsequently forgotten. Besides, there was nothing interesting enough up there to hold his attention.

Then he tried to study his fingernails, a scar on his thumb, the whorls in the kitchen tabletop against which he flattened his palms—all of it just to be polite. He was seated at the table, one he gave the witch last week as payment for a month's worth of mixtures of sage, ginger, and nettles to cure a cold, a sore throat, and other assorted ailments he didn't have. The village's carpenter, moments ago he had promised her two matching chairs as payment for his next several sessions and for whatever additional herbs he could coax from her today.

"Elspeth," he said, his gaze finally leaving the table and meeting her ice-blue eyes. He put on a doleful, pained expression. "I'm still feeling a bit untoward. My stomach gives me fits and keeps me up at night. Do you have something to quiet it and set me aright? So I can get some proper sleep?"

Before she could answer, his gaze dropped to her considerable bosom.

Elspeth Linn of Skarnhold Shire was more than well endowed.

And try as Willum might to look at her unblemished face or her beautiful hair or to glance about her immaculate kitchen, he couldn't long keep his eyes away from her cleavage.

She sat opposite Willum at the narrow table, the surface of which gleamed in the sunlight that came through the window. Studying him, she tried to determine if he truly had a malady and thereby decide what mixtures and poultices might best treat him.

"Is there a sharp pain, Willum?" Elspeth's voice showed her concern. "This pain in your stomach? Or is it a dull ache?"

He didn't answer, just continued to stare, his eyes widening.

"Does the pain spread up toward your neck? How long does a bout linger? Is it every night? Or just after evenings that end with big meals? After certain foods?"

It seemed he hadn't heard her.

"Willum?"

Perturbed by her visitor's fixation with her chest, she sucked in so deep an irate breath that she threatened the seams of her bodice. As a result, Willum's eyes grew wider still and a thin line of drool spilled over his lower lip.

"Or is it nothing at all that bothers you, Willum Smithson? Nothing but what rumbles 'round in your empty head each time you visit? Like always, you look as healthy as the village ox."

Again no answer.

"Willum." She repeated his name louder, then louder still. "Willum!"

"Huh?" He didn't lift his eyes. "So do you have something to ease my stomach, Elspeth?"

He didn't see her lips stretch into a threadlike line and her icy eyes narrow tetchily.

She rose and retreated to a cupboard at the back of the kitchen, one he had made for her, rummaging around amid the jars and pouches, measuring something into her hand and putting it in a small clay cup.

"Charcoal powder," she pronounced. "Just in case you really are feeling untoward. If you're not ill, neither will this bother you." She put some dried parsley into a small cloth packet and returned with both to the table. "The parsley should help settle you."

He looked up, his eyes not quite able to reach her face. "Charcoal?" He forced the word out through a mouth that had somehow gone dry. "I should eat charcoal?"

"Put it in something," she instructed. "Pudding, tea, soup. It will chase the toxins right out of your system and thereby ease your stomach problems so you can get proper sleep at night." And in the process likely get the scours, she added to herself.

She thrust the cup and packet at him and he shook his head to clear his senses.

"Thank you, Elspeth. Thank you mightily." Reluctantly, he got up and turned to leave. "If I have any other troubles, I can come to see you again? Next week?"

The witch opened her door each week on the middle day for the villagers to visit and seek her counsel and remedies. She made no exceptions to this rule and did her best to avoid them all other days, keeping to her garden and herself.

She nodded halfheartedly. "Of course, Willum. Next week on the middle day. And you'll bring those chairs?"

"Aye, Elspeth."

She was quick to close the door behind him.

Elspeth sighed. She had hoped this village would be different than the last one, and the one before that. She had hoped that the folks here would come to her for honest ailments and problems. Not just to . . . to . . . look.

"By the goddess!"

Oh, some did come to her when they were truthfully feeling ill, and for this she was grateful and quick to help. But most of the men who visited—and it was mostly men who did come to her door—were only interested in ogling her. She knew Willum only came to stare, and she knew she should turn him out. But he was a good carpenter, and she needed the chairs and another cabinet. And there was always the possibility he was ailing, and therefore her oath demanded she aid him.

A slight possibility. Very slight.

"By the goddess!" Elspeth hissed.

She wasn't a young woman anymore. It had been worse when she was, all the attention she got then from men of all ages, even boys. She turned the head of any man in her young years—when she was in the waxing time in the first aspect of the threefold goddess' energies. And she turned down one offer of marriage—or companionship—after another and another and another.

But she wasn't an old woman yet either. Not yet. She was a good stretch of time from that, she told herself. Matronly, she decided, on the lean edge of her middle years, only a few strands of gray weaving their way into her auburn mass of curls. No real wrinkles yet, just a sprinkling of faint lines around the edges of her eyes and at the corners of her mouth. And no one seemed to notice those imperfections, or had spied the one brown spot on the back of her left hand. Folks were always looking at her other . . . features.

"Maybe when I am an old woman and I sag. Maybe when I'm flat, then they'll pay more attention to what I say and brew and will look elsewhere about me. And maybe in the meantime I should look elsewhere for another home." She'd been in this village called Skarnhold Shire only a year. The place had caught her eye because it was nestled comfortably at the mouth of a low valley, the farmland spreading rich and away from it, a thick stream close and musical. All of it lovely. "Or maybe this time I'll stay for a long while and the ogling be damned. Stay until I'm old and flat. Be buried where I plant my herbs."

It was the nicest home she'd made for herself so far, occupying a cottage that had been abandoned when the old man who owned it died, buying it from the village in exchange for helping with their crops last spring. Last fall's harvest was impressive, and they begged her to stay and help again this year. It was a good feeling to be wanted.

Elspeth took in her kitchen. It was tidy and simple, with the table Willum had fashioned and two old chairs that matched an old table since turned into kindling. There were three large cupboards, one filled with dishes and pots, the others with herbs, roots, and various things she'd gathered for brews and infusions. And there was a high counter on which was neatly placed her athame, or spirit blade, the knife she used to prepare not only her magical and medicinal concoctions but her meals as well. There was a grinder for powdering roots, and a strainer for teas. And there was a soapstone mortar and pestle that she hoped to replace with a marble one when a traveling merchant who sold such things came through. Marble would serve better for crushing and bruising herbs. Her possessions were few enough that they could be carried on the back of a donkey or in a small cart—in the event she could no longer stomach the ogling.

But she was adding to her possessions each month. The carpenter, blacksmith, cobbler, and chandler were among the villagers trading her goods for spiritual sessions and medicines.

A light woolen blanket, festooned with an embroidered leafy design and used as payment from the village weaver, hung in a doorway that led to a small bedroom—where there was a heavier woolen blanket from the weaver and soft pillows from a man who kept fowl. Propped up against either side of the doorframe were twin brooms she'd fashioned herself. A lovely village and a lovely home. Lovely people—for the most part. Even Willum was tolerable, she decided.

"Wouldn't hurt to sweep again, I suppose." Elspeth started toward the brooms, but was stopped by a firm knock on her door.

"Elder Kendal." She greeted him with a smile.

He tipped his hat and nodded, stepping past her on bowed legs, clumsily striding to the table and sitting down.

"What can I do for you this afternoon, Elder? Does your wife know you're here? You know she disapproves of . . ."

He thrummed his fingers and made a show of settling in more comfortably.

"I've only come to you a handful of times since you moved into the village," he began, " 'cause of my wife's wishes. And 'cause the other elders think I'm being a fool consulting a kitchen witch. Not that they haven't consulted you themselves. Renald comes here often enough."

"I prefer hearth witch," Elspeth said as she took her place across from him. "Or hedge witch if you must."

"Kitchen witch," he repeated, taking a quick look around her kitchen before resting his eyes on her bosom. At least Elder Kendal occasionally raised his gaze to meet hers.

She crossed her arms in front of her, which only served to deepen the crease between her breasts and cause Elder Kendal to sharply suck in a breath. "All right, yes, I am considered a kitchen witch, as you say. The kitchen is, perhaps, the most basic approach to the craft."

Elder Kendal raised an eyebrow, perhaps out of interest in her talk.

Elspeth continued, happy for a chance to discuss her profession. "Food supports the circle of life, you see. A meal brings families together and nurtures them. Festivals are filled with food. Praying in advance of a meal is honoring the goddess. And in turn a rich harvest is seen as a gift from the goddess. In preparing food and spices, I work in rituals and direct positive energy. Community, health, food—these are things I devote my magic to."

"So, witch, can you tell me the future?" Elder Kendal met her gaze, then returned to his staring. "I'm getting up in the years, and I was wondering the other day just how long I might have left. Only curious, you understand."

She shook her head, a mix of disappointment and amusement flashing across her face. "You call me a kitchen witch, Elder Kendal, and then you ask me to look into your future? How can you possibly think that . . ."

"A witch is a witch, ain't it? 'Sides, I ain't got no

ailments today, kitchen witch. Wife ain't sick neither."
He looked into her eyes again, but only briefly. "Corn
and beans are in, and no weeds are showing yet. So I
ain't got no other reason to come see you 'cept to ask
about my future, how much of it I have left. An' I
know well enough that you'll be more than busy when
the sun starts going down. The fellas done with their
work and coming by here for herbs and the like and
a look at you before going home. So I figured I'd best
ask about my future now before you get busy."

Elspeth noticed his breathing was in time with hers,
and that his head bobbed slightly with the rise and
fall of her chest. "Elder Kendal . . ."

"I give you beans come harvest, you know that from
last year. Corn if you want it."

The air hissed between her teeth as she edged away
from the table and went to her altar shelf. She selected
two tapers and some incense, a small dish, and a pol-
ished piece of granite.

"A hearth witch isn't the sort of witch who stirs
cauldrons and casts spells, Elder Kendal. I use my
brooms for sweeping, not riding through the night
sky." She returned to the table and arranged the incense on the dish in a star-shaped pattern, set the
granite in front of her, and lit the two tapers. "I focus
on the kitchen and home. I do not perform banish-
ments or cast shielding spells. I have been known to
brew love potions, as that relates to family. But I cannot divine your future."

He pointed a calloused finger at the candles. "What
do you use those for?"

"Candle magic and color magic combined," Elspeth
replied. She scowled to note he hadn't looked her in
the eyes for a few minutes. "The white candle symbol-
izes purity and healing."

"Said I ain't sick."

"And the blue is water, peace, and tranquillity."

"So what do I need with peace and tranquillity? I got me enough of those things."

"Elder Kendal, I thought that since you are here, and since no one else has yet come to my door, I might try to sooth you. Chase your worries away, so to speak."

"Ain't got any worries," he said. "Got my corn and beans planted, I say. Left my nagging wife to her cleaning. Just was wondering about the future."

"I can't help you there."

"Some witch you are." He shook his head, his eyes only leaving her bosom for a moment, and that to give her a stern look. "A witch is a witch, or should be. Well, I suppose I'll come back next week and see if you can tell me the future then." He sat there for several moments, still staring, not saying anything else.

"Next week then," she said finally, sucking in another perturbed breath and again menacing her seams.

"Next week," He was slow to rise and slower to the door. A tip of the hat and a nod. "You think about my future in the meantime. All right?"

Elspeth didn't quite get the door closed behind him before there was another rapping. This time insistent and soft. She stepped back to admit her next visitor.

"Anna Cla . . ."

"You . . . you . . . witch!" The retort came from a comely young woman in a well-worn skirt and peasant blouse. She and her clothes were clean and smelled of lilacs, and there was a hint of rouge on her cheeks. A spot of flour on her arm and a trace of cinnamon indicated she'd been baking. Her dark eyes danced angrily. "Witch!"

Elspeth opened her mouth to say, *Yes, I am a witch, and you well know that* but thought better of it. She simply regarded the young woman, breathing quickly in her ire, balled fists set against her narrow hips.

"Witch. Witch. Witch."

"Anna . . ." Elspeth slid to the side and opened the door all the way. She gestured to her table. "Would you like to come in and talk about what is troubling you?"

The red spread from Anna's cheeks to the rest of her face. "You're what's troubling me, witch. Troubling me and Dela and Huberta and even Isamu. Poor Dela, I know her Willum was here a little while ago. I saw him coming out your door."

"I don't understand what you're upset about, Anna."

"Upset? Yes, I'm upset. You're what's troubling us—me and Huberta and Isamu, Dela especially. Look at that table Willum made you! You're troubling us fiercely. Have been for some months now. You and the twins."

"Twins?"

Anna thrust a finger at Elspeth's bosom. "The twins."

Elspeth looked down. Rising above the edge of her bodice, she had to admit her large breasts resembled the bald heads of infants suckling.

"The twins," Anna repeated, pointing with her finger again at each one. "Misery and Woe I call 'em. The twins. Misery and Woe." She made a huffing sound and tossed her head, her dark eyes wide and wild. "Our men visit you almost every week, getting potions and whatnots, claiming to feel sick, claiming we're sick and needing your herbs. But what they're really doing is just getting a look." Another huff, this one so loud it sounded like dry leaves shushing across the ground. "When you go to the market, they stare at you. When you tend your garden, they just happen to stroll by. It's not that the rest of us don't have what you have, witch. We just don't have near as much of it."

Elspeth stared slack-jawed at Anna's tirade. "I'm no threat to you."

"Threat? Misery and Woe there certainly are threatening our happy homes." She slammed her fists against her hips. Spittle flew from her mouth. "I've stayed quiet until now, just talking with Dela and Huberta and Isamu, cursing you. I've kept my tongue all these months. But last night my man was chattering in his sleep. I heard him say your name quite plainly."

"I'm sorry, Anna. I mean no . . ."

"I thought you kitchen witches were supposed to help families, not tear them apart. I thought . . ."

It was Elspeth's turn to be angry. "I've caused no trouble here. I've nurtured the fields with my spells. I've healed the sick. I've . . ."

"Drawn the attention of our men, who bring you the bread we bake and who make furniture for you, who repair your roof . . . who come by to get a good, close look at Misery and Woe." Anna made another huffing sound. She balled her fists so tight her knuckles turned white. "You and the twins aren't welcome here. Not welcome by me or Dela or Isamu or Huberta. Not welcome by other women either, I'm certain. You threaten our homes. You and the twins threaten this entire village, you . . . you . . . witch! And you haven't heard the last from me."

With that, Anna spun and nearly bumped into the chandler, who was striding up the walk, bundle of candles in hand.

"No," Anna said, as she stomped off. "You and the twins haven't heard the last."

For an instant, Elspeth considered packing up and leaving this very day. But only for an instant. To give in when she'd done nothing wrong would not be honoring her craft. This village was lovely. Her home was lovely. The candles Ordney was thrusting at her were lovely and scented with vanilla. She liked it here.

Witches were persecuted elsewhere, Elspeth knew.

It seemed to be part of their lot in life. People were suspicious and fearful of them, wary of the magic, and hounding them because they were not of the same cloth as a commoner. Persecution was rife. But she suspected few were victimized because of being so well endowed.

"And what can I do for you today, Ordney?" Elspeth accepted the candles and gestured to her table. "Oh!" Her breath caught when she noticed the still-burning tapers. The white was burning properly, little of the wax had melted, and the candle was straight. But the blue had burned down far more than it should have in the scant time, and it was bent and twisted like a gnarled tree branch.

"Looks like you needed these new candles," Ordney said. "Never seen one of 'em burn quite like that. Odd."

"Indeed," Elspeth hushed.

That night she studied the remains of the twisted blue candle. It was an omen of some sort, she decided. Water, peace, tranquillity—that's what blue stood for. And candle magic? In general, to Elspeth, it represented the power of fire. A candle could burn away bad influences and could release positive energy. The chandler used beeswax, the finest kind.

"A bad omen to be certain," she pronounced. "Perhaps Anna's tirade shattered the tranquillity and so ruined the candle."

Elspeth selected the broom to the right of the doorframe. It wasn't used for sweeping dust and catching spiderwebs. The other broom served that purpose. This broom was blessed during its making, and she used it to sweep out the negative energy that collected in her kitchen. And there was always some trace of negative energy on the middle day of the week when the villagers came to call. The residue of their problems—when they actually had problems—gathered under her table and settled in. She swept them out.

Tonight she swept the floor again and again, getting into every corner and into every crack. Then she swept one more time, her arms heavy and tired from the task.

"Perhaps it was Anna," she mused, as she climbed into bed and pulled up the cover. Her head relaxed into a thick goose-down pillow. "Perhaps she brought so much dreadful energy to my home that she indeed ruined the candle and disturbed my peace."

In the morning, Elspeth lit another blue candle and watched it burn. Next to it she lit a green one, for luck, and again a white one for healing and harmony and protection. Within moments the blue candle twisted.

"By the goddess!"

She added a yellow taper that symbolized clairvoyance. And as the blue continued to burn unevenly, she stared at the yellow's flame. Perhaps she *could* look into the future as Elder Kendal intimated. Other witches could, and in her earliest days in the craft she'd studied under a matron who had such ability and tried to teach Elspeth the same. But at the time Elspeth was interested in other things and was determined to specialize in hearth magic.

The flame grew brighter as she placed her thumbs against the base of the taper.

"Does something threaten the peace and tranquillity of this village? A force other than jealous Anna Clayborn?" She edged closer to the candle until her face became warm. A trickle of sweat rolled down her cheek. But she saw only the fire and felt only the increasing warmth.

The blue candle she lit the following day also warped. And another yellow taper provided no clue that she could discern.

*   *   *

Twice more before spring ended Anna came on the middle day to complain about the twins and to spout her wrath. Perhaps in response Elspeth worked in her gardens in the early morning, wearing filmy skirts and blouses with skimpy bodices, bent over in her weeding so she was facing Anna's house. On more than one morning Elspeth caught the young woman staring angrily at her. Elspeth offered a friendly wave.

In the spring afternoons, save on the middle days when she accepted villagers into her kitchen, she strolled through the market in her finest clothes, hair tied up with ribbons to show off her neck. Sometimes she saw Anna and Isamu there, glaring at her. The men never glared. Stared, yes, and with either smiles on their careworn faces or mouths hanging open in appreciation. She talked to none of them, save the few vendors with whom she dealt.

There'd been little rain throughout the spring, and so early evenings found Elspeth and her handcart at the creek, filling ceramic bowls and jugs so she could water her herbs. Some of the farmers also gathered water, and most of these did so at the same time of day as Elspeth. Ogling her as they toiled. But the majority of the village farmers had fields too large to be helped by a few jugs of water.

Elspeth's herbs were growing, though not as vibrantly as they had the previous year.

It was the beginning of summer and the days were hot, almost fiery.

When was the last time it had rained? she wondered. The herbs weren't getting enough water. The water she drew up from the stream wasn't sufficient. The farmers' crops were doing no better, and the men were coming to her on the middle days seeking remedies while still seeking to stare at her cleavage.

Water, Elspeth thought.

The blue candle represented water. The tapers had twisted months ago trying to tell her something, to show her a future with no rain and a dying stream. Elspeth's eyes flew wide. When she was at the stream last night, she noticed how it had been shrinking away from its banks. It was no longer the thick creek that made music. It was struggling. Like the crops were struggling.

"Blind," she cursed at herself. "The candle was trying to tell me something months ago. Warn me. Elder Kendal asking about the future . . . the goddess was speaking through him, trying to warn me of the dry weather to come."

She paced in the kitchen, her long skirt sweeping the floor. "I could have advised the farmers to plant differently, to draw water from the stream and hold it in barrels for the drought. To conserve their food, to pray to the goddess for rain. I could have done things differently. I should have . . ."

There was a knocking on her door. It wasn't the middle day, but Elspeth answered it nonetheless.

"Anna."

"He talked about you in his sleep again last night." The young woman thrust her finger at Elspeth's bosom. "You and the twins aren't welcome here, I say. Misery and Woe and . . ."

Elspeth brushed by her and hurried down the walk, heading straight toward Elder Kendal's. "There's still time to conserve," she said. "If we all work together, we can save the crops and get through this. We can . . ."

"How dare you ignore me!" Anna sputtered. She caught up to Elspeth and shook her finger wildly. "How rude!"

Elspeth sped up, leaving the younger woman puffing behind her and taunting the "twins."

"There's time, I know it," Elspeth told herself. "We'll take from the stream now, before it completely goes. Fill every container we have. Take mud from the bank and set it around the melon mounds and around the carrots. We can meet this challenge."

She vaguely registered the men staring at her as she went, eyes fixed on what they usually were fixed on, smiles on the faces of some, mouths hanging open on others. Her breath came ragged, and she was jeopardizing the lace on her bodice. She gleamed with a thin layer of sweat by the time she reached Kendal's.

He'd been smoothing at a rail on his porch and had seen her coming, strode forward on his bowed legs to keep her in the yard—where his wife wasn't. He beamed at her.

"Elder Kendal!"

"Kitchen witch! So good to see you. And what a surprise. It's not a middle day. I don't think you've ever . . ."

"I need to talk to you, Elder."

He looked into her eyes for a moment before dropping his gaze. His breathing matched hers, and his head gently bobbed up and down in time with her heaving breasts.

"Elder, you asked me to look into the future."

"That was months ago." There was a trace of drool at the corner of his mouth. "Thought you said you weren't a diviner. Thought you said a witch wasn't a witch."

She tried to calm herself and slow her breathing. Elder Kendal's head bobbed slower in response.

"I am a . . ."

"Kitchen witch. Yeah, I know. Glad you came for a visit. Want to sit on the porch?"

She shook her head. "This weather."

"Hot, ain't it? Burning my beans. I ain't faulting you for it. You can't make it rain."

"No," she admitted. "But about the future."

He raised an eyebrow, perhaps a reaction to her comment.

"It seems I can tell enough of the future to know that this drought is going to continue for some time. The stream is going to dry up. It's just a matter of days perhaps. We need to take water from it, while it's still running. We need to . . ." Her words trailed off. "Elder Kendal, are you listening to me?"

He nodded, eyes still fixed, drool more noticeable.

"You need to speak with the rest of the elders, and all the farmers in the village. Hold a meeting. I'll be happy to talk and explain what we must do."

Another nod.

"So you'll set up this meeting?"

Elder Kendal stroked his chin. "Don't see where's we need one. Sometimes this happens, kitchen witch, this lack of rain. It's the valley, you know. The mountains stop the wind and rain on either side. Sometimes. We'll get past it. We always do. Nothing for you to worry about. Hey, maybe you need to light one of those blue candles for yourself, get you some peace and tranquillity."

Elspeth drew in a deep breath, preparing to repeat her request.

Elder Kendal's eyes swelled.

"Jon! Jon Kendal you come inside this very minute!" This came from Elder Kendal's wife, who was standing in the frame of the front door, nearly filling the space. Her eyes were daggers aimed at Elspeth. "Jon! You get away from that witch. It's not a middle day, and you've chores to tend to. D'ya hear me? You get away from that witch and the . . ."

Twins, Elspeth knew she was going to say. Misery

and Woe. So Anna's wagging tongue had made its way around the entire village.

Elder Kendal took a last look at Elspeth, before shrugging and turning toward his wife. His shoulders stooped as he shuffled toward the cottage.

"Think about a village meeting. Please," Elspeth said. Her voice was thick with urgency, but she doubted it registered on Elder Kendal.

Then he was swallowed by the shadows in the cottage, and his wife firmly closed the door behind him.

Elspeth visited the other village elders, and Willum and the chandler. At each stop she explained that the drought would continue—perhaps throughout Lammas, or Lughnasadh, the witch festival of the First Fruits, the First of the Three Harvests.

"There might not be a harvest," she told Willum, who couldn't seem to raise his head high enough to look her in the eyes. "This drought could wipe everything out and seriously cripple this village." *This lovely village in this lovely valley.*

Willum mumbled that he'd be sure to tell his farmer friends. And would she like another shelf in her kitchen . . . in exchange for some herbs to help his achy joints?

The chandler and weaver paid her insufficient heed, though both were elated by her visit. The fowl tender offered her a goose-down quilt come the fall, as trade for some oils for his hands and a potion or two. It seemed he "didn't quite catch" what she was trying to say about this unforgiving summer.

At last she stopped by Anna Clayborn's cottage. She hoped to find both Anna and her husband at home. But there was only irate finger-pointing Anna.

"So the witch and her twins have come to pay me a visit. You've been stepping up on the stoops of everyone else, why should I be left out, eh? Well, I'll not invite you in. Misery and Woe have no place in my home, I say!"

Elspeth squared her shoulders, inadvertently better displaying her chest and causing something worse than anger to scud across Anna's face. "I need your help, Anna Clayborn." Before Anna could offer a retort, Elspeth continued. "This summer is fierce and will get no better. The stream is dying and there is no rain. This village needs its crops, and they are withering in the fields. I need your help. People listen to you. The goddess knows you have every woman in town referring to my . . ."

"Twins," Anna hissed.

"Yes, my . . ."

"Misery and Woe."

"They listen to you, Anna, the people of this village. They hang on your wagging tongue, it seems. We need to gather water. We need to take the mud on the banks. We need . . ."

"You need to leave my property, witch. Misery and Woe have no place here."

The summer grew hotter and the grass around the village cottages became dry and brittle. Elspeth's herb garden was barely surviving, and yet it was faring better than the crops in the fields. The witch had gathered water, as she'd begged the townsfolk to do . . . and as she repeatedly told each man to do who came to visit her on the middle day.

It was past the time of the first harvest. Lammas had passed and there were no crops to cull. There were only stumpy dry cornstalks and withered bean shoots. The villagers were living by slaughtering the sheep and cows. All the geese were gone, their meat dried and spiced to serve in the coming desperate months.

Elspeth feared there might not be enough meat to

take them through the winter. She would be all right, as she'd started putting things aside when she realized the drought would continue. But the others were only now starting to plan ahead. And it could well be too late.

"Misery and Woe you've brought upon us," Anna told her again one day. "The men cared only about watching you, mouths all agape. They didn't pay enough attention to the weather and the fields. It's 'cause of you we're suffering so!"

That night, the thatched roof of Elspeth's cottage caught fire.

In her heart, the witch knew it was Anna's doing, the young woman's desire strong enough to drive her out of the village. But there'd been no wisdom in the gesture, only anger. And like the flame of Elspeth's red candle, the one that by its color symbolized fire and energy, the blaze grew.

With everything so dry, the fire spread down the walls and leaped to the quilts and blankets the weaver and fowl keeper had given her. Elspeth managed to grab her mortar and pestle, a change of clothes and a few jars of herbs. These and a lone blue taper she threw in her handcart and started away from the village.

This lovely village, she thought. *This lovely valley.*

The fire spread from her cottage, an angry red beast racing across the brittle grass to the next cottage and the next. The flames danced up barns and across fences. And from a distance Elspeth watched. There was no water to put it out, and a breeze had picked up to aid the conflagration.

"Misery and Woe you brought upon yourselves," she said, as she finally glanced away and looked to the south. There would be another village where she could make her home. And then another and another after that.

She'd settle for good, she decided, "when I am old and flat." She breathed deep, threatening the threads in her tight blouse. The air was hot and filled with the smells of Skarnhold Shire. "When I am flat, then they will listen."

IN SIGHT
by Charles de Lint

Charles de Lint is a full-time writer and musician who presently makes his home in Ottawa, Canada, with his wife MaryAnn Harris, an artist and musician. His most recent books are *The Blue Girl*, *Medicine Road*, and *Spirits in the Wires*. Other recent publications include the collections *Waifs & Strays* and *Tapping the Dream Tree*, and *A Circle of Cats*, a picture book illustrated by Charles Vess. For more information about his work, visit his Web site at www.charlesdelint.com.

I DON'T KNOW WHEN it was that people first started dropping into the Rainbow Tavern Grill after their gigs. They've been doing it for longer than I've been in the biz, and I've been making music since the late seventies, when "folk" was a four-letter word in more ways than one. Around two AM, when the late night crowd starts to drift in, Stan shuts off the outside lights and the place is officially closed for business. He keeps the kitchen open, and he'll still serve beer and drinks, but the alcohol's all on a tab now. You can't pay until regular business hours.

If it ever went to court, I guess it would be a fine point for the lawyers to argue, but until someone lodges a complaint, the cops leave Stan alone. They know he's not running some speakeasy. After hours at the Rainbow really is a social club. No one gets too drunk and there aren't any fights, though I've seen feuding couples shoot looks that could kill across the room.

If you don't have a gig, and your apartment's getting

to feel claustro, the Rainbow's a great place to just hang out at any time. People bring instruments and sit in the booths or around the tables and swap songs. I've seen it used as a rehearsal hall during the day, and sometimes in the evening a band'll set up their whole kit and jam with whoever wants to sit in.

So it can get a little noisy, but in a musical way, and with everything nearby closed at six, there's no one to bother. And sure there's a pecking order—all you need is three or more people together and social politics take over—but here, it's not such a big deal. The Rainbow's a cool place to hang, but it's also a bit of a dive, so there aren't too many of the really big egos coming out to be seen. What's the point? It'll only be other musicians and it takes more than a record deal or a hit song to impress most of us. And besides, it's big enough inside so that if you don't like what's going down on one side of the room, you can just find a seat on the other.

I spend a lot of time here—more than I should, maybe, but it's a way to get out of my apartment and be social without actually have to participate much if I don't want to. Company without obligations.

I had a gig at the Casement tonight, which is why I'm here early. Rubin always starts his shows right at eight with an open mike—three performers, each gets fifteen minutes—then the headliner's on at nine. By eleven you're packing your gear, collecting your check from Rubin or his sister Justine, and you can be on your way home. Or do like I did and come by the Rainbow.

There was a girl at the open mike tonight that I took a shine to. I invited her to meet me here after the show and since she stayed through both my sets, I figured she was coming. But by the time I got packed up and paid, she was gone. I chalked it up to the

usual: I'm never the person people think I'm going
to be.

There's something about a black woman playing
folk music that just doesn't make sense for most people. At least not the kind of folk music I play. There
aren't any blues, or soul, or R&B influences. No Afri-
can rhythms or hip-hop street cred. There's just me
and my guitar, doing our Joni Mitchell thing.

I've had criticisms leveled at me—usually in reviews,
but sometimes in person—about how I shouldn't be
ignoring my heritage, but I don't know what that's
supposed to mean. Growing up, I never knew anything
about the projects or the streets. Woodforest was a
mostly white, middle-class suburb. Maybe I was lucky,
or maybe I just had real people as neighbors, but I
never had any personal experience with racism until I
moved to the city.

I grew up listening to people like Joan Baez and Judy
Collins and Joni Mitchell—hell, I wanted to be Joni
Mitchell. When I started to play guitar, I wasn't looking
to learn Bessie Smith's blues riffs or those soulful rendi-
tions of old folk and blues songs that Odetta does. I was
trying to figure out Joni's weird tunings.

But people see a black woman with an acoustic guitar and they figure they already know what I'm all
about. Even my name works against me. Ruthie Blue.
Right off, they're thinking twelve-bars. It was hard at
first, let me tell you. But later on, Tracy Chapman
opened a lot of doors in the folk field for people like
me—just like Charlie Pride did in the country field—
but you still didn't see many blacks just playing folk
music. And now . . . well, somehow I missed the boat
on the whole Lilith Fair phenom. So I do what I've
done all along: work at the library four days a week,
play around town on the weekends, and make the odd
self-produced low-fi recording to sell at shows.

I'm not complaining. Maybe I never hit the big time—I came close, just before the seventies ended, which gets me a footnote in the history books—but at least I'm still getting gigs and people will pay to see me. And with the Internet, my CD sales are up. If I had the nerve to quit my day job, I could probably get by on a low scale tour. I've seen it work for others, using their Web sites to build up the interest for the actual gigs, even if most of them would be house concerts. If I was doing it, I know it would be under the media radar—like pretty much anyone who doesn't sing with *American Idol* pyrotechnics—but I could maybe make a living.

Except I don't have the nerve, so I play it safe. Not so much in what I write—I'm always trying to push the boundaries with my music—but definitely in how I live my life. It's a young person's game, anyway. I'm in my mid-forties now and unless menopause sends me spinning out of control the way it has some of my friends, I'll be doing this for pretty much as long as I can. And you know what? It's not so bad being a medium-size fish in a small pond. When I play in the Newford area, I get the headline gigs.

I glance at my watch and decide to stay a little longer, so I go to the bar, get another Corona from Stan, then return to my booth. It's not busy yet, so no one's complaining about me taking up this much prime real estate. Later on, I'll be sharing the booth—if I stay after this beer. I haven't decided yet. It's a slow night. Someone's playing with a keyboard at a table by the door—got a funky little rhythm going, pulled from the on-board styles and he's trading sampled trumpet riffs with a girl picking a beautiful Archtop Gibson. It's so quiet I can hear every note.

I look out the window, my foot tapping to the music.

It's too bad Tina didn't show. That was the blonde

at Rubin's open mike tonight—Tina Wallace. A tiny little thing with the kind of translucent white skin that'll never take a tan. She was sitting at a table by herself, guitar at her feet, when I got to the Casement for my gig. I checked in with Rubin, talked with Billy the soundman, and did a quick soundcheck—that's a luxury the headliner gets; the opening acts get their sound adjusted through their first song, though it's not as bad it sounds. Billy's aces with his board, and really, how hard is it to get a good mix on a guitar and a voice in a room you probably know better than your own apartment? Because I swear Billy lives in the Casement.

I had time to kill after my soundcheck, so I went and sat down with Tina because she looked a little lost and nervous and I can still remember how that feels.

"Are you playing tonight?" I asked.

She nodded. "They tell me I was lucky to get on the list."

"You were," I told her. "This is a good place to showcase your stuff. You never know who's going to show up." I waited a beat, then added, "Belinda Samms got her start here."

Everybody knows Belinda now, thanks to her getting songs on a couple of good soundtracks which she's managed to parlay into a more than decent career. But back then she was just another young songwriter starting out, trying to downplay a bad case of the jitters.

Tina smiled and introduced herself before asking, "So are there any big shot Hollywood directors in the house tonight?"

"Not that I can see. Just folks with a love for acoustic music. Don't worry about playing for them. The Casement gets crowds that are big on supporting anybody who shows she's serious about what she's doing."

"I don't know if that makes me more nervous or

less," Tina said. "I'm used to playing in bars where nobody's really listening."

"Around here?"

She shook her head. "Mostly up the line. I'm from Hazard originally, but we moved to Tyson when I was twelve."

Which meant she'd played the county seat and pretty much every little town between it and Newford.

We talked some more, me working at putting her at her ease, her grateful for the distraction from her nervousness, though, once she played, I didn't see what she had to be nervous about. She had a big voice—I mean a *big* voice—and played her guitar like she'd been born with it in her hand.

The funny thing was, looking at the two of us, she should have been doing my material and I should have been doing hers—if somebody was into stereotypes, that is. Because her music was nothing like mine. It wasn't quite like anything I'd heard before: a kind of funky hip-hop folk, liberally spiced with jazz chords and happy ska beats. The verses were spoken rhymes, the choruses these seriously hooky melodies, like something from an old Motown record.

She had a sound and she was going far, and I told her as much after her fifteen minute set. I felt sorry for the guy who was up after her—she was a hard act to follow. Truth is, I felt a little sorry for myself, because while the new guy was playing, bits and pieces of her songs were still stuck in my head, the hooks were that good.

I'd already told her about the Rainbow, and I repeated it before I got up to do my first set. She told me she'd come by—all she had was a room at the Y to go back to tonight—but like I said, by the time I was ready to leave the Casement, she was gone and now I'm sitting here by myself with a half-empty bottle of Corona for company.

I'm just trying to decide whether to get myself another beer or go home, when Tina slides her guitar into the booth, and then follows suit herself.

"Hey," she says and smiles.

Just that, with no word of explanation, but then I guess we don't know each other well enough for one to be needed.

"Hey, yourself," I tell her. "You want a beer?"

"Sure. But let me get this round."

Before I can say anything, she fetches a couple of Coronas from Stan and brings them back to the booth. She pushes one of the beers across to me, the bottle leaving a streak of condensation behind it.

"So tell me," she says. "Were you coming on to me back at the Casement, or were you just being friendly to someone who looked way out of place?"

Was that the reason she took so long to show up?

I decide to focus on the last part of what she said.

"You didn't look out of place," I tell her. "Any venue that offers up great music, that's where you belong."

She takes a pull from her Corona, but doesn't say anything.

"And I'm not gay," I add.

I get the sense that wasn't the answer she was hoping to hear.

"So you're just nice," she says.

I shrug. "You looked like you needed a little encouragement, though, like I told you, after hearing you play, I don't know why."

"Oh, I needed it," she tells me. "The idea of opening for you . . . I was sure I'd get up there and not remember a single word or even how to play my guitar."

"Now you're being a shameless flatterer."

Not to mention a little flirty.

I'm surprised to find that I kind of like it, but maybe

that's because I haven't been out with a guy for a couple of months. I know, musicians are all supposed to lead this wonderfully promiscuous life—in your dreams. For my part, I think the brothers don't know what to make of me, those that actually show up to hear me doing my introspective thing at the kinds of places I play, while the white boys . . . well, I'm guessing they're expecting someone hotter—you know, where it's all about the booty—and I disappoint them, too. I'm tall, black, and big enough in the right places, but I speak softly and I'm a conservative dresser. It must be the librarian in me, though some of my co-workers can party heartier than any clubber half their age.

"No, it's true," Tina says. "I have all your CDs."

I smile. "Even *The Bedroom Demos?*"

"That's one of my favorites. I love 'Valentino.' And that early version of 'Rock Czar' is way better than the one that came out later on *Pointed Interludes*. I think some of the tracks on that album were a little overproduced. You have such a beautiful voice and occasionally it got lost behind the synthesizers."

"It *was* the eighties," I say.

Though I have to admit I agree with her. It was an experiment I didn't repeat.

"Oh, I know. And I didn't mean to sound critical. I don't think you could write a bad song if you tried."

I have to shake my head. "Careful, you're edging into stalker territory."

But I smile to let her know I'm not serious and she smiles back.

"Did you ever think that people were supposed to meet?" she asks.

I'm about to reconsider the stalker angle, but I give her the benefit of the doubt. After all, I'm the one who invited her to meet me here.

"I'm not sure what you mean," I say.

"Well, back at the Casement. I really *was* nervous. It was getting so bad I actually considered leaving before it was time for me to go up on stage. But then you came over and talked to me and all my nervousness went away. You'd never even heard of me before, but you were still so supportive."

"Well, I'm not into being competitive. And seriously, the people who come to a venue like the Casement, they're rooting for you. They want you to be good. Some of the people only show up for the open stage segment, looking to run across their next personal discovery."

Tina grinned. "I know. While you were packing up, this A&R guy from a local label came up and gave me his card. He wants to meet with me tomorrow." Her grin widened. "I can't believe I just got to say 'meet with me' and it wasn't a joke."

"That's terrific news," I tell her. "And having heard you, I'm not surprised."

And I have to admit, if only to myself, that I'm pleased that it was something so important that had her arriving late. It's getting to the point where you can't much count on anybody—though I suppose that's asking a lot from a total stranger. Call me old-fashioned, but I just think you should do what you say you will, no matter who you're talking to. If you're going to blow somebody off, don't tell them you're going to show up.

"But see," Tina's saying. "That's what I mean. If you hadn't taken the time to encourage me, I might have left and it never would have happened."

"Don't make more of it than it was. Any serious interest you get in your music is because of what you're putting into it, not because of anybody else."

She shakes her head. "No, I think everything we do depends on the people around us. How we connect to where we are and who we're with."

"Well, I hope it works out for you—your meeting tomorrow."

"Me, too."

She cocks her head, then asks the really hard question that I can't answer to other people's satisfaction, never mind my own.

"You were kind of a star on the rise at one point," she says.

I have to smile to myself. When she was in diapers.

"So why did you put your career on hold?"

"I didn't. I just redefined my priorities."

"You didn't like touring? Because I love the idea of going to new places, meeting new people."

"It has a surface appeal," I tell her, "but it didn't click for me. I could get the gigs—small, but steady—and I did do some touring in the late seventies, early eighties. Maybe it's different now, but I didn't enjoy it at the time. It's hard enough being a woman alone on the road, without being black as well. I guess I had a sheltered childhood because being black was never a problem growing up. Moving downtown from the suburbs was when I got my first inkling of how it could be, and later, when I did travel . . ." I shrug. "I just had too many bad experiences."

"That sucks."

"And now I'm too set in my ways. I like working at the library and my cat would hate me if I abandoned him to go touring."

"What kind of cat?"

"A very needy one."

I smile, thinking of Crosby. Right now he'll be perched in the front window of my ground floor apartment, studying the street for me to come home. These days he's the only man in my life.

"What would make you happy?" Tina asks.

I just look at her. I wonder if the way she jumps around in a conversation is some particular facet of her personality, or just comes from her youthful energy—she's part of the generation that grew up with the five-second soundbite, after all.

"World peace," I say.

It's always a safe answer.

"No, I mean, you personally."

"Where are you going with this?" I have to ask her.

"Well, it's just that you know how in fairy tales people are always being rewarded for their selfless kind acts, so I was just wondering, if you could have anything, what would it be?"

"I don't want any reward and I really didn't do anything."

"But that's the beauty of it. It doesn't come because you want it, or expect it. It's because you did something kind—because that's just the sort of person you are. So you help the old lady, or the talking spoon, and the next thing you know, they're turning straw into gold for you, or teaching you the language of birds."

"I take back what I said about your going far," I tell her, smiling. "I just don't see much of a future for a girl who thinks she's a piece of cutlery."

She laughs. "I know, I know. It all sounds silly, but work with me here. What would you wish for if you could?"

"Now you're a genie offering me a wish?"

"It's not about me granting wishes. It's just what my gran taught me, how you have to articulate things and put them out into the universe to give them the chance to happen."

"And now I feel like I'm trapped in the New Age section of the library."

"Come on," she says. "Humor me."

"Okay. If I could have anything I wanted? I guess it'd be to write a song that'll still be around long after I'm gone."

"You've already done that," she says.

She starts listing songs, counting them on the fingers of one hand. The funny thing is, all the ones she picks are among my own favorites.

"Try again," she tells me.

I don't say anything for a long moment.

Did this ever happen to you? You're still in high school, or maybe you're at college, and people start talking about whether or not you have a soul. Then somebody pulls out a twenty, lays it on the table, and offers to buy the soul of whoever's protesting loudest that we don't have one.

Nine out of ten times, they won't do it. They won't take the twenty to sell something they don't even believe they have in the first place, and you can't get them to tell you why, either. But I know. It's because their assurance in how the world works has suddenly been gripped by a niggling little "what if?" that they can't shake.

That's what happens to me, sitting across the table from Tina. Her eyes are so blue and serious, with just the hint of a twinkle. That humor isn't coming from her pulling a fast one on me. It's coming from a shared joke, even if she's the only one who gets it so far.

So I think about wishes.

What if, what if . . .

I think about impossible things that could be done. Or undone.

"When I was on the road," I finally say, "before I settled down here with my job at the library, I picked up this teenage hitchhiker. This was down south, in the early eighties. She was in pretty bad shape—not physically, so much, or at least not that I could see. But inside she was warring with demons. It was in her eyes, in the way her hands trembled where she had them folded on her lap.

"I asked her where I could take her and she wanted

to go home, but she said it in a way that told me it was the last place she wanted to be. I tried to talk her into letting me take her to a shelter instead, but she wasn't very responsive to the idea and I didn't try very hard. In the end I just drove her home and went off to my gig."

I can remember it like it happened this afternoon.

"What happened?" Tina asks.

"I got a room in a motel on the edge of town and went to play my gig. The next morning the TV's on while I'm getting ready to head back on the road and the face of my hitchhiker from the day before appears on the screen. She was shot by her brother, who also killed her sister and her mother, before turning the gun on himself."

Tina doesn't say anything for a long moment.

"So you'd go back and fix that?" she asks when I don't go on.

I shrug. "I don't know. How do you fix something like that? Yeah, it would have been great if I could have gotten her to a shelter, but her sister and mother would still have died."

"Then what would you do?"

"I'd like to know why—*really* know why—people do this kind of thing to one another and then figure out a way to stop it before they hurt themselves or anybody else." I hold her gaze. "Can you do that?"

It's a stupid question. Of course she can't. But she's put me in this funny mood where it feels like anything is possible. As though, if I can just say the right thing, she can make it happen.

She shakes her head. "No, I'm sorry. That's like world peace—too big an issue." Then she adds, "Why didn't you become a social worker instead of a librarian?"

"A librarian is a kind of social worker, sometimes," I tell her. "We have homeless people coming in. Kids needing a safe place. Lonely, messed-up people just looking for some kind of company because they don't get it anywhere else in their lives. And we do what we can while we go about our work. A kind word here. Maybe spot them a snack or a drink from the vending machine. Recommend books that'll maybe help them, or at least let them forget what's going on in their lives for a few hours."

"Books change everything," Tina sang softly, quoting from my song "These Books Do."

"They changed my life," I tell her.

"For me, it was music."

"Okay, books and music."

"But I know what you mean about libraries being safe places," she says. "I knew a girl back home who used it to get a breathing space. Her parents were awful to her and the kids on the street seemed to have made it their personal duty to torment her whenever they could. The library was the only place she could be okay."

"We get too many kids like that."

I look past her. The tavern's filling up. I recognize a lot of faces and nod when Sid, the bass player for this retro band called The Everlasting First, gives me a wave.

"I thought about social work," I go on, looking back at Tina, "But I didn't think I'd have the stamina for it. I'd just be part of the lives of too many people I couldn't help. *Really* help, I mean. So I write songs for them instead."

"That's what I'm talking about," Tina says.

I give her a puzzled look.

But instead of explaining, she asks, "What would you say if I told you that there are people who hold the gift of possibilities and that I'm one of them?"

"What do you mean?"

"If someone wants something enough, I can give them the possibility of making it happen."

"You mean like . . . magic?"

She shrugs. "You do it with your songs—is that magic? When a song changes somebody's life?"

"I guess . . ."

"So that's what I can do, except it's more direct. It's the face-to-face promise that it can and will happen. They just have to decide what it's going to be."

"So you just walk around giving people wishes?"

Now I'm wondering what kind of drugs she's on. I mean, she seems sweet, and I doubt she's dangerous, but, come on, really?

"Not exactly," she says. "They need to be worthy of the gift. It doesn't work on the big scale, and it's got to be about putting something good into the world. Also, I can't do it all the time. The ability to do it just comes and goes at its own whim. It kind of sleeps inside me until I meet the right person."

"I don't know, Tina. This sounds—"

"Crazy. I know. But you don't have to make up your mind right this moment. Just humor me and think about it."

"And when I decide, you'll know?"

She shakes her head. "No, you will." She leans her elbows on the table. "So tell me. What should I be looking out for when I talk to this guy tomorrow?"

It takes me a moment to shift gears. How can she be so spacey and so practical, basically at the same time?

"I think I need another beer," I tell her. "Do you want one?"

"Only if you promise to walk me back to the Y after, because I've already pretty much had my limit."

"We don't have to drink beer."

"I'll have a coffee, then—regular, not decaf."

"It doesn't keep you up?"

"Just the opposite. Caffeine calms me down."

I start to get up, but pause to say, "You can stay at my place if you like."

She raises her eyebrows.

"No, I'm still not gay."

"Too bad. You should try it."

I smile. "It's been long enough since I've been with a guy that I'm finding it hard to remember what it's like, but I'm definitely into them, no question."

She toasts me with her empty beer bottle.

"To whatever turns us on," she says.

"Let me get our beverages and I'll drink to that."

Later, Tina's curled up in the bed I've made up for her on my couch, sleeping the sleep of the innocent, while I'm lying awake in my own bed, staring at the ceiling. I don't have anything to feel guilty about—at least nothing that I know of—but any kind of sleep seems to be eluding me, innocent or otherwise.

Crosby jumps onto the bed and settles in beside me. I put my hand on him and rub the hair around his chin. His purr is loud in the quiet of my bedroom.

I think about something Tina said when our conversation briefly returned to this gift of possibilities business of hers.

"It's not what we know," she said. "It's how well we share it with each other."

She was talking about how communication gets so messed up between people because half the time we're talking different languages. The kindest thing can be misinterpreted. And instead of taking what people say at face value, we spend too much time trying to guess what we think they really mean.

It happens with songs all the time, which is both good and bad. It's great that a song can mean so many different things to different people. But sometimes the things they get out of a song are so diametrically opposed to the songwriter's intent it's like they're living on different planets.

Like this song I wrote about the confusion of staying in an abusive relationship, how the woman still has all this love mixed up with the hurt she's being dealt on a daily basis. It seemed pretty clear to me, and I worked hard to just tell it as a story, not a diatribe. And it touched a lot of people. But then I had a guy e-mail me, thanking me for writing a song that shows how screwed up women are and why sometimes they needed to be slapped around a little, just to knock a little sense into their heads.

I sit up against the headboard and Crosby makes a complaining sound, but quiets as soon as I start to stroke his fur again.

Think about it, Tina had said.

I don't know if she had this in mind when she said that, but it's what works for me. And it just goes to show you that wisdom doesn't necessarily come from the old wise woman, like some of the authors and singers I turn to for inspiration. It can also come from a twenty something kid who seems more suited to a career that will be lauded by MTV than the folk festival circuit.

Because if the gift of possibilities is real, then I want people to get exactly what I mean from what I say, whether it's in conversation or song. I want my communication to be clear.

I smile. Which is pretty much what everybody wants, isn't it? Everybody wants to be understood. Not to simply speak clearly—we all think we do that anyway—but to actually be understood.

And that would invest a person with so much responsibility. You'd always have to speak the truth. And if you couldn't, you'd have to keep your own counsel—which is something all of us should probably be doing anyway. Who needs to know what you think, if it's going to be hurtful? Maybe if you want to change some injustice, but it's not relevant in our day-to-day lives. Thumper's mother's advice—echoed by my own, when I was growing up—is always going to hold true.

Life's full of unhappiness and disappointment. It's so easy to be brokenhearted by the atrocities, the stupidity, the greed—all the things that fuel the endless litany of bad news that scrolls across the bottom of the screen on the news channel.

So, yeah, if you had a voice that was always going to be understood—and maybe even believed—it would be important to speak out about that. But it would also be important to *generate* some happiness, on however small a scale it happens to be. Even if that means shutting up at times.

I can do this, I think.

No, not that magic of being understood. That belongs in the fairy tales Tina was talking about earlier. But doing something more with my life. Using the communication tools I have to make the world a better place—not just in songs, but in my everyday life.

I realize this is something I've been struggling with for a while, I just wasn't able to articulate it to myself in a way that I could do something about it. I've been going through my days without direction, and I'm the kind of person who needs a direction if I'm going to do anything meaningful.

I wouldn't call it magic. It's just insight, which, when it clicks for you—when it finally does come *in sight*—feels like magic.

I get up from the bed, generating another cranky response from Crosby.

"I'll be right back," I tell him.

I know Tina's asleep, and I'm not planning to wake her, but I just want to . . . I don't know. Look at her, I suppose. Make sure she's real.

But the couch is empty. Her duffel bag is gone. Her guitar isn't by the door.

I know she didn't leave, because I would have heard her. And that means . . .

I guess I was expecting this all along.

Strangers don't come offering insight out of the blue. Not in real life. In real life we have to create that kind of a situation in our imagination.

It's funny. I don't think I'm crazy. But I am curious as to whether I generated the whole thing in my head, or if there was some modicum of truth in my having met her.

Did she play at the Casement, or did this little fantasy of mine start there?

If she did play the Casement, did she ever come to the tavern?

If she came to the tavern, did I walk her to the Y and leave her there?

I turn on my computer and Google her name. If she's real, if she's gigging around, she might have a Web site—everybody does, these days.

But the first link that comes up is about a tragic death last year in Tyson. I click on the link, but I don't read the story. I just look at the picture of the victim. It's Tina, with that blonde hair and those blue eyes of hers that seem to know so much, but haven't forgotten how to smile.

"Of all the people in the world," I ask the image on my computer screen, "why did you pick me?"

Though maybe she didn't just pick me. Maybe her spirit just goes around, randomly bringing a bit of fairy-tale wisdom into the lives of those she meets.

Bits and pieces from our conversation back at the tavern return to me:

Did you ever think that people were supposed to meet?

I'd never thought about it before, but I guess in this

case, she was right. I *needed* to meet her at this time of my life, to get me thinking about all of this.

And when I decide, you'll know? I'd asked her.

She'd shaken her head then, saying, *No, you will.*

And I do.

"Thank you," I tell the image.

Then I close the browser window, turn off my computer, and go back to bed. Tomorrow's the first day of the rest of your life, as the cliché goes.

But you know what? It's true.

And I'm going to make it count.

THE GIFT
by Jody Lynn Nye

Jody Lynn Nye lists her main career activity as "spoiling cats." She lives northwest of Chicago, with two of the above and her husband, author and packager Bill Fawcett. She has published thirty books, including six contemporary fantasies, four SF novels, four novels in collaboration with Anne McCaffrey, including *The Ship Who Won*; edited a humorous anthology about mothers, *Don't Forget Your Spacesuit, Dear!*; and written more than seventy short stories. Her latest books are *The Lady and the Tiger*, third in her Taylor's Ark series, and *Myth-Taken Identity*, cowritten with Robert Asprin.

"THE BEST GIFT is the one you give away," Demetra's mother had always told her. Anganeta was full of those funny adages. Demetra generally let them go in one pretty ear and out of the other. She far preferred receiving presents, like the fur robe that Haskel was presenting to her on bended knee.

"Accept this, lovely one," he pleaded. The steel-gray fur matched the flinty blue of his eyes and, she had to admit, went well with her own inky black flowing tresses. "I killed the mighty wolves with my own hands. The clasp is the purest gold and bears gems from my family's own mines." He spread it over her silk-draped lap and gazed upon her with adoration.

Demetra loved the tickle of the rich fur between her hands and smelled the musk that rose from it. "But it's spring," she complained, letting the pelts drop. "It's too warm to wear it."

Haskel looked crestfallen. For a moment he was

speechless. "Then keep it in case the nights grow cold. You will surely enjoy it when winter comes again."

Demetra laughed, flicking a slender hand. "Winter is so far away!" She bounded up and away to the window and leaned through it. In the distance was the faint sound of music. She held out her hand to the young man. "Come and dance! I can hear Father's musician piping in the meadow. It sounds wonderful, doesn't it?"

But Haskel's face had turned sulky. "You're heartless, Demetra."

"My, who left his manners at home!" Demetra exclaimed. She had passed into womanhood only a few months before, and suitors were beginning to appear beside her at public feasts and celebrations. She liked the way boys stared at her newly-formed breasts, small soft globes pressing against the fabric of her tunics. She liked the new sensations of her maturing body, wondering how as a child she had never suspected they existed. She knew her father hoped she would be drawn to Haskel. He was handsome and wealthy and sweet, most of the time, but he was so *dull,* only interested in hunting and the pleasures of the outdoors, while she loved music and dance and epic stories of gods, which made those new bodily sensations tingle. Haskel had come to ask her to the Festival of Maidens, a celebration to be held in the city agora that very evening, on the first new moon of spring. One more dull feast where she would end up giggling in a corner with her unbetrothed friends. But it would be better than spending the evening with a boy who had insulted her. "Me, heartless!"

"I am sorry," Haskel muttered, his tanned cheeks darkening to rosewood. "But you care not for my gift. You don't know how dangerous it was to pursue these beasts! And all through it I thought of you. I seek to please you, and you don't care."

"Just because I'm practical?" Demetra turned again. The music drew her like a spell. She must go and dance to it or explode! "It's spring. Can't you feel it in your bones?" He didn't reply. "Well, come along, or don't." She twirled past him, stopping only to muss up his sleek russet hair with careless fingers. She ran out of the room, heeding little whether he followed her or no.

The gentle breeze carried the melody to her, along with the gorgeous scent of blooming lilacs and lilies. Demetra adored lilies; their perfume overpowered all senses, defying one to look upon the day and not love it. She ran lightly toward the sound, enjoying the feel of her leaf-green chiton brushing her legs and the whisper of her thin sandals over the meadow grass. Away with winter clothes and winter sorrows!

She stood at the top of a gentle crest, peering around her for Paolos. Normally on a fine day he liked to sit in the herb garden overlooking the vineyards, but it was empty. Light, feminine laughter overwhelmed the music for a moment. Paolos was entertaining an audience. Who could it be?

Demetra followed the sound through the burgeoning vineyard to a dell that lay on a sunny slope on the other side.

"Paolos," she called, waving. But the brown-and-gray head that turned toward her was not Paolos. The upslanted eyes were more goatlike than the gentle old man's whose legs had failed him and whom Demetra's father now kept on to entertain the family. This man was much, much younger, with a wild beauty that Demetra envied. A tunic clung to one shoulder and draped down a muscular, tanned chest. He was a stranger. For a moment Demetra felt shy.

She would have studied him further, but her attention was drawn to the laughing girls swirling in a circle. Demetra knew them. One was her friend, Phoebe, who lived over the river, and many of the rest were serving girls and the children of farmers who worked for her father, Ganymedes, and her friend's father Otrius. At the moment no hint of the difference in class existed. Demetra could resist it no longer, and hurried to join the group.

"Demetra!" Phoebe shouted, holding out her hand to her friend. Another hand clasped her free hand, and drew Demetra into the circle. The steps the girls were doing were unfamiliar. Demetra felt clumsy at first, but the music seemed to cast a spell upon her feet. Within minutes she was laughing and stepping with the rest of them.

She turned to smile at the girl on her other side, and stumbled over her own feet. The maiden was the most beautiful woman Demetra had ever seen. Demetra thought her own hair was black, but this maiden's was blacker still, lit with malachite-green and lapis-blue glints. Her lips were rose-pink, and when they parted in laughter, as they often did, her teeth were as white as the snow that Demetra saw on the tops of mountains. At that moment the maiden noticed them, turning her gaze fully in their direction. A flash of her eyes made Demetra forget all else and run toward her. They were grass-green, and clear as pure water. In them, Demetra felt she could see the breadth of spring, of all things she worshiped. She wanted to be part of this girl's circle, to impress her somehow. She tried to let the music reclaim her, to dance better than any of the others. Hop, slide, step, slide—she put her left foot down directly on Phoebe's, tripping her into the girl on her other side. The beautiful maiden threw back her head and let out a peal of laughter. Demetra felt her cheeks grow hot.

"Who cares?" she muttered, letting go of the others' hands.

"Don't go," the girl said, catching at them. "We are just beginning. Don't take your beauty away from us."

Demetra stopped, astonished. Was the girl teasing her with such open flattery? But the clear green eyes were guileless. She allowed her hands to be recaptured, and the song began again. This time her feet found the rhythm. She skipped and twirled with the others. The music blended like an elusive perfume with the aroma of the flowering shrubs that dappled their beaming faces with shade. It was all so perfect. She was enjoying herself as never before in her life.

Suddenly, Demetra caught sight of a gloomy face. Haskel. He sat in the shadow of the trees, watching them, immune to the power of the music.

To her surprise, he was not alone. First she spotted a slender lad not much taller than a girl, with a pointed chin and a prominent forehead. He would be bald before he was twenty! He was watching the redhead across from Demetra, a half-Circassian slave whose father had been taken in battle when he was a boy. Then she recognized Stefanos, from a villa clear across the valley. His eyes were fixed upon Phoebe. Demetra was surprised. Stefanos had seemed immune to the charms of any girl. Did Phoebe know he was there? Did she care? In fact, in the brush were many young men, as many as one for each girl in the circle.

Haskel's cold blue eyes spun into view again. Demetra was so annoyed at his expression of disapproval that she decided to forget all about him. She threw herself into the dance with all her effort.

"Come, my sisters!" the black-haired girl called, pulling the whole circle with her toward a huge laurel bush as the sun began to tip toward the horizon. The tiny crescent moon, already up in the deep blue sky, glowed brilliant white. "Come share the joy!"

The group broke apart, tripping behind their hostess, laughing and hugging one another. Demetra and Phoebe embraced.

"I am so glad you found us," Phoebe said, as they collapsed onto a pale blue cloth spread on the grass. Bowls of fruit, cheeses, and loaves of fresh bread on platters awaited them. "I heard piping. I couldn't resist. I had no idea . . ."

"But who is she?" Demetra whispered. She ran her fingers over the rich weave beneath them. It was the softest fabric she had ever felt. No craftsman in Thessaloniki had such fine stuff for sale. Her father would never have denied it to her.

"I do not know," Phoebe replied. "But she is fun, isn't she? I don't even want to go to the festival tonight. I don't want this party to stop!"

"Neither do I." Demetra accepted a cup brimming with garnet-red wine from the smiling maiden. She nodded her thanks. "We won't go. We'll stay here."

"Isn't your father one of the hosts? He said he is bringing twenty lambs for the feast!"

"What of it?" Demetra replied. "He didn't ask me how I would like to spend my Festival. This is better."

"Sisters!" the hostess called to them, raising her own cup, a gold goblet chased with figures of fawns and lambs. "To youth!"

"To youth!" the girls echoed, and drank. The wine tasted finer than any other vintage Demetra had ever tasted. The warmth flowed along her throat and belly, then spread out to every part of her body, tickling and caressing nerve endings. She felt her face flush with pleasure.

The maiden refilled her cup and held it out to the ill-concealed men.

"Will all of you join us?" she asked. The boys stared at her, then glanced at one another uncomfortably. "It is not wise to refuse my invitation."

That brought a round of scoffing from the young

men. What could a mere girl do to warriors and hunters? Demetra felt the insult to her hostess.

"I wish I could beat you all until you cry for pity," Demetra exclaimed. "You arrogant rabbits!"

The boys laughed.

"Rabbits," the maiden said, with a wicked expression upon her fair face. "Now, that is a good notion." She stretched up her hand and plucked the new moon from the sky. She brought it down to her with a tail of stars dangling from one end.

Demetra fell to her knees. The other girls collapsed, some covering their eyes in fear. They were in the presence of a goddess.

"Who are you?" Demetra whispered.

"I am Youth," the maiden replied, with a quirk of her lips. "You should know. You ought not to fear me. You are one of my sisters who has come to join me here to celebrate the Festival of Maidens."

Hebe! Demetra let her lips form the name, but she could not produce any sound. The maiden straightened out the string of stars and affixed the free end to the other side of the crescent. She plucked the glistening string. It vibrated with a sound like a calling woodcock, and sparks flew from it.

"But the celebration is in town," Demetra managed, grasping the one ordinary fact she could.

"For those whose time is past," Hebe said, with a toss of her mane of hair. "I am sorry for them. You should be, too. We shall have the true celebration here! Make ready, girls!" she called out. Suddenly, Demetra found a bow and a quiver in her hands. "Our revelry is about to begin! We seek prey among the very heavens tonight!"

Hebe drew back the string of the bow, and suddenly there was a gleaming silver arrow in it. She aimed at the first boy, and let it loose. He gaped in astonishment as the silver bolt exploded in a shower of stars.

When the sparks cleared, he was still gaping, but the face was that of a hare. The others began to run away, but the merciless bolts, glistening with their own blue-white light, blazed their way through the woods and struck each fleeing shadow in turn.

"No!" Phoebe cried, as Stefanos dropped to four legs and began running.

"What do you care?" Hebe trilled, loosing another arrow. Her eyes gleamed with terrible power. "They are men! We shall make them pay for their scorn."

"That's right," Demetra cried, strangely excited. She put it down to the wine. "Let them run!"

Hebe took the lead, pursuing the leaping hares through the woods. Demetra hurtled down a slope behind a trio of white scuts barely visible in the gathering darkness, heedless of her fine skirts or her thin sandals. She seemed carried by an unseen force that prevented her from taking harm. No matter how far or fast she ran, she breathed easily, with no stitch forming in her side. So that was what it was to feel immortal!

The woods fell away at the bottom of the slope, near the stream, dappled with thin moonlight from the gleaming bow in Hebe's hands. The hares struck out across the water, their ears laid back against their heads. Demetra pelted them with an endless stream of arrows, never hitting one. She laughed to see them scramble up the slope on the other side. With her sisters, she bounded across the stream on pebbles no larger than her big toe and galloped upward after them. She was the fastest, and soon left the others behind her. The ground leveled into an open field, and the hares spread out across it. She sighted along the arrow on the string and let fly at the hare-that-had-been-Haskel. He jumped to one side at the last minute, and it struck the ground just behind him. Wily! Demetra laughed. The prey's elusive maneuvers only made her enjoy the chase more. She began to understand why Haskel liked hunting. Perhaps he was not so dull as she thought. In the meantime, she would teach him to call her heartless!

The wind picked up as the sun slipped below the horizon. It sleeked her hair back and plastered her dress against her body. It should have been cold, but Demetra drank it in like wine. The maiden's arrows were diamond-spangled comets, arching ahead of the hunters and lighting up the sky. Eight of them flicked out in rapid succession, one on top of the next like the rungs of a ladder. The hares ran upward along it as if the silver shafts were a flight of stairs. Demetra hesitated as she reached it in their wake. Would the fragile staves hold her? But Hebe ran ahead, her silver sandals twinkling. Demetra followed, determined to catch up with the hares.

As she made to step off the top arrow, she stopped, her breath caught in her chest. Nothing lay beneath her but air. The tops of the trees waved in the wind twenty or thirty feet below. Her heart pounded, closing her throat. Hebe ran on through the sky ahead, but she was a goddess. Demetra, a mere mortal, would fall to her death. She started to turn back. The other girls were climbing up after her.

"Hurry up!" Phoebe urged her.

"I can't," Demetra whispered.

"Come on!" Hebe called back to her. "Come ahead! Take the chance! You will be safe!"

Demetra had no choice but to hold her breath and leap out onto the void.

It held her! The footing was spongy, like running on moss, but it held her. She stood on the sky! Demetra shouldered her bow and leaped after Hebe, now fast disappearing into the night. She had no time to wonder at the miracle, when all around her were more miracles than she could ever have imagined.

Now that the sun was gone, the stars had come out to play. She had always seen the constellations as clusters of brilliant pinpoints on the sky. It took the imagination of one such as Paolos to show her the shapes they made and the stories about them, but now she saw them as he must, the lines filled in and colored like jewels. The Twins gamboled together high overhead between the snorting Bull and the furtive Crab. The Lion prowled, flicking his mighty tail. The Bears, both Great and Small, browsed among fields of smaller stars as earthbound beasts would root for something tasty in the grass. And striding along, upside down to her, was great Orion and his silver-coated hound Sirius, of whom she could normally see only the star that represented his eye. He looked at her, and she knew he saw her. Another miracle.

The shooting stars of Hebe's arrows seemed closer to her now. She spotted the goddess' perfect form silhouetted against an endless river of tiny stars. The cluster of hares quivered just beyond her.

"Come and drink!" Hebe shouted to the girls.

Phoebe was fitting another arrow to her bow as she ran to join the goddess. Hebe set her hand down on top of it.

"No," she said. "The chase is over." The girls groaned in disappointment.

"But what about the kill?" Phoebe asked. The hares quaked and moved closer together.

"Tonight is about beginnings," Hebe said, her green eyes gleaming, "not endings. You got to experience the thrill of the chase. Did you not enjoy it?"

"Oh, yes!" Demetra exclaimed. Shamefacedly, she put away the arrow she had been preparing to shoot. She didn't know if she could have shot; the sad brown eyes of the animals touched her heart. It *had* been exciting, more exciting than anything in her life so far.

Perhaps she would join Haskel on a hunt one day. She combed her tangled hair with her fingers. Suddenly she felt tired, and why not? She had traveled over a quarter of the night sky.

"You must be thirsty," Hebe continued. She gestured to the cataract of stars behind her. "This is your night. You become women with the turning of the new springtime. Drink of the river of life, and come into your power. You first, Demetra."

Demetra felt suddenly shy at being singled out. She came forward, and with the goddess' hand resting on her hair, she knelt to scoop up stars. They trickled out of her hands just like water. She gathered up another double handful and brought it to her lips. The liquid light tingled through her body, not like the wine, but like a shock, but gentler, and extended in duration. She quivered like the hares. Light glowed from her hands, her skin, her dress, until she had become a star herself.

"Phoebe."

Demetra felt disappointment when Hebe's hand left the top of her head, but she was left with the wonder of drinking stars. She caught up another handful, and another. This was her power, hers! It coursed through her like the tumbling waters of a waterfall, opening awareness to a world so much larger than the one she had known growing up in her father's house. She had visions of the beginning of the world. The first man and the first woman stood together before the gods, humble creations yet important in their own right. Around them ranged all the beasts and monsters, the birds and fish, the plants and trees, all singing with their own unique voices. She could *understand* them all, thanks to the draught of stars. There was so much more beauty and excitement than she knew. So many gifts from the gods, freely given to her. Was this what it was to be an adult? She thought of her mother, and for a moment was ashamed how carelessly she had pushed aside her words.

She became aware of a presence beside her. One of the hares stood on its hind legs with one paw reaching towards the pool. It beseeched her with its eyes.

"You are thirsty, too, aren't you?" Demetra asked. It leaned closer. "You can have only what I permit you, isn't that so?" It bowed its head in assent. For a moment she felt like denying it, just because she could. Then she relented. She had had her triumph, of being the huntress, of being blessed by the goddess. She could afford to be generous. Demetra moved aside. "Then, drink."

The hare crept forward, humbly, and lapped at the pool of stars. Demetra was surprised how satisfied she was at having been kind.

The faint music of the stars was drowned out just then as Hebe's piper struck up a merry dance tune. Demetra went to listen.

The rest of the girls stood in a circle, clapping and laughing. The hares, all of whom had drunk from the pool, were turning back into young men. Stefanos, glowing with light, stepped forward and bowed deeply to Phoebe, holding out his hand. Beaming, the star-girl joined him, and they swirled together on the soft sky like a couple of comets. The other young people began to dance to the piper's melodies. Demetra joined them. Slowly, the others paired off. Demetra danced with them for a little while, but the couples gazed at one another and did not look at her. She suddenly felt the chill of the high, thin air, and shivered. She wrapped her arms around herself, wishing now she had the thick cloak she had scorned.

"I am all alone," she said to herself.

Hebe seemed to hear the sorrowful thought, for the green eyes flashed before her for a moment.

"You are not, and never will be alone, beloved," the trilling voice said in her mind. "Share the joy."

Demetra felt a whisper of warmth just before hard arms encircled her from behind. At first she felt like the hares she had been hunting, her heart beating strongly in her chest. Her body warmed, and she stopped shivering. A gentle breath touched her ear.

"Is that better?" Haskel asked, leaning closer.

"Yes."

"Thank you for letting me drink. You didn't have to. It was your choice."

"I didn't know," Demetra said, turning her head to smile at him. "But I'm glad that I did."

"So am I." He shifted his arms to envelop her more closely. "I didn't want to be a hare forever. I don't like being the prey, at the mercy of creatures more powerful than myself."

"Were you afraid?" she asked.

"No," he replied. "Yes. For a moment. I was helpless. I'm not used to being weak. It gave me something to think about. I know now what my prey feels when I pursue it. It made me think of a song my father's poet recited one night. But then it was fun. I could run so fast."

"But I could see why you enjoy the chase," Demetra admitted. "That was fun, too."

"Can you?" Haskel asked. She turned in his arms to see the surprise on his face. "I never thought . . . Will you come with me one day? There is a wolf that is killing my father's sheep. Come help me seek it out."

"I will," Demetra promised. "I will enjoy seeing you in the field. I am sorry I did not thank you for the gift. It was cruel of me not to see how much effort it took you to accomplish."

"I didn't mind," he said, his light eyes shining. "It was for you."

Demetra's bones almost melted with gratitude. He forgave her, both for her brusque treatment, and for chasing him halfway across the heavens with a deadly weapon. What gift could she possibly give him in return for his kindness?

His lips were so close to hers. She stood on tiptoe to kiss them, touching his soft warmth with her own. His arms pressed close, lifting her off her feet. She let her arms wrap around his body. He deepened the kiss. She felt the power of the stars shoot through her again, inflaming parts of her body with yearning she had never felt before. Her newly awakened womanhood responded to his maleness. A part of her worried that she was making decisions too fast, in the heat of passion that she didn't want to control.

"Enjoy one another," a voice whispered in her ear. "Think not of tomorrow, but of today. Here. Now. Find the balance between you."

Demetra smiled, and kissed Haskel again, with all the gods-given passion inside her. She looked forward to finding that balance. She could make the hard decisions tomorrow, or someday. Not now.

The stars' light formed a globe around them, sealing them apart from the world.

"Here's to youth," she whispered.

BEARING LIFE
by Devon Monk

Devon Monk lives in Salem, Oregon, with her husband, two sons, one dog, and a colorful assortment of friends and family. Her fiction has appeared in *Rotten Relations*, and *Year's Best Fantasy* anthologies and in magazines such as *Realms of Fantasy*, *Amazing Stories*, *Black Gate*, *Talebones*, and *Lady Churchill's Rosebud Wristlet*. In addition to writing short fiction, she is currently working on several novels. The idea for this story came to her when she was asked what three words described the concept of "maiden, matron, crone," and she replied, "dream, endure, succeed."

THERA WORE four silver and five gold rings on her right hand—two on each finger except her pinky. The silver were for the daughters she had borne and watched die—wasted away by the coughing plague before they had done little more than learn to speak. The five gold were for her sons who were dead—three to infections—and the last, the only ring on her thumb, for Gregory who had bled out all eighteen years of his life on the northern border with Balingsway in one of many, unnecessary skirmishes.

On her head she wore her husband's crown. She had worn the black and gray of grieving for so many years, some called her the grave queen and, a few, woman of stone.

Thera tapped her right hand—the ringed hand—against the arm of her husband's throne and tipped the parchment to better catch the light from the glass sconce that burned over her shoulder.

"Majesty?"

Thera glanced over the yellow edge of the parchment to Johnathon, her husband's—and now her own—loyal adviser. His walnut-colored hair had gone gray with streaks of brown, and his face carried grim but not bitter lines. Johnathon still knew how to laugh.

"Do you understand what the summons outlines?" he asked gently.

Thera nodded, the crown on her head heavy. *Endure,* Johnathon had said when he removed the crown from her husband's cold brow and placed it upon her own. *Endure,* her husband had said as they stood above their last child's grave. *Endure,* the midwife had yelled at her through the birthing pains. *Endure,* her mother had whispered when she sent her, thirteen years of age, to be married to the king easily twenty years her elder.

"The Mother Queen of Harthing is asking for my surrender," Thera said in a matter-of-fact tone. "And that I supplicate to her and her lands. That I give over the valley, the crops, and the shipping route to Balingsway." Thera tipped her head to one side, only so much as the crown would allow, and felt the sting of metal breaking the blister it had worn upon her temple. "Have I missed anything, Johnathon?"

His eyes, still warm and brown after all these years, narrowed at the corners.

"By the Seven, Thera. She wants your lands. Your people. She wants word by dawn tomorrow that you will step down and stroll to the gallows so she can pull the rope. Where is your fire?"

Thera took in a breath and wanted to yell, to scream, to beat at the walls, the throne, her own body until something broke. To Johnathon, likely her closest friend, she said, "Fire does not solve every ill, Johnathon. Let us see if the Mother Queen has the forces she claims. Are the slave tunnels still open?"

Johnathon looked shocked, something Thera had seen rarely in their thirty years together.

"You know of the tunnels?"

"Johnathon, I am the queen. Of course I know. I was there when Vannel," her voice caught, and she swallowed quickly. Had this been the first time she had spoken his name since his death? "When he closed the slave trade route eighteen years ago."

Johnathon let his breath out in a rush and raised his hands to rub at his face. "You know of the slave trade, too. It wouldn't have hurt you to have told me so, Thera."

"Nor would it have hurt for you to ask me about it, if you thought it important. I am your queen."

"And I your adviser," he replied with faint annoyance.

She raised an eyebrow.

"Yes, yes," Johnathon said, "point made and taken. I thought since it was done and over, it was not worth your worry. You have had too many hardships in your years."

Like a blow to the stomach, Thera felt all the blood drain from her face. Her vision closed in at the edges, crowded out by memories. So many last breaths, warm little bodies going cold in her arms. She had thought her heart could break no more. Had sworn she had no tears left. Until the next child died. All of them. All of them gone.

She gripped the arm of the throne, carved wood inlayed with metal that never warmed to a palm. A reminder of the steel a ruler must keep in their decisions, their heart.

"Thera," Johnathon reached out for her, his hand pausing before resting on top of hers.

"I am your queen," she said, sharply. Too sharply. "As such, all matters of import to this kingdom's well-being will be brought to my attention." She pulled her hand out from beneath his, unable to endure the warmth of his touch any longer. "That, Adviser, is your job. It can be another's if you are unable to keep your personal feelings separate from your duties."

Johnathon stepped back and folded his hands in front of his tunic. His expression was blank, his lips a severe line.

"I swore duty to the throne," he said, and it hurt all the more for how softly he spoke. "That duty I will uphold regardless of who sits as ruler upon it."

Thera nodded. She wanted to untake her words, to draw the pain out of what she had said. But of all the matters before her, one man's hurt feelings were surely the least important. "The tunnels are open, then?"

"Yes, Queen Thera Gui." Flat. Nothing more than duty required.

"Johnathon," she began, but could not bring herself to apologize. If she admitted she was wrong, hurt, confused—if she admitted the pain was too much for her to bear and continue breathing—then she would have to admit it all, face it all. Every senseless, painful death.

No. She promised her mother she would endure. She promised her husband she would endure. And she had never broken a promise in her life.

"Take me to them," she said.

Johnathon nodded. "You may want your cloak, Your Majesty." At her look of annoyance, he sighed. They were both too old to hold grudges for long, a happenstance for which Thera was grateful.

"It is cold beneath the mountain, Thera," Johnathon said, "and damp. You may also want to bring a guard or two in case the old gates have rusted into place."

"Agreed," she said. "I'll leave it to your discretion

whom to bring. I will meet you at the well house in the apple orchard within the hour."

Johnathon bowed, and waited as she walked behind her throne to the door that led to her private hallway. She paused at the doorway.

"Johnathon," she said.

"Yes, Majesty?"

"Thank you."

He nodded. She opened the door and entered the hallway lit with the rare blown-glass globes Vannel had spent a small fortune on to line this hallway, their room, and their children's rooms. The wicks burned brightly over globes of refined oil, the globes themselves doubling the flame's radiance.

Beautiful, rare, Thera remembered when she had looked at them with wonder and delight. Now they lined the dark paths of her duty, and her confinement.

Two turns and a gradual curve brought her to her room. She closed the door behind her. She did not allow serving women to help her dress or bathe, though occasionally someone brought tea, or changed the goosedown quilts of her bed. If she was strong enough to rule a kingdom alone, she was strong enough to tie the lacings on her own boots.

Thera walked behind her dressing screen that was set close enough to the fire that she gained a bit of its heat as she disrobed. Out of her official black-and-gray gown and layers of underskirting, Thera wrapped her arms around her rib cage, holding still, holding herself. For a woman who had borne nine children, she was thin, the bones of her ribs and hips barely hidden beneath her flesh. Her stomach still carried the lines of pregnancy—ghostly finger-width scars across her empty belly. She never looked at her body in a mirror anymore. It was not a queen's body that a land most needed. It was her spirit and her will.

She took a breath, steeling herself. She donned Vannel's fine black wool shirt, and a pair of his breeches she had asked the tailor to shorten and sew down to her size. To that, she added her heavy cloak, with a hood that would help ward off early spring's chill. Lastly, she donned her calf-high, hard-soled boots that were laced with the same sinew the archers used on their bows.

She stepped out from behind her dressing screen and picked up the gloves from her bedside table. The mirror across the room flashed with her reflection. Black hair gone gray like frost over stone was pulled back in a severe braid to reveal the blue eyes of a younger, laughing woman. Her lips were unpainted and deep lines marked her forehead and the corners of her eyes.

She looked away from her reflection, and walked out the corner door, down a spiraled wooden stair, and finally entered the rear room where a guard stood his watch.

She tried to remember the man's name, but had long ago given up on memorizing the faces of men who so quickly left to battles, borders, and death.

"I will be going to the apple orchard," she said. "Come with me."

"Majesty." He crossed the room to the bolted outer door, opened it, and took a lantern from a wall peg before stepping through the doorway. He held the door open as she crossed out into the cold night air.

The moon flickered behind moody clouds, giving and taking of its light like a beggar flashing sorrowed eyes for coin. Even though the air stung her cheeks and lungs, Thera felt her shoulders relax at the simple act of moving, of doing, of being anywhere but upon the throne.

It took little time to reach the well house—a squat brick-and-thatch structure. Johnathon and two guards, who were both as gray-haired as he, stood by the well house.

"You may go," Thera told the guard who had accompanied her. The man bowed and offered her the lantern, which she took.

"This way, Majesty," Johnathon said. He led the way through trees, following a path Thera could not discern, and finally stopped by a rise in the hill where a fall of rocks was covered by brambles and vines nearly two stories high. The guards made quick work of pushing aside the leaves, uncovering an open space between the stones.

One guard stepped into the gap between the stones and Thera watched as light from his torch cast a yellow glow against the bellies of leaf and vine and then was swallowed altogether.

"It's clear," the guard called back, his voice muffled in the cold night air.

"Go ahead, Majesty," Johnathon said.

The path was covered with slick leaves and rotted berries over thick loam. The path was longer than she expected and she had the uncomfortable sensation of the stones closing in above her, like a hood pulled over her head, darkness over her eyes, a death cowl cinched to strangling around her throat.

This is what it is like to be buried, swallowed by earth and all the weight of the world, she thought.

She tried to keep her breathing calm as she followed the path, squeezing between stones, and finally stopping in front of an iron gate set into the mountainside.

Her heart hammered. How many people had been dragged this way, to be sold to distant lands, knowing only despair before death? The stones seemed to constrict around her, and she could taste the fear and hatred of the souls who had crossed this way.

"Open it," she said.

Johnathon stepped forward, so close to her she
could smell hearth smoke upon him, leather and oil,
and the spice of cloves. He placed a key in the fist-
sized lock and pulled a vial of oil from his pocket. He
poured oil into the lock and worked the key until the
lock gave way with a grating clack.

It took both guards to pull then push the gate back
upon its hinges.

"Tarin and Beir, first," Johnathon said, "then you,
Majesty. I'll follow. If that is your will," he added.

Thera nodded and followed the two guards into the
tunnel of dirt and stone braced by timber and iron.
The tunnel was damp and cold, the air so still, she
thought she would choke on every breath. All the
while the ceiling seemed to drop lower and lower, and
she struggled not to panic, not to imagine the earth
collapsing, crushing. She forced her feet to lift and lift
again, her eyes on her own boots or the back of the
guard before her.

Endure.

After an hour, they came upon an opening in the
tunnel where a natural chimney exposed the glint of
star and clouds. Dusty remains of fire pits scattered
the small chamber, and though the light breeze did
little more than stir the smell of mold and bat guano,
Thera inhaled deeply, grateful for even that small reminder of the outside world. They drank from water-
skins and moved quickly onward, hoping to reach the
opening of the slave tunnel above the border of the
Harthing lands within the hour.

"How many?" Thera asked.

"Majesty?" Johnathon said.

"How many slaves did we drag through this
tunnel?"

He considered his answer. "The tunnel was built in
Vannel's father's father's time."

"Hundreds?" Thera asked, "thousands?"

"Thousands," Johnathon said. "Easily that."

"All taken from the Harthing lands?"

"Not all. Many of the slaves were from the lands south and east of Harthing. All came through Harthing, then this passage, and up the Kilscree River to be sold in Balingsway, and from there to distant shores."

Thera had known of the tunnels a scarce few months before Vannel shut them down permanently. She had seen the papers he drafted to cancel the long-standing contract with Harthing. But only now did she understand the deep and undoubtedly financial rift it had caused between their two kingdoms. Without the river route to the northern ports, all merchandise, even human, would have to be marched over the spine of the Riven Mountains, or sailed around the southern edge of the continent itself. Taking slaves and other goods through these tunnels, or even through the pass and upriver was only a short journey, but sailing the seas could take months.

Thera paused and turned so that she could watch Jonathan's expression in the light of her lantern. "Why did Vannel shut the tunnels down?"

Johnathon's gaze held steady, but she had known the man for enough years to know when he was telling less than the truth.

"Vannel thought the slave trade abysmal. He would not continue his father's trade in flesh, once his own child had been born." Johnathon held her gaze, and she had the distinct feeling he was waiting for a reaction from her, an admission of knowledge.

"Majesty," one of the guards called out. "This is the opening."

Thera approached the guard. This door was the exact match to the iron door Johnathon had worked loose, and as before, he stepped forward, placed the same key in the rusted lock, and worked it with oil until it gave way. The guards lifted the heavy bolt—a beam of timber reenforced by rods of iron—and put their shoulders to the door.

It gave way and cool air poured into the tunnel.

The guards extinguished their torches in the dirt and Thera put out the wick of her lantern. With no lights to give them away should anyone chance to look up at the mountainside, the guards stepped out, Thera and Johnathon on their heels. The moon was lowering to the west, only a few hours from the horizon line. The tunnel opened onto an outcropping of rocks that looked down over the sloped valley to the expanse of Harthing's outermost lands, given mostly to wheat crops and sheep. Even in the uncertain light, Thera could make out the distant, glossy black towers of Harthing Keep, banners catching like strands of silver in the moonlight. But in the valley itself, Thera saw the glittering orange jewels of campfires and the dark hulk of tents. Enough for an army readying to march the Riven Mountains to Gosbeak's Pass, and then to her kingdom proper.

"How many?" she asked.

"Five thousand at least," one guard, perhaps Tarin, said.

"Near enough," the other guard agreed, "with more at the keep, I'd wager."

Thera felt the cold of the night sink through her flesh. "Five thousand here, an equal amount at the keep and a likely alliance with the East. How many men do you think Harthing can muster?"

The guards looked at Johnathon. She, too, glanced at her adviser. His face was grim, pale. "Forty thousand, with the aid of their southern borders, which seems likely since the trade route has been closed to them also."

Thera took several deep breaths. "We have twenty thousand soldiers at best, and most of them two weeks' ride at our northern borders. The skirmishes have taken too many men, the plague has taken too many babies—" Her voice took on a high, frightened tone and she shut her mouth.

"I would like your advice, gentlemen," she said evenly.

"We could come at them by the river route. They wouldn't be expecting that," Tarin said.

"Meet them at the pass with archers," Beir mused.

"And what of the other thirty thousand men who would descend upon us?" Thera asked. "We are already too short on human life. How many can we lose before we no longer have the people to run the kingdom or defend it?"

Johnathon spoke into the silence. "If we are in a position of defeat, let us preempt their attack with negotiation. Perhaps we can come to an agreement for the trade route, placing our own profit upon it. If," he added, "the trade route is what they want."

"Agreed," Thera said. "I'll send a request for negotiation to the queen in the morning." Thera turned back toward the tunnel. The steel rasp of a sword pulling free of a scabbard stopped her.

"Hold," an unfamiliar voice called out.

Behind her, Jonathon paused. Over the edge of her hood she saw Beir shift, his hand going to the weapon on his hip.

"Hold or you'll take your last breath," the voice warned.

Beir cursed. Thera tipped her head so she could see over her shoulder. Two archers held heavy crossbows aimed at them. The sound of movement told her there were at least two others she could not see.

"Do not draw your weapons," the voice said to her guards. "You two, turn around."

Thera and Johnathon turned. Thera's heart sank.

Six men clothed in cloaks the color of the rock and scree stood on the outcropping. Five held crossbows, and one, likely the leader, held a sword.

Sentries, scouts. How could she have been so foolish? The Mother Queen had not forgotten about the slave tunnels in all these years. And now Thera had just opened the surest route of attack into her own kingdom. Her heartbeat raced. There had to be a way to solve this, to undo the damage.

Johnathon stepped forward, his hands spread wide. "Peace. Let there be no bloodshed between us. We bear news from the Midlands."

"Of course you do," the leader, taller and thinner than the other men, said. "Spies. Assassins."

"I assure you that is not so," Johnathon said. "Allow us to speak to your commander."

The swordsman grunted. "If it were up to me, Midlander, I'd carry your head to the queen herself. But the captain wants spies questioned before they're killed." He sheathed his sword and smiled coldly. "You'll have your say, but I'll have your weapons."

Johnathon inclined his head in a bow.

"These two first." The leader pointed at Tarin and Beir. Two sentries came forward and stripped them of their swords and knives, then pulled their hands behind their backs. Beir's shoulders bunched and his hands clenched, but neither he nor Tarin resisted as the sentries bound their wrists. A sentry turned to Johnathon, tied his hands, then approached Thera.

The man smelled of wild onions. His eyes were dark and narrow, his face unshaven. He pressed his hands against her hips, then his eyes went wide.

"Well, look what they've brought along." He pushed her hood and cloak back, revealing her obviously female form, though she wore shirt and pants.

The man smiled, showing crooked teeth. "Let me make sure you don't have anything sharp under your clothes, girl." His hands lingered over her breasts, hips, and slid up her thighs.

The other sentries chuckled.

Thera grit her teeth and stared straight ahead. He pulled her close and ran his palms over her rear.

"You feel safe enough to me." He bit the lobe of her ear.

Anger filled her in a flash. Though she would endure many things, she was still the queen.

Thera shifted her weight and ground the heel of her boot into his insole.

The man howled and slapped her across the face. Her vision tunneled to a point of darkness and her ears rang. When her head cleared, she heard Johnathon's voice.

"Enough! She carries no weapons. Men of the Midlands don't need women to fight their battles."

Thera blinked until her eyes focused. "Do not—" she began.

The sentry holding Johnathon drove a fist into his stomach. Johnathon bent at the waist, breathing heavily, his hood hiding his face.

"Let him be!" Thera commanded. She tried to move, but her wrists were behind her back and a rope bit into her skin.

The swordsman glared at Thera, looked at Johnathon, then at Thera again. "Which of you is the leader?"

Thera drew a breath, but Johnathon spoke first. "I am." He straightened.

The swordsman strode forward and punched him again. Johnathon groaned.

"Tell your people to obey us," he said to Johnathon, "or they will receive twice your punishment." He looked over at Thera. "Do you understand?"

Johnathon straightened, slower this time. "We will listen," he said. Thera nodded.

"Good," the swordsman said. "The captain will not

want to be kept waiting. Move." He pointed to the
thin trail that led down the mountain side.

Johnathon started down the path, Tarin and Beir
pushed into place behind him. Thera was last. Her
head hurt and her right eye was swelling. The anger
that had filled her seethed below the surface of her
thoughts and with it, fear.

The men behind her muttered and made wagers.
More than once, she heard them say "the woman"
was the prize. Hands tied, weaponless, she felt vulnerable as a naked child. She pushed that thought away,
and kept her gaze on the uncertain footing among the
rocks. What mattered now was finding a way to save
her lands. Everything else, she could endure.

The trail ended at a dirt road that brought them
along side the encampment. They stopped in the middle of the road and one of the sentries jogged off
through the maze of tents, returning with a cloaked
and booted woman beside him. The other sentries acknowledged the woman's arrival with a nod.

"Tell me," she said. Her voice was a soft alto, her
unhooded face a pale oval with high cheekbones and
deep-set eyes that were colorless in the moonlight.
Her hair was pulled back in a peasant's knot, yet she
held herself with confidence and poise. Royalty, but
too young to be the Mother Queen.

"Midlanders from the tunnels, Captain," the sentry
said. "They say they have news for the Mother Queen."

"And the tunnels?"

"I left two behind to see."

The woman—the captain—nodded. "Bring them."
She strode into the encampment.

In a voice they alone could hear, the swordsman
said, "You have come to the wrong place this night,
Midlanders."

They were marched into the encampment, past tents
where Thera heard gambling, snoring, and soft pray-

ers. In one tent, the only sound was a blade drawing again and again over a whetstone.

That, Thera thought, *is the sound of my land's death, and I their only shield.*

The sentries pushed them through the door of a small tent surrounded by torches. The torchlight outside and within the tent fouled Thera's night vision and made her eyes water and sting. Johnathon, the guards, and she stood shoulder to shoulder, crossbows still aimed at their backs.

The woman, the captain, sat in a chair behind a dark wooden table that held a plain clay cup, parchments weighted by a rock, and a lantern.

The captain looked perhaps twenty years of age. Her cloak was drawn back to reveal the collar of a simple green tunic trimmed by gold thread and tiny jewels that winked as she breathed. But it was her eyes that caught Thera off guard.

The girl's eyes were the unmistakable deep-set green Thera had seen reflected in each of her children. The one trait each child had inherited from their father, Vannel. A clear and mark of his royal blood in their veins.

Thera's thoughts whirled. Johnathon had said Vannel closed the slave route when his first child had been born. Was it for Thera's first son, Gregory, or was it because of this girl, the link of royal blood between two kingdoms, that Vannel had broken the slave trade with Harthing? The girl was old enough she would have been conceived in the early years of Thera's marriage to Vannel.

He had betrayed her. He had fathered a child, who was now a maiden, fully old enough to claim his throne. To take his lands. To take Thera's lands.

Thera looked over at Johnathon. He nodded in silent apology.

The only child the Mother Queen had borne survived. All of Thera's children had died, and now, too, the certainty of her husband's faithfulness.

Thera felt sick, dizzy. Angry. *Endure.*

"Who are you, and what brings you to my lands?" the captain asked.

Thera stepped forward. "I am Queen Thera Gui of the Midland Kingdom. I came to answer your summons and negotiate peace for both our lands."

The girl's eyebrows shot up. "Truly?" She held very still, her bright eyes never leaving Thera's face. "Let me hear your offer."

What could Thera offer this girl? What one thing would join both lands in peace? Looking at the girl's eyes, Thera knew what she must do.

"I will step down from my rule, given certain conditions are met. The first of which is that you and I negotiate this peace alone."

"My Queen. Please reconsider," Johnathon said.

Thera did not look away from the girl. "Are you willing to speak for your lands or shall I speak with your mother?"

The girl scowled. "I am not such a fool to bring a woman claiming to be queen in front of my mother. Guards, take the men from my tent, but do not harm them yet."

"As you wish, Captain."

The guards and Johnathon were escorted away by the sentries.

"Can you prove you are, indeed, Queen Thera Gui?" the girl asked.

"No."

The girl studied her, gaze flicking to her hair, the faint red line that marked the place of Vannel's crown upon her brow, her mouth, and then her eyes. Something there made the girl nod.

"As I could not prove that I am Rynell Harthing if

I stood bound and tied before you." She stood and pulled a long knife from her belt.

The girl walked behind Thera and cut free the ropes that bound her wrists, then stood in front of her, close enough she could easily strike with the knife. "Tell me what peace may be found between our lands."

Thera pulled her hands forward and resisted the urge to rub her wrists.

"I am no longer a young woman, nor is your mother," Thera said. "The dispute between our kingdoms could end if another woman ruled in both our steads."

"You ask me to usurp my mother's power?"

"I ask you to take what is rightfully yours."

They stood, eye to eye, silent.

"The invasion will cost your lands dearly, as it will cost mine," Thera said. "There is little to gain but bloodshed. If I give you my throne, it will be on the condition that you rule with me for one year so that I may guide your hand, give you counsel."

"And if I refuse? If I spill your blood now and take your lands?"

"Even with the tunnel open, even with my death, my kingdom will not fall easily." It was more of a bluff than Thera liked, but there was truth in it. Her people were fiercely loyal. Peace would never be held in hearts crushed beneath Harthing's rule.

"People you love will die," Thera said quietly.

The girl's eyes narrowed and she bit her bottom lip. She looked so like Vannel that Thera's heart caught, ached.

"Child," Thera began.

"Rynell."

"Rynell, you are the hope of both our lands. My people will follow you if I so bid them."

"You are so sure of this?"

"Yes. They will see their king in your eyes."

Rynell blinked and looked as if Thera had just slapped her. *Surely the girl must know who her father was,* Thera thought. *Anyone who saw her eyes would know.*

Rynell walked behind the wooden desk.

"I have heard I resemble him greatly," she said quietly. "Was he ashamed of me? Of a daughter?"

"He was proud of all his children," Thera's voice caught, but she pressed on. "He would have wanted the lands in the hands of his own blood."

"Perhaps he would have," Rynell said, "but I do not understand why you would want such a thing."

"For my lands. For my people. For peace."

"What of my mother?"

"She shall rule these lands in peace with you until her days end."

"And you?"

"I will find my own peace. I have seen enough death."

Rynell nodded. With the brisk formality of a captain, of a queen, she withdrew a sheet of parchment and picked up a quill.

"Let us put to ink that you and I wish peace between our lands."

"And then?" Thera asked.

The girl looked up with a grim smile. "Then we will ask my mother to agree."

Thera had met the Mother Queen only once, when Thera was being married to Vannel. She remembered the Mother Queen to be a stern, mid-aged woman whose scowl worsened the longer the marriage celebration continued.

Thera followed Rynell to the large tent at the east of the encampment. The moon had long gone down and false dawn caught indigo on the horizon. They strode past the Mother Queen's guards and ducked through the wide tent flaps.

The Mother Queen was a dried-up husk of a woman reduced to muscle and bone, her hands like bird claws upon the arms of her padded throne. Her dress and the heavy blanket across her lap were the color of dried blood. Her eyes were iron gray, her face narrow. Prominent cheekbones stuck out like blade edges, though they had lent her remarkable beauty as a younger woman.

Her voice was jagged with age, but still strong. "Who is this, Rynell?"

Thera pushed back her hood. "I am Queen Thera Gui of the Midland Kingdom."

"She has come with an offer of peace," Rynell said.

"Peace?" The Mother Queen's face hardened and her voice was like steel. "King Vannel made it clear he would not negotiate with our lands, on any matter."

"Vannel is no longer king," Thera said. "The lands are mine, the decisions mine. Let us make decisions queens alone can make. I am willing to step down if your daughter will rule the land as her father would have wished her to."

"Her father, Lord Frederick," the Mother Queen said, "died just after her birth. He had no interest in your lands."

Thera gave the Mother Queen a stony gaze. "We both know the matter of which I speak, do we not?"

The silence between them was charged with anger. Thera wanted to strike her, hurt her for her part in Vannel's betrayal. Instead, she waited.

Finally, the Mother Queen spoke. "Did he tell you?"

"No," Thera said honestly. She felt suddenly tired. She had spent her life on a lie, and now there seemed little reason to continue it.

"Did you love him?" Thera asked.

The Mother Queen kept her gaze steady, but Thera could see pain, such familiar pain, in her eyes.

"I loved him, too," Thera said.

And there between them was the shared knowledge of a man, of love given, of love lost. With that pain, Thera felt something else, a weary kinship with a woman she did not know, and for all accounts, should hate.

"I am an old woman," the Mother Queen said. "And ill. There are few days left to me."

"Mother."

"Quiet now, Rynell. Let me speak."

The girl nodded, but cast a worried look at Thera.

"I never asked anything of him," the Mother Queen said. "Not even after Frederick died. But before my death, I will see my daughter's future secured."

"Then let Rynell become Queen of the Midlands in my place. I have no children to give the throne to." Her voice, thankfully, did not waver. "I would give the throne to Vannel's child so long as she rules with me for one year. Passage up the Kilscree River shall be evenly given to both lands, as well as the share in profit from that source."

"And in return for this?" the Mother Queen asked.

"You will not invade the Midlands, nor spill the blood of my people. Your lands will be joined to mine, coruled by Rynell, and your forces and allies will help us end the border skirmishes to our north. Lastly, you shall agree to abolish the slave trade."

"And you, Queen Thera Gui, where will you reside?"

"On the western shore. A small manor I can tend on my own. I will expect a stipend to repay my years of rulership and see me through to my grave."

Thera was shaking. Here, in her enemy's tent, she bargained away all that her mother had expected of her, all that Vannel had given her. Lands Vannel had died for. A peace he did not want, into the hands of a woman who had loved him, and the child she had borne.

The Mother Queen looked at Rynell. "Do you want this? Two lands will be a heavy burden."

Thera felt a pang of envy. No one had ever asked her if she wanted the life she had lived, they only expected that she would.

"I want peace," Rynell whispered. "Yes, I will rule both lands."

The Mother Queen nodded, and her whole body lost its strength. She leaned back against her chair and Thera wondered at the will and determination it had taken for her to appear so fierce. The Mother Queen looked over at Thera and Thera saw it was not determination that gave her strength, it was endurance.

"I will call my scribes," the Mother Queen said in a much smaller voice.

"We've begun the treaty already." Rynell handed the parchment to her mother who tipped it to better catch the light.

"Two guards and my adviser came with me," Thera said. "I ask that my adviser also see the contract."

"Yes, then." The Mother Queen handed the parchment back to her daughter and Thera had no doubt she had read it all. "While our advisers finish the papers, perhaps you would care for a cup of tea?"

"Tea would be welcome," Thera said.

"I'll see to it." Rynell pulled a plain wooden chair Thera had not noticed from the corner of the tent and brought it over for her. Thera sank down onto the chair, her entire body trembling. When she placed her hands on the arms of the chair, the smooth wood was cool, but slowly warmed beneath her palms.

Thera tucked another piece of wood into the stove's firebox and checked the loaf of bread baking in the oven. The gold and silver rings on her right hand flashed as she pulled out the loaf with a large wooden spatula. She had added two rings to her right hand, a gold to replace Vannel's crown she no longer wore and, given to her as a parting gift, a silver ring with a green stone that represented Rynell—her daughter of heart, if not of flesh.

Satisfied that the bread was rising, but not yet brown, she pushed it back into the oven and turned from her small kitchen. She stepped out into the living room where she had left her shutters open to the cool autumn breeze that carried the salty tang of the nearby ocean.

It had been a year and three months since Rynell took over the rulership of the Midlands. So far, the girl had proven to be a quick learner and a compassionate soul. The Mother Queen had been true to her word, sending their forces to secure the northern border. And Rynell stood firm on the agreement of abolishing the slave trade.

Thera had journeyed to this small manor on the edge of autumn's rainy season, and did not regret one day of her solitude.

She walked to the window that looked over the grass and stone hill to the ocean below. Waves caught in blue and gray beneath the cloudy sky. Dark clouds crowded the horizon. Rain would reach land within the hour, and by the bite in the wind, winter would be early this year. She'd need more wood cut before the snow set in, and might need to restock her larder.

The sound of horse hooves echoed off the fir trees that lined the path to her manor. Thera took the stairs to the foyer and opened the door.

Three horses were approaching her yard. The riders all wore plain green cloaks, hoods drawn up. But a hood could not disguise the man who rode in front. She lifted her hand in greeting and Johnathon raised his in reply.

The riders stopped at her split log fence, swung down off their horses, and strode up to her. Johnathon, pushed his hood back, revealing gray-and-brown hair and warm brown eyes.

"Johnathon. I hadn't expected you," Thera said.

He nodded. "We bring news." The wind gusted cold, shook rain out of fir boughs, and plucked at their cloaks and the skirt of her dress.

"May we come in, Thera?"

She looked over his shoulder and smiled at the two familiar guards. "Tarin, Beir. Welcome all of you. Of course you can come in."

"We'll stable the horses and tend to the tack first," Tarin said.

"Majesty," Beir added with a bow.

"Not here, Beir. Not ever, really," she said with a smile.

"Still and always," Beir replied, but there was nothing in his voice to indicate he planned to forsake his duties to the new queen.

"I'll put the kettle on," she said. "Come, Jonathon, warm yourself." Thera walked back into her home. Once the door was shut behind him she asked: "What news brings you out during the rain?"

"The Mother Queen died three days ago," Johnathon said.

"Ah," Thera said. "She is done, then." She was surprised at the compassion in her voice.

"Yes. The burial will be at the new moon, three weeks away."

"How is Rynell?" Thera led Johnathon up to her living room, then to her kitchen where the warm, yeasty smell of bread filled the air.

Johnathon sighed. "She took it much like you did, though I'm sure she grieves. Her mother has been sick for so long, longer even than Rynell had known. Her suffering was great."

Thera pulled the kettle over the firebox of the iron stove and fished clay mugs out of the cupboard.

"I will try to come to her burial. Will it be held in Harthing?"

"Yes, at the royal crypts there."

"So, now Rynell will truly be the queen of both lands." Thera handed him a cup. "I'm glad you have stayed on as her adviser, Johnathon."

"Hmm. Well, about that . . ."

Thera raised her eyebrow. "What have you done?"

"I retired."

"What?"

"There are other, younger men who can advise her as well as I, Thera."

"I doubt that," Thera said. "What happened to your vow to serve the throne and anyone who sat upon it?"

Johnathon held her gaze. "She had the throne burned."

"What?" Thera said again.

"She said it made her cold and had a throne carved of heartwood instead. It's padded. Tapestried. Beads and tassels. Quite a grand thing, actually. Vannel would have hated it."

Thera laughed for the first time in a long time.

Johnathon's smile led to a warm chuckle. "I'm glad you see the humor in all this, but I am, after all, without a job. Unless perhaps you have need of an old adviser?"

Thera's heart skipped a beat, then drummed faster. "Is that why you came, Johnathon? Are you asking if I need your advice?"

"If you want it. Ah," he added, warm brown eyes resigned at her expression, "perhaps not."

Thera tipped her head to one side, considering him, considering her own heart. "I don't need advice today," she said, "but I could use a hand chopping wood if you'd like."

"I would like that," he said.

"It might take a while," she said.

Johnathon nodded. "I hope so."

Thera held her hand out for him. He took it in his own, and together, they stood before the window to watch the rain rush upon the shore.

ADVICE FROM A YOUNG WITCH TO AN OLD PRIESTESS
by Rosemary Edghill

Rosemary Edghill's first professional sales were to the black & white comics of the late 1970s, so she can truthfully state on her resume that she once killed vampires for a living. She is also the author of over thirty novels and several dozen short stories in genres ranging from regency romance to space opera, making all local stops in between. She has collaborated with authors such as the late Marion Zimmer Bradley and SF Grand Master Andre Norton, worked as an SF editor for a major New York publisher, as a freelance book designer, and as a professional book reviewer. Her hobbies include sleep, research for forthcoming projects, and her Cavalier King Charles Spaniels. Her Web site can be found at http://www.sff.net/people/eluki

We were dreamers, dreaming greatly, in the man-
*   stifled town;*
We yearned beyond the sky-line where the strange
*   roads go down.*
Came the Whisper, came the Vision, came the Power
*   with the Need,*
Till the Soul that is not man's soul was lent us to lead.

   —"Song of the Dead" by Rudyard Kipling, 1893

I WAS TWENTY-FIVE in the Decade of Excess, living under conditions of harrowing drama only sustainable by the young in the place that's half city and half predicament: Manhattan. I'd come almost a thousand miles for the Goddess, following her the way you'd follow a jilting lover. Our connection was that tenuous in those days, even though nobody'd done much jilting yet. The Real World had me as dazzled as the headlights of an oncoming truck, and I hardly needed Supernature to stick its oar in to really fuck up my life.

I was in my twenties, and I was almost in love.

His name was Elwyn. Everyone called him Lark. It was his magical name: Witches had them.

And I wanted to become a Witch more than I'd wanted anything in my entire life.

I'd met Lark at an Open Beltane in a bookstore called The Serpent's Truth. It was crowded, shabby, and reeked of incense. There was actually no sign of any kind displaying its name on either the window or over the door—I'd found out the name of the place I'd wandered into the first time I bought something there. I'd gone in because of the books I'd seen in the window (I'd ignored the wizard hats and the light-up and patently fake crystal balls). I'd gone back because of the lectures, and the open Circles, and the fact I hadn't bankrupted myself yet.

That day, after the ritual was over, I'd been buying some books I couldn't afford and visiting others; Lark saw what I'd picked out and recommended more. We struck up a conversation. In those days I had a fourth of a tiny apartment in a neighborhood worse than I'd used to be able to imagine, and I was working two jobs to pay for it. Everything left over I spent on books—Gardner, Valiente, Leland, the Farrars. Lark said that every Witch should read Crowley. The book he picked out cost a third of my weekly salary. I bought it anyway.

"Only a Witch can make a Witch"—that's how the saying ran in those days. I was looking for training, but it wasn't easy to find. The notice board at the Serpent's Truth was covered with notices of groups forming. Some were outdated. Some groups were full.

Some were in New Jersey, or Connecticut, or Long Island. Those might as well have been on the Moon—given my state of financial health and the cost the commute would involve—but I still wrote to them.

I was not credulous, even back in the day, and even then I knew that the Craft I so ardently wished to espouse—in the most archaic meaning of the word—did not operate upon faith. But faith was needed: faith that there was something there to find.

And so I steered clear of the groups and people who made claims too good to be true—the ones that made claims of lineages dating back to ancient Atlantis, or that required darker avowals and more unreasonable sacrifices than anything research and my admittedly limited common sense had prepared me for. I read books; I went to the public events I could find and the lectures I could afford.

And I talked to Lark and his friends. We never did agree about Crowley. In revenge for being made to read *Magick in Theory and Practice*, I made him read *The White Goddess*. He was voluble in his pejoratives. I threatened him with *Seven Days in New Crete*, and all of Margaret Murray. He countered with Israel Regardie, holding Mathers and Waite in reserve. We compromised in the no-man's-land of Dion Fortune.

I imagine other young revolutionaries feel the same way: to be drunk upon ideas, intent upon remaking the world out of books. But we had more than books.

Of course, every revolutionary thinks so.

Lark and I turned out to know a lot of the same people—the New York Craft community was an insular thing in those days, not yet—quite—having become grist for the popular culture's mill. At the end of the summer, we moved in together, in the sense that he and I and eight other divergent fellow travelers all moved to a four-bedroom apartment in Brooklyn overlooking Prospect Park. Lower rent, better neighborhood than the one I was leaving, and by then I was only working one job that paid more than my previous two had.

I was on the fringes of what I wanted. I knew Witches, now, and knew there were several covens in the city. But I was no closer to getting into one. Badgering the people I did know would only have pushed me farther away—I had picked up that much Occult Etiquette.

Lark's coven was called Steelstone. It met in the room in the back of the Snake (as I'd learned to call it) in what was the "secret temple" when the O.T.O. used it and the lecture room when it was open to the public. He never said anything much about it. I never asked. You didn't in those days.

But Lark knew what I wanted, and how much I wanted it. He came home one night after his coven had met and told me he'd heard there was an Outer Court forming up near Inwood. He gave me the number to call.

It took me a week to work up the courage. Wanting was better than being turned down. Ignored. Told that for some reason I couldn't understand I just wasn't good enough to have the only thing I wanted.

But I couldn't *not* try. I made the call.

I got an answering machine that told me to leave a brief message with my name, number, and the date and time I called. I hung up and called back three times before I could figure out what to say, and by then I was sure this would be yet another dead end.

Instead, three days later, I got a phone call in return.

The woman told me her name was Belleflower. Later I found out her mundane name was Isobel Singer, but by then I couldn't think of her as anything but Belleflower. She said we could meet, if I was still

interested in her Outer Court. I said I was, and so I
met her and a man she called Daffydd at a Chinese
restaurant near Columbia.

She explained about her Outer Court—the training
group for people who might become Witches. She told
me about her tradition and its history, and asked me
what books I'd read. She explained that the Outer
Court would meet at her house once a week. Its members would study the Craft. Membership in the Outer
Court might lead to Initiation. It might not.

And over dinner, she asked me the simplest, and
the hardest, question in the world:

Why did I want to be a Witch?

To this day, I'm not sure what I said.

Because I do. Because I have to. Because it's right.

She made no guarantees.

She made no promises.

When dinner was over, I had no idea if I'd ever
hear from her again.

That is power, to have what someone else wants,
and to be able to choose whether to give or withhold
it. In those days, I only felt one side of its blade, but
the blades of the Craft are double-edged for a reason:
to remind us that the blade of power always cuts two
ways, whenever it is wielded. I know now what I didn't
know then: that Belle felt its sharpness that night as
much as I did.

Two weeks later she called me again, and told me
when and where the Outer Court would meet, and
what I would need to bring.

If I was still interested.

I felt relief and delight—as if I'd accomplished
something, though I knew it was false even at the
time. I'd accomplished nothing yet. I knew that much
from listening to Lark and the others at the Snake.
Finding an Outer Court was hard. Staying with one
was harder.

The Craft is not for everyone. Your own fears and desires can pull you elsewhere—as near as another tradition within the Craft, as far away as another spiritual path altogether. What I thought I wanted might not be what I wanted at all. The community has its own version of campfire tales: this person got all the way up to the night of their Initiation before realizing they were about to make a dreadful mistake: that person was actually Initiated before realizing the Craft was not for them.

You fool yourselves. You fool your Teachers. But you do not fool the Gods. They know.

The first official meeting of Changing Coven's Outer Court was the middle of November. Seventeen people all crowded into Belle's living room to begin to learn the basic Paganism and practical ritual that would someday, if we wanted it enough, be transmuted to the practices of Initiatory Craft.

By February only nine of us were left. The others were too tired, too busy, too bored with what Belle had to teach them. They wanted other mysteries, more blatant ones, mysteries that matched their preconceptions.

I wanted what was behind the Veil.

I knew there was something there—something more than was in my books, something more than I touched in my private devotions. Perhaps I was too busy to be wise. Certainly I was too tired between job and study and the extension classes I was taking at the New School. I finally had someone to ask questions of, and all my instincts told me I had come home.

Those of us who were left drew closer together. We chose magical names for ourselves, names to call up something from deep within ourselves and make it manifest.

I chose Bast.

My feet—I told myself—were firmly set upon the

path that would lead me to Initiation, and Lark and I made hopeful plans for a time, somewhere in the indefinite future, when we would run a coven together. It seemed inevitable to us that as our mundane lives intertwined, so our magical ones would as well.

Lark was more interested in Ceremonial Magic in those days, and one of our housemates was a Thelemite, a follower of the philosophy of the self-anointed Great Beast, Aleister Crowley, whose work formed the foundation of twentieth-century Ceremonial Magik. Belle didn't include CM in her curriculum, but I ended up studying it essentially in self-defense. Its systems were as ornate and dispassionate as mathematics, as rigorous as dance.

Ideas can be as dangerous as drugs—as empires have discovered to their cost.

As I found out, that year.

Initiation purifies. Lark knew that already. Belle had begun to warn the rest of us—seven now—that spring, giving us the first of our last chances to leave. To accept Initiation, to become Priests and Priestesses of Wicca, was not a trivial matter, so she said over and over; it was just fine if you felt it was appropriate to remain a Pagan instead of becoming a Witch. So she said.

I doubt any of us really understood. And I, at least, was in love.

I don't think, looking back with the judgment of years, that it was ever with Lark, though we were lovers. My love affair was with the Goddess—with the Gods and the Craft. Lark was caught up in the limerence, gilded by the glory with which I saw everything in that season of Becoming. The consequences were just the same.

We made a plan, Lark and I, to bind ourselves together on the night of my Initiation, invoking a Karma Dumping Run that would (surely) turn us into the

deific clergy that the New Age required. We would
enact a ritual that would cause all the life Life Lessons
we were ever slated to learn to be condensed and
intensified into this one incarnation, burning away all
the dross, and we would sail above the wreckage
strong and wise. We had the tools, we had been given
the wisdom; we weren't worried about emotional en-
tropy.

We should have been. But in those days we all
wanted to be psychologically invulnerable, and assumed we were.

Did it work? I've never been completely sure. Magic
is a craft of will and possibilities: there are other possible explanations for what followed. If it did nothing
else for me, it taught me to distrust fashion—it was a
fashionable ritual to do, that decade, or at least to talk
about. Everybody swore they'd done it, or were going
to do it, or knew someone who had. In the stories
that were told of Karma Dumping Runs past, everything had ended favorably, or that the ritual that had
been done was the justification for everything bad that
happened later—which is also a happy ending of a
sort, since being free of all personal responsibility for
your own life is, in its way, a liberation.

But that was only my future. My present was daz-
zling. With six others I stayed the course. Belle initiated me into Changing Coven on a full moon a little
over a year after I'd started attending her Outer
Court.

The ritual of Initiation draws from the oldest symbols humanity has made for itself, rites and promises
that were old before we left the caves. It's a powerful
thing. It was designed to be.

But it wasn't the transcendent experience I'd been
hoping for. I stood outside myself during the ritual
itself, half terrified that I'd get something wrong, half

indignant—once it was over—at the sense of anticlimax.

Belle told me afterward that my reaction was normal; that in a day or two I'd wake up and everything would have "dropped into place." She told me not to worry, and cautioned me to be careful.

But I was in no mood to be careful. I went from that ritual to Lark's, and there we did a ritual of our own.

Craft folklore holds that personal disasters, major and minor, follow one's Initiation, as one settles into being Priestess and Witch, but oddly, that winter, the disasters seemed to follow Lark, not me. His band broke up, several of its members having found better-paying gigs elsewhere. He lost his day job. There were no auditions to go to.

Nothing happened to me in the most complete sense of the word: I'd come no closer after Initiation to feeling that sense of belonging to the Gods that I'd expected to feel.

I wondered if I was supposed to quit. If the Initiation hadn't "taken." If I was supposed to go to Belle and explain to her that I was one of the ones that didn't belong here, and I was just too stupid and stubborn to actually know it.

But I didn't want to. I was in love, even if I didn't *feel* loved. Changing was home to me now. And if she wouldn't throw me out, I wouldn't leave.

Not yet.

And there were times I could actually forget that I felt incomplete. As long as I wasn't actually standing in a Circle.

But the worst thing that happened that winter in terms of displaced post-Initiation fallout—from my perspective (and I assumed, at the time, from Lark's)—was that Steelstone broke up.

Steelstone had been meeting in the back of the

Snake for about two years, and before that in an illegal Williamsburg loft that wasn't there any more. Trismegistus, the Snake's owner, was a man of volatile and obscure likes and dislikes. One day he told Steelstone's High Priestess that they couldn't meet at the Snake anymore.

So they stopped meeting entirely.

There was more to it than just losing their space—I know that now, with the hindsight of more experience. There were things they could have done to keep the coven going. But covens can be fragile things, driven apart by clashing personalities, or simply by the unspoken sense that their time is done. Lark didn't volunteer any more information than that Steelstone was dead, and after a few thoroughly discouraged questions, I let it go.

I did ask him what he was going to do now. He told me he was taking care of things. That was something I should have questioned further. But I was in love—however seemingly unrequited at the moment—and not with Lark.

He had to have known I'd find out. The Community does not keep secrets well, except the ones that really matter. I was at the Snake one Saturday—alone—when I heard a Welsh Trad named Sirius complaining about Lark's new student.

"—been coming to my OC for six months. It isn't fair. That's coven raiding. Coming in and promising to initiate her—that's the last time I let Lark come to an Open Circle!"

I was behind the center rack of books and she was on the other side. The Snake is a typical downtown retail space of a certain age, about fifteen by thirty, after Tris' various modifications. The Santeria section was yet to be added, so the back wall of the store was still bookshelves. The right wall of the store was herbs and storage, and the left wall was a haphazard and by no means orderly collection of more shelves and random display cases holding (at various times) do-it-yourself voodoo doll kits, Magic 8-Balls, wishing mirrors, scrying glasses, gargoyle bookends, stained-glass pentacles, fluffy stuffed unicorns, bumper stickers, blank books, CDs, cassettes, and less immediately explicable objects. The majority of the actual books were on a shaky free-standing bookshelf about six feet tall that ran down the center of the store, and right now I'd never been more grateful for its existence in my life.

I moved a couple of books and peeked through the gap. Sirius and two of her coveners were retelling the latest gossip for a small but interested audience, including Tris' latest find in the hired help department, a leather-clad Kemitic Pagan named Ammit. Tris only hired royalty, as it were, and under the combined influences of that and his particular Path, Ammit bore a startling resemblance to Liz Taylor circa *Cleopatra,* only with slightly more eye makeup. I was not distracted.

It had, I told myself, to be a coincidence of names. Lark was the same degree I was, and as such, neither of us would be training anyone for years yet. Second, walking into somebody else's Open Circle and promising someone you met there to initiate them—bad form on so many levels I couldn't begin to count them.

I turned my back and pretended deep interest in Tris' collection of mummified herbs in their antique flint-glass jars until Sirius and her crowd had moved on, and then braced Ammit.

"Who were they talking about?" I asked. "The coven raider?"

"Some guy named Lark," he said. "You know, used to be in Steelstone?"

Everybody knew that Lark and I were a couple.

But Ammit hadn't been here long. Maybe he didn't recognize me. Maybe he was using what passed for tact below Twentieth Street.

I thought that was the worst. It wasn't.

I was waiting for a good time, a private time, to bring up the issue with Lark, but living in a house full of people with interlocking schedules, that wasn't easy, or maybe even possible.

What I learned from that—though I didn't realize it until much later—was not to wait for the easy and the possible when things are important.

And then it was Thursday, and we still hadn't talked.

I was taking night classes in graphic design at the New School. Lark misjudged the time. Or he didn't care.

I came home and found them together.

Not in bed. That wouldn't have mattered as much. I'd never expected Lark to be faithful. We were in the sunset years of casual sex then, still giving body-worship to counterculture social mores current around the time most of us had been in kindergarten, though soon even Pagans would have to take monogamy seriously as the death toll began to mount.

They were in a circle.

I'd opened the door to our bedroom before I realized it would have been far better to leave it closed. I stood there, smelling sex and incense, watching the candles gutter in the draft from the open door.

It was not Craft. Not *my* Craft. Not the Craft that Lark had trained in. What they were doing was some fake Hollywood Dennis Wheatley/Paul Huson version. Goblin fruit.

I closed the door and went into the kitchen.

For proper drama the apartment should have been

dark, echoing, and empty. It felt as if it were. But it was nine o'clock at night and ten people lived there. Some of them were in the warm, brightly-lit kitchen.

"He said you were okay with Tiphanie," Patti said, when she saw my face.

I looked at her. Ron put a hand on her arm, shaking his head at her.

By the time the tea water boiled, I was alone in the kitchen.

Until Lark came in.

Lark and I fought: he said I was too serious about things. I told him he took them far too lightly. By the time he got to the word "experimenting," everyone in the apartment could hear us, and probably people in the apartment next door.

It wasn't about the infidelity. It was never about that. Monogamy was Old Order evil and we all meant to rise above it. It wasn't Lark's "infidelity" I was objecting to: it was his magic. If anything I'd over-heard from Sirius was true, he was using the power Tiphanie thought he had to impel her into sex.

"She knows what she's doing," Lark insisted, after we'd fought ourselves to exhaustion. "It isn't Craft. I wouldn't do that. It's just sex magic. Look . . . I'll stop if you want."

But I wouldn't ask him to stop.

Did I refuse to take the power he offered me because I knew it was empty? Or because it was dangerous?

"Do what you choose," I said.

I slept on the couch that night. I didn't sleep well. Changing was meeting the following evening and I had to go into our bedroom that morning to get my working tools so I wouldn't have to backtrack after work.

All the evidence of the night before was gone. Lark was gone. Only a faint smell of incense remained. I could pretend it had never happened.

But I'd still know.

I wrestled with my convictions all day. People left Outer Courts all the time. I'd seen that myself. Tiphanie might have left anyway. She might have been looking for an excuse to leave. Or help to leave. Lark and I had made no claims of fidelity to each other.

If Lark had been telling the truth— If Sirius had been massaging the facts in favor of a good story (not impossible)— If Tiphanie had indeed known exactly what sort of relationship she was entering into, with full knowledge and consent—

If and if and if.

Did I trust Lark not to lie to me?

Did I trust Lark?

Once I would unhesitatingly have said yes.

I didn't tell Belle about it, though I had ample opportunity that night when our coven met. I was ashamed, as if I were the one who'd done something wrong, not Lark, and at the same time I couldn't work out exactly why I thought it was wrong, or whether it really was. But it left a bad taste in my mind.

That night in the circle, I felt more alone than ever before.

Not just alone. Lost.

Not only did I not feel what I thought I ought to feel, for the first time I wondered if any of the others felt anything at all. That night the words were no more than words, and everything seemed faintly ridiculous, a shadow-play for overgrown hippies, containing nothing of value.

Somehow I had managed to sustain a mortal wound of the spirit, something that would grow, and spread,

and fester—because if Lark could do something so
contrary to everything I had so far learned, what hope
was there for me? Steelstone had broken up, Lark
seemed to have given up; wouldn't I simply go the
same way—if not now, then in a year, or two years,
or three?

And then there would be nothing left.

I left Belle's that night not certain if I was going to
go back to the apartment, but where else could I go?

Walking down the hill to the subway, I felt the desperation that defines suicide, but it wasn't Death I was
seeking, it was Life.

I had come to New York to find the Gods of Wicca.
Everything I had read, everything I had been taught,
had told me that Initiation opened the door to Their
Presence.

But I had been Initiated, and I was still no closer
to Them.

I refused to accept that.

I will not be left, I thought, standing on the subway
platform. Or perhaps it was: *I will not leave.* In the
Shadowlands, in the face of the Gods, the two con-
cepts are much the same.

And there, in pain, in loss, was the beginning of
wisdom. I had gotten what I had been foolish enough
to ask for on the night of my Initiation after all. It
had come in secret, in silence, and in disguise, as all
proper magic does.

I stood alone in the deserted subway station and
flung myself upon the Goddess the way a metalhead
throws himself into the mosh pit, as careless of my
vulnerability. I let go of the world, of everything outside of the moment. I thought of my desire, my love,
my need. I stopped expecting anything at all.

And I felt at last, absolutely, what I had only had
in hints and reflections before: the true and absolute
presence of the Goddess. She bore me up, but that

mercy does not come without cost. Taking Her help, I gave Her power over me.

It was not deliverance I found, or absolution. We do not deal in these things. My only faith—still—was in myself, and the evidence of my senses. To experience the Gods is to know, not to believe.

What She gave me—what I gained—was the courage to endure.

I understood power that night, or began to. To give it is to take it, among the Gods as among Wicca. It is the true price of Initiation: knowing the cost of power. It is a high cost, but I thought that night it was what I wanted: to be a partner in that dance that defines Creation. I have never changed my mind.

But it doesn't come without cost.

When I got home that night, Lark was gone. He'd taken all his things. Ron told me he'd moved in with Tiphanie. He'd be back, over and over until we were finally over, but after that night it wouldn't be the same.

I'd chosen my path, he'd chosen his. Someday they'd converge again, but not without a lot of the pain we'd so lightheartedly conjured on the night of my Initiation.

Lark didn't believe in magic, and didn't understand power.

But he'd learn. One day.

As I was already beginning to.

THE THREE GEMS OF THE FIANNA
by Fiona Patton

Fiona Patton was born in Alberta and grew up in the United States. In 1975 she returned to Canada and after a series of unrelated jobs, including electrician and carnival ride operator, she moved to rural Ontario with her partner, one tiny dog, and a series of ever-changing cats. Her Branion series which includes *The Stone Prince*, *The Painter Knight*, *The Granite Shield*, and *The Golden Sword* has been published by DAW Books and she has just finished the first book of a new series tentatively entitled *The Silver Lake*, also for DAW.

THE HOT SUMMER SUN blazed down on the palace of Tara, traditional seat of the High Kings of Ireland, causing the pale, silvery flagstones of its main courtyard to shimmer with an almost otherworldly glow. Nothing stirred in the heavy summer heat, not a bird in the sky, nor a cat hunting by the granaries; even the flags and banners which decorated Tara's many high towers and turrets hung limp and heavy in the still air. It was almost as if the entire palace had been placed under a spell. And in a way it had, for the country was at peace and neither High King Cormac mac Art and his retinue nor Captain Fionn mac Cumhaill and his battalions of Fianna were in residence. The latter was off hunting in the cooler forests of Ulster while the former took his ease in his bright and airy palace at Clifden in Connacht. Only a small garrison remained to guard the king's capital from the heat and the dust.

Seated by a small, reedy pool to the east of Tara's

stables, Brae Diardin of the Fianna sat on a wide, flat stone by the water's edge, listening to the sounds of wrens and larks singing in the hawthorn trees as she worked a small whetstone along the blade of her sword. It was quiet and peaceful. And incredibly dull. Leaning the sword against a nearby tree trunk, Brae gave a loud sigh, causing the brown-brindled hound at her feet to raise its head hopefully before dropping it down again with a sigh of his own. Dropping her own chin into her palm, Brae stared out at the invitingly cool woods beyond the pool.

A hard, driving thunderstorm had forced Brae's company of twenty-eight Fianna to seek shelter at Tara two weeks ago and, knowing full well that no one could deny hospitality to the traditional protectors of the land, their Sub-Captain Cunnaun mac Morna had brought them to King Cormac's shiny new Court of Learning, much to the dismay of the Court's senior Druids. They'd been expecting a quiet summer of contemplation and study without a rambunctious band of hunters eating them out of house and home.

Brae gave an uncharitable snort. *She'd* been expecting an *exciting* summer of hunting and tracking in the forests without being glared at by a flock of toothless old men and women, but since Cunnaun showed no sign of leaving any day soon, boredom had forced her to agree to help train her headstrong young cousin Etaine—here by the leave of her mother to learn the twelve books of poetics that she needed to join the Fianna.

Brae shook her head. The girl had Sidhe blood from the otherworldly deer folk on her grandmother's side and was as skittish and easily distracted as any young hind. It would have been as easy to teach Brae's hound poetics—but Etaine needed them if she were going to join the Fianna, so she was stuck in a hot and stuffy lecture hall while Brae was stuck cooling her heels until the girl was released from lessons and they could get on with the more important elements of her training: like running.

Retrieving her sword, she drew the whetstone along the blade again, feeling her own otherworldly blood tingle as it sensed the iron beneath her fingers. The echo of baying dogs sounded in her mind and the sudden urge to give in to it came over her. Brae was of the hound people, the guardians and hunters of the Shining Folk and she hated being inactive almost as much as she hated . . . well, being inactive. And the woods were so . . . tempting.

Sensing her thoughts, the hound whined at her, and she rubbed his belly with one booted foot to quiet him.

"Later, Balo."

With a reproachful woof, the dog dropped his head down again and Brae scratched his rump sympathetically. They'd gone rabbit hunting after the noon meal, and although Balo was still as keen-sensed and eager as any whelp, he was nearing nine years old and needed a longer rest in between exertions than he used to. The gray along his muzzle and the thickness about his ribs told her that he would soon be bound for her mother's hearthrug and a quieter life than chasing the Fianna across the country.

"But not yet, eh, boy? You still have a few good travels left in you, don't you?"

A thrush flitting past his head caused the dog to snap irritably at the air, and Brae chuckled. "We should have run off to Tir Na n'Og when we were younger," she said fondly, reaching down to rub his long, flopping ears. But you're still as fast as you ever were, aren't you, boy?"

Which was entirely untrue, but his tail began to thump against the ground beside her foot anyway as she returned her attention to her sword with a nostalgic expression. She'd been eight years old when she'd first come to Tara to begin her own training for the Fianna, and fifteen when she'd been admitted into their ranks. Balo had been a squirming whelp of just ten weeks, a gift from her Aunt Tamair after she'd passed her final test: diving under a knee-high hawthorn staff held by the Captain of the Fianna, Fionn mac Cumhail himself.

It had been a good day. An exciting day. *Not* a dull day.

A soft fox call alerted her to someone on the path and Balo began to growl low in his throat until they saw Matha Cunnaun pushing through the trees above them. Laying one finger on the dog's nose to quiet him, Brae watched the other warrior negotiate the thick underbrush with a mischievous smile.

She and Matha had a somewhat thorny on-again-off-again relationship, mostly because Brae kept forgetting that when it was on it was supposed to be off with everyone else. They were of an age, half a year past twenty-four and much alike in looks: tall and lean, muscular without being heavyset, with thick copper-colored hair worn long and generally loose, and dark brown eyes framed by thick lashes, but where Brae was otherworldly pale, Matha was tanned almost bronze by the sun. The fastest of her generation, the youngest daughter of Cunnaun mac Morna was often used by her father to carry long-distance messages and she rarely bothered with either horse or hat.

She did not, however, have the best eyesight of her generation. Struggling and cursing, she finally broke through the underbrush to stand, sweating and scowling, at the edge of the woods.

"Brae?"

"Matha."

The other woman started in surprise to see Brae so close, then gave her an exasperated look as Brae began to laugh.

"Grow up," she muttered. Picking her way carefully down to the water's edge, she paused to let her own hound, Derkame, maneuver around her. Balo raised his head and whined at the other dog who trotted over to flop down beside him and immediately begin licking his ears.

"Did Cunnaun send you?" Brae asked, trying to school her expression. "Are we leaving today?"

Crouching beside her, Matha shook her head, the grimace replaced by an expression of concern. "Is Etaine with you?" she asked instead.

Brae snickered. "No."

"Was she?"

"This morning early. We ran through the north woods together at dawn, like we do every morning. *Training,*" she added in case her words might be repeated to some interfering Druid who wanted to steal away Etaine's mornings as well as her afternoons.

"Do you know where she might be?"

"Well, she's *supposed* to be at lessons with Moifinn this time of day," Brae answered unnecessarily because it was probably Moifinn, the senior Druid in charge of Etaine's training, who'd sent Matha out looking for her.

"She never showed up."

Brae just shrugged. Moifinn had been in charge of stuffing poetics into her own head a decade ago. She'd been old and cranky and pushy then and was even more so now. Brae could understand why Etaine might be ducking lessons. "Would Moifinn like me to go and find her?" she asked, again unnecessarily, because even if Moifinn didn't, Matha probably did.

"Moifinn would *like* you to stuff her in a sack and send her home to Nenagh."

Brae brightened. "That's a thought. I could go with her. You could come, too."

Bending to the water's edge, Matha drew up a double palmful of water. "Don't pack our saddlebags just yet, it's a *passing* thought only, I'd wager," she warned, bringing up her hands to drink. Brae watched the water trickle down her throat, feeling her own mouth go suddenly dry. "Barring that, yes," Matha continued, wiping her hands on her tunic. "She wants you to track her, find her, and herd her back here, but you're *not*—and she said not very loudly, by the way, Brae—*not* to go running off together until the sun sets."

Brae leaned back, her head supported against her palms. "What's in it for me?" she asked with an evil grin.

"I'll give you a biscuit."

"Ha, ha."

"All right. How about the next time you sleep with Duail, I won't try to knife her. Or you."

"Don't make any promises you know you won't keep," Brae answered mildly. Standing, she stretched her arms toward the overhanging branches above, while at her feet, Balo raised his rear end in a stretch of his own. "Are you going to be busy later tonight?" she asked.

Matha glanced up at her from under her lashes. "Why? What did you have in mind?"

"Getting my biscuit."

"Come by after moonrise. I'll see if I can find you one in my bedroll."

"I'll be there."

"Just don't forget or you'll find yourself both biscuitless and alone; I'll go after Duail myself."

With a careless laugh, Brae blew her a jaunty kiss. "C'mon, Balo," she said, "Let's go have some fun hunting down a delinquent fawn." With a whistle, she and the hound plunged into the woods beyond the pool.

*   *   *

Several miles away, Etaine Caileigh was running through the nearby woodland, weaving and dodging, coming as close to the grasping branches of the thickly growing oak, ash and thorn trees as possible without actually touching them. She'd been running full out for over half an hour, pushing herself as hard as she could, and her hide tunic and breeks were damp with sweat. Small and dark, with long, delicate limbs and glossy black hair and blue eyes, she seemed more like some woodland creature than a girl of fourteen and, as she broke from the trees, the afternoon sun shone across the shimmering outline of a young hind that covered her like a fine mantle.

Cutting through a small meadow, dotted with wild-flowers, she made for a line of dolmans in the center. The thick summer grasses tried to impede her progress and she put on an extra burst of speed and, reaching the largest of the portal graves, leaped into the air, landing nimbly on the top of its sun-streaked capstone. But before she could catch her breath, the baying of a hound in the distance jerked her to her feet. Her heart pounding in her chest, her hand dropped instinctively to the long knife at her belt, but the brown-brindled hound that burst from the trees was familiar and she relaxed, feeling stupid. It was only Balo.

A heartbeat later, her cousin Brae broke through the trees after him, and Etaine could almost see the red-eared, white hound of the Shining Folk overlaid like a mystical pelt across her shoulders as she ran. When she and Balo flopped down into the grass on the shaded side of the dolman, Etaine joined them as Brea took a long pull from a waterskin at her belt, then poured some into her palm for Balo.

After a long moment of silence, Etaine tugged at one of the hound's ears with a grimace. "Before you ask," she said haughtily, "I am not ducking Moifinn's lessons, I am in the latrine."

Brae's copper brows raised in an unspoken question.
"All right, I *was* in the latrine. Now I'm . . . on my way back."

"Taking the long way back, are you?"

"I needed to talk to you, but I couldn't find you."

"How hard did you look?"

"Well, not very. I knew you'd find me eventually."

"You mean you knew Moifinn would send me out looking for you eventually."

"Yes, that's what I meant."

Kicking off her boots, Brae leaned back against the dolman.

"So what did you want to talk about?" she asked.

Scratching absently at Balo's muzzle, Etaine frowned. "I got my first flows today."

"I heard."

The girl's brows drew down in a dark vee. "From who?" she demanded.

"Conlach."

Etaine scowled at the mention of her brother's name. "Conlach should mind his own business," she snapped.

"True enough."

"Does everyone know?"

"Probably."

"Jerk." She glared at the general direction of Tara until Balo swiped one large paw at her hand and she moved it down to scratch his chest. "It makes me feel all fat and heavy," she continued. "And the blood was brown and dark. Not like what I was expecting at all. Shouldn't it be brighter?"

Catching up a handful of grasses, Brae began to twine them around her fingers. "It'll be brighter next time," she answered.

"So, I'm not dying, then?"

"Did you really think you were?"

"Well . . . no." Drawing her legs up, Etaine leaned

her chin against her knees. "As soon as they found out, all the old lady Druids were on me like a pack of dogs on a kill," she complained. "They say I'm an *adult* now."

"Mm-hm."

"Am I?"

"If the Learned Ones say you are, why are you asking me?"

"I dunno. 'Cause you know things. *Real* things. Not just things from stories."

Tossing the grasses aside, Brae shrugged. "You've set foot on the path to adulthood, anyway," she allowed. "I wouldn't say you'd traveled very far, though."

Etaine frowned. "What would you know about it?" she grumbled half under her breath.

Brae just shrugged and after a moment Etaine gave a long, drawn out sigh. "What if I'm not ready to be an adult?" she asked.

"Are you?"

"I don't know."

Brae stretched out and laid her head back into the cool grass and closed her eyes. "So why worry about it, then? Just be who you are until you do know."

"What if I never know?"

"Then you never have to worry about it."

"I suppose that makes a twisted kind of sense."

"There you are."

The two of them sat in companionable silence for a long time until Etaine glanced shyly over at the older woman.

"Were you ready? To be an adult, I mean, when you got your first flows?"

Brae snorted. "Not hardly."

"How old were you?"

"Your age."

"The Druids seem to think that every goddess of

sex, birth, and hearth is going to take an interest in me now."

"Well, just keep away from anything sporting antlers and you should be safe."

"That's not funny."

"Sure it is," Brae chuckled but said no more, and after a moment Etaine stretched out in the grass as well, giving an involuntary grunt as Balo dropped his head onto her chest.

"Lugach says we're going to have a party to celebrate my adulthood," she said, watching a hawk circling high above them in the almost painfully blue sky.

"Lugach likes parties."

"It seems . . . foolish to me."

"Don't *you* like parties?"

Etaine frowned. "It's not that. And no, not particularly. I like being by myself. It just seems foolish to have a party because I got blood all over my breeks."

"There's more to it than that. There's that whole adult thing, remember? It's symbolic."

"Oh, right." Etaine raised herself up on one elbow, ignoring Balo's grunt of reproach. "I don't feel like an adult," she groused. "I don't feel any different at all." She dropped back down again. "Except for that whole bloated, fat, and cramping thing. Of course," she added in a happier tone, "Lugach also said that Conlach can't come to the party, so that's something."

"It's for women only," Brae agreed, swiping at a fly that kept trying to land on one ear. "In this case, for women warriors, Druids, and bards in the Fianna only."

"I'm not in the Fianna yet," Etaine pointed out.

"You soon will be."

"What if I fail my test?"

The plaintive sound in her voice caused Brae to

glance over at her. "Is that what this is all about?" she asked.

Etaine jerked a buttercup up by the roots and began to shred it compulsively until Balo whined at her and she reached over to scratch his muzzle again. "Maybe," she allowed. "Conlach says I'll fail. He says that I should go home now before I make a fool of myself and shame our whole family."

"Since when do you listen to anything Conlach has to say?"

Etaine just shrugged.

"Well, never," Brae answered for her. "You don't listen to older brothers, or to younger brothers either for that matter. You should know that by now."

"Sure, but Conlach passed," Etaine insisted.

"Barely. I remember his test. My spear came within a hair's breadth of gelding him."

"Exactly, barely." Etaine said, ignoring the joke she might otherwise have laughed at. She stood abruptly, bouncing Balo off her chest. He glared at her in sleepy annoyance and scooted over to lay his head across Brae's legs instead. "He's faster and he's stronger than me," she continued, waving her arms. "He'll probably catch me just because he can."

"He probably won't be chasing you at all; family usually doesn't."

"Will you be chasing me?"

"Maybe."

"*You're* family."

"*Second* cousins."

"Still. And you've got hound blood, *Sidhe* hound blood. How'm I supposed to outrun that?"

"By calling on your own Sidhe *deer* blood, like everyone in your family does, like Conlach did, only he manifested antlers, so he got a little distracted."

"Antlers?"

"Well, little antlers," Brae allowed. "Single prong."

This time Etaine snickered. Sitting back down, she glanced over to see if Balo would return to her, then sighed as he ignored her.

"But I probably won't be chasing you either," Brae continued, "because Fionn might suppose I'd let you get away on purpose."

"Would you?"

"Maybe at first, but when I run, the hound blood comes up and I forget things. I might even try to bite you," she added, showing her teeth at the girl.

Etaine ignored the threat with casual élan. "You never have before," she pointed out.

"You've never been in front of me before. But don't worry," Brae continued before Etaine could take offense at the comment. "You're fast and you're fleet. You'll be fine."

"But what if I get a spear through the head right at the beginning?"

"Then you'll have nothing more to worry about."

Etaine frowned at her for a moment and then nodded. "Yes, there is that," she agreed, watching as the hawk suddenly dropped into the grasses beyond a small hillock. "It's a stupid test, anyway," she muttered, glancing over at Brae to see the effect of her words, but Brae was watching a bumblebee buzz about the clover by her right foot.

"Really stupid," she added.

"Hm?"

"The test. It's stupid."

"Oh." Brae shrugged. "It's the test."

"Even if I die?"

"Even if."

"Think I might?"

"Hard to say."

"Think there'll be cake? At the party, I mean?"

"I imagine so."

"Think it'll have a red filling?"

Brae just snorted.

"Think there'll be cake at my funeral? You know, if I do get a spear through the head right at the beginning?"

"No. Likely there'll just be biscuits."

"Good thing I shan't be wanting any of them, then."

"Yes, good thing; more for me." Mention of biscuits made Brae think of moonrise and Matha and then dinner and biscuits and Matha again. A lazy smile played across her face and Etaine frowned at her.

"My mother doesn't like it when I talked about death," she said. "She lectures; so does Moifinn. But you don't."

Brae opened one eye. "What?"

"Lecture. About death. You don't."

"Oh." Digging a pebble out from beneath her shoulder, Brae shrugged again. "Why should I?"

"They think I don't take it seriously enough."

Brae shrugged. "Why should you? It happens to everyone eventually, so why worry about it?"

"Is that your answer for everything? Don't worry about it?"

"Yes."

"So, it doesn't scare you? Death, I mean?"

"I suppose it might if I thought about it, so I don't."

"My mother says I think too much."

"Oh?"

"Moifinn says I don't think enough."

Brae snickered. "She's probably talking about specific things; like the poetics."

Etaine gave a disdainful sniff. "I have dozens of verses memorized all ready," she retorted, "both spoken and sung, from Togla, Forbaisi, Tana, Echtrada, Catha, Aideda, *and* Airgne," she said picking each one off on a finger.

"Well, that certainly covers all your martial choices,"

Brae agreed, "so if you're called on to recite a poem about sieges, battles, and plunders you'll be fine."

"And destructions, cattle raids, adventures, *and* tragedies," Etaine pointed out.

"You don't like feasts? I always liked feasts. All those long lists of meats." She licked her lips.

"I'm working on Fessa."

"What about Aitheid and Tochmarca?"

"What about them?"

"Well, I know elopements and courtships aren't as exciting as destructions and battles—there's less bloodshed for one thing . . ."

"Sometimes there's bloodshed," Etaine interrupted.

"Yes, and sometimes there's just wooing and kissing. You need some of that, too."

"Did you?" Etaine challenged.

"One of each."

"Fine, I'll learn one of each." She paused. "Which ones have the most bloodshed?"

"Ask Moifinn."

"In other words, you don't remember."

"In other words, I don't *have* to remember." Blinking up at the late afternoon sun, Brae gave a great yawn and beside her Balo yawned as well. "And don't forget the others," she said almost as an afterthought. "You need navigation, which one was that? Imrama, and . . ." she yawned again. "Whatever the other one is."

"Uatha," Etaine supplied primly.

"Right, caves." Brae shook her head remembering her own lack of interest in anything that didn't involve horses, dogs, or swordplay. Or meat. "If you get called on to recite one of those and you can't, you'll fail as surely as if you did get a spear in the head right at the beginning."

"I'll know them when I have to," Etaine answered

testily. "And it's not like I haven't got lots of time. Fionn isn't due back to Tara for weeks."

"Maybe, but Garbhcronan has the authority to convene the testing in Fionn's absence and he's due back *next* week."

"Oh." Etaine chewed uncertainly at her lower lip. "Do you think he might?"

Brae snapped at the returning fly. "No, so stop *worrying;* you won't be tested until you're ready, which won't be until *all* your teachers say you are, including Moifinn. And maybe even me. But probably not," she amended.

Etaine watched a wren chasing a raven away from its nest then frowned again. "I had a dream last night, Brae," she said suddenly.

"Oh?"

"I was running in unfamiliar woods—to the west, I think, because I seemed to be following the sun. I was running fast, so much faster than I'd ever run before, and then I realized I was running on all fours like a deer."

"*Were* you a deer?"

Etaine cocked her head to one side. "I think perhaps I must have been. *Anyway,* I was running because something, some *things* were chasing me and I was afraid. I ran faster and faster, but they kept coming, and just when I thought they would catch me, I came upon a huge gnarled oak tree with three animals sitting in its branches: a white whelp with red ears, a fat, brown hare, with, you know," she gestured absently at her chest, "teats like it had been nursing, and a crow so old its feathers were turning white and soft. And beneath it I saw a woman. She was small and dark, and had flowing black hair. She wore a red cloak about her shoulders and a golden torque around her neck and she carried a bronze sword in one hand

and a rowan branch in the other. She seemed familiar, but I couldn't think who she might be. She motioned, and the three animals drew me up into the branches so that when the things that were hunting me came upon us . . ."

"What'd they look like?"

Etaine frowned at the interruption. "I couldn't really see them too well," she answered stiffly, "but I saw that they were carrying spears, and as each one threw their spear at me, a different one of the animals caught the spear and hurled it back, killing the . . . whatever they were. But as the animals caught the spears, they got their hands, or paws . . . or wings, whatever, nicked and a drop each of their blood mingled with a drop of the hunter's blood and they turned into three red gems, like rubies only brighter." She paused. "So, what do you think it means, Brae? And don't tell me it has anything to do with my flows, or being an adult, or having sex, because I've already rejected those possibilities as being *completely foolish*. Do you think it might mean that I'll pass my test?"

"Maybe. What did Moifinn say?"

Etaine stared up at the sky. "Well, I haven't *actually* told her yet."

"Why not?"

"Well, I haven't *actually* seen her today."

"Didn't you have lessons after our run this morning?"

"Sort of . . . not."

"Sort of not, why?"

"Well, I sent her a message saying I needed to talk to you and then I got busy."

"So, in other words you tried to use me as an excuse to duck out on lessons, then didn't even bother to warn me that you had."

"I would have warned you if I could have found you," Etaine replied. "I mean, if I could have remembered to actually look for you," she added sheepishly. "But it was just *too nice a day.*"

Brae sighed. "Yes, I know."

"But I did find Cnu Deireoil, and he said I had an aisling dream and that the woman I saw was a speir-bhean."

"Well, he ought to know, he's a Sidhe. And a bard."

"But he didn't tell me what it meant."

Shaking the dried grass from her hair, Brae reached for her boots. "I think it means we're going on a journey," she said cheerfully.

"We?"

"We. C'mon; we've managed to avoid lessons long enough and we have to talk to Moifinn about this before we make any real plans."

"We?"

"We."

"You're a woman now, Etaine."

"I know."

"You can't just run off and play whenever the mood takes you. You have responsibilities and duties."

"I *know.*"

"*And* now that you've had your first flows, you really have to buckle down and prepare for your test."

"I . . ."

Moifinn shot her a warning glance from beneath her steel-gray brows and Etaine shut her mouth with a snap, wishing that she and Brae had decided to head off on that journey alone instead of waiting to speak to Moifinn. But it was too late now. The senior Druid had been waiting for them both when they'd returned to the Court. Etaine had immediately muttered some excuse about the latrine, but Brae had caught her by the back of the tunic, effectively cutting off her escape. Now she gave her teacher a halfheartedly apologetic look.

"I *do* know it," she said.

Moifinn crossed her arms. "Really?" she asked, her voice dripping with sarcasm. "Because you certainly haven't demonstrated that fact lately, and that is *your* fault," she added, turning on Brae.

"*My* fault?"

"You encourage her." As Brae made to protest, Moifinn glared her into silence. "You're always running off whenever a scent catches your nose—you're like a half-trained puppy—and Etaine follows your lead. She's a daughter of kings, Brae. You know what that means? One day she might represent Sovereignty. That's a huge responsibility; if it happens, she won't be able to use you as an excuse to avoid it."

"I did tell her that," Brae protested. "Didn't I, Etaine? Sort of. Except that bit about Sovereignty, which I didn't think about."

"Are either of you planning on listening?"

"Yes."

She turned to Etaine.

"*Yes.*"

"But in the meantime we have a bigger problem," Brae continued.

"Which is?"

"She's had a dream."

"I don't have time for this," Moifinn groused in a tone very similar to Etaine's. "I have students and responsibilities of my own, you know; I can't just drop everything to go wandering off on some girl-child's vision quest."

Brae just shrugged. Pulling the wing off the boiled chicken between them, she chewed at it reflectively. After explaining Etaine's dream, the two of them had allowed the girl to join the other students at supper while they sought a quiet meal in the Druid's Hall. "There were three animals," she reminded the older woman unnecessarily. "Three champions, one for each of Maid, Mother, and Crone."

"You think so?" Moifinn snarled at her. "Because the symbolism had escaped *me* utterly."

"Well, the whelp is obviously me for the Maiden . . ."

"No! Really?"

"And the crow is you for the Crone."

Moifinn's eyes narrowed. "Why me?"

"You're her teacher."

"Hmph." Pulling a clay pipe from her pocket, Moifinn stuffed a pinch of dried catmint into the bowl and caught up a candle, pointedly ignoring the disapproving glare from the old man at the next table.

"Now, what about Macha?" Brae prodded.

"What about Her?"

"Any ideas?"

"None whatsoever. You're the scholar today, you figure it out."

"What about her mother?"

"Her mother's in Nenagh. What about *your* mother?"

"She's in Wales. Maighneis?"

"Crone."

"Since when?"

"Last year."

"I didn't think she was that old. What about Cainche?"

"Maiden."

"Lugach."

"*Maiden.* Tamair, Camma, all of your sisters save Imaris in Wales, the same."

They fell silent. Brae passed Balo a strip of chicken under the table while Moifinn sucked peevishly on the stem of her pipe.

"You know the problem," the older woman observed after a moment, drawn in despite herself, "there's precious few female Fianna who follow the Mother."

Brae shot her an incredulous glance. "Well, are you surprised? Who wants to go to war with a baby hanging off the tit?"

"I did."

"Did you actually want to?"

"Well, no, not *actually*. They kind of snuck in under my guard."

"On a river of beer from the tales I've heard."

Moifinn chuckled. "Those were good days. Of course, these are good days, too," she added reflectively, "all the appetite and experience with none of the yowling consequences." She blew a smoke ring into the air. "Oh, yes, the Crone gives the best gifts," she observed.

"Does that include the bad knees, cantankerous attitude, and loss of any real sense of humor or adventure?" Brae said sarcastically as she tore off another wing.

"Yes." Moifinn swallowed the contents of the very large tankard in front of her before thumping it down on the table. "And let's be honest, we're stalling. There's only one real candidate and we both know it."

Brae nodded with a resigned expression. "Creidne. She won't like it."

"She's had three children. She qualifies, and she's the daughter of kings, a representative of Sovereignty."

Brae winced. "If I were you, I wouldn't remind her of that part."

"Me? Oh, no. I only represent Death; you're supposed to be Challenge and the Vigor of Youth. *You* don't remind her."

"Thanks a lot."

"You're welcome; if you're going to drag an old lady from her studies, you deserve what you get.

Speak to Creidne, then get some sleep. I imagine we'll have a long, bumpy ride ahead of us tomorrow."

"But I have a . . . courtship tonight," Brae protested.

"Too bad."

"Yes, it is." She rose with a sigh. "Oh, well, maybe Creidne will kill me before Matha leaves me for Duail." Whistling to Balo, she caught up a drumstick before heading for the door. "C'mon, boy, let's go risk our lives in the name of family."

The sound of Moifinn's harsh, unimpressed laughter followed them from the hall.

"Are you sure this is a fairy mound? It looks a little . . . tatty to me?"

Etaine peered at the low hill before them with a dubious expression.

The four women had ridden out from Tara early the next morning with Balo and Creidne's dog, Grier, following along behind, and had ridden quietly westward—or as quietly as Etaine could ride—keeping the River Boyne more or less in view. An hour after noon they'd come upon a clearing with a huge, gnarled oak tree growing beside a low mound in the center.

Dismounting, Creidne shot Etaine an exasperated look. "What did you expect?" she snapped, "ribbons and gold lace hanging from a magical portcullis?"

Etaine started guiltily. "Well, yes, actually."

"You think too much."

"That's what I keep saying."

Behind them, both Moifinn and Brae rolled their eyes.

Creidne had been as unthrilled to represent the Mother Aspect as they'd expected, but had finally agreed after Brae had promised to catch her a brace of coneys. The greatest resistance, however, had come, surprisingly, from Etaine who, after learning of their preparations, had practically bolted from the room.

"What if it doesn't mean that at all?" she'd demanded in a shrill voice. *"What if we get lost, or eaten by wild boars, or drowned in a mystical lake, or lured off to Tir Na n'Og?"*

"Then you'll die forgotten, skewered, soggy, or happy," Brae'd answered bluntly. *"We're going."*

"Why?"

"Because I'm bored!"

"Fine. Whatever. You don't have to shout."

She'd sulked for the first few miles, but as a warm summer breeze began to weave playfully through her hair, she forgot her pique and begun to sing the latest song Cnu Deireoil had taught her. Now, however, as Moifinn and Brae joined Creidne on the ground, she hung back again.

"What if the speir-bhean lays a geis on me," she asked worriedly. "Because, from the stories *I've* heard, they seem awfully inconvenient. Imagine never being able to refuse anyone's hospitality no matter how busy you were or how terrible the food was reputed to be or, worse, not being able to talk from dawn to dusk or some such other *foolish* piece of nonsense."

"Yes," Moifinn said dryly. "Imagine that."

"What?"

"I said, imagine running away and accounting yourself a coward who couldn't face her own vision quest?" the Druid answered sweetly. "How's that going to appear to Fionn mac Cumhaill?"

"Etaine," Brae interjected before the girl could respond. "Neither Balo nor Grier is sensing anything otherworldly or dangerous here, and you know that they'd be the first ones to react, right?"

The girl glanced over to see the hounds in question happily rolling in what appeared to be a large pile of . . . droppings.

"Oh, yes," she muttered, "They're on guard all right; I'm so relieved." Dismounting, she followed Creidne while Brae took the horses to a small stream and Moifinn pulled out her pipe with a sigh.

They made one or two cautious inspections of the mound and the tree, and Etaine was just about to announce that she was certain the entire journey was foolish when Brae, Balo, and Grier suddenly froze.

Creidne immediately drew her sword.

"What?" Etaine asked in a strangled whisper.

"The birds have stopped singing," Brae answered quietly. "Someone's coming."

"Someone or something?"

"I don't know."

They turned to see a small, dark, ebony-haired woman emerge from the trees to the west and Etaine's jaw dropped.

"Well, I can see why you thought she looked familiar," Brae said jokingly as she and the dogs relaxed. "She's you."

"Only older," Moifinn noted. "That makes sense."

The older Etaine stopped ten paces away, casting a peevish glance at the four women. "You're late," she accused and Creidne gave an explosive snort as she resheathed her sword.

"Well, it's nice to see you haven't changed," she replied.

"Three creatures will challenge you to single combat. You must choose a champion from the three who ride beside you, one for each aspect of Maiden, Mother, and Crone."

"Told you," Brae said to no one in particular.

"Shut up," Creidne snapped. "Or we'll be here all night."

Standing before the older version of herself, Etaine frowned. "But if I'm going to be attacked by three monsters," she insisted, "shouldn't the Maiden deal with all three of them?"

Creidne ground her teeth together. The two Etaines had been arguing like this for the last half an hour and she was getting very annoyed.

"I never said *monsters*," the older Etaine retorted, "and I never said *attacked*, though if you choose wrongly, both will likely be the case."

"Wrongly?"

"Wrongly. It's a druidic term. *Everybody* knows that." The older Etaine turned to Moifinn with a baleful expression. "Was I really this obtuse?" she demanded.

"Yes."

"Hey!" the younger Etaine shouted. "Standing right here with perfectly good hearing, you know!"

The older Etaine swung her attention back. "Oh, right. Sorry. But it's still three creatures, three champions, and three combats. That's the test; take it or leave it."

"But . . ."

"And here comes the first one now."

They turned and Brae leaped forward instinctively but came up short against an invisible barrier as Etaine let out a tiny shriek of alarm.

The creature that came rushing from the trees had a huge, sinewy body covered in a mottled gray-and-green pelt and three triangular heads that snapped and snarled and tore at each other even as they lunged toward the women on the mound. Both Balo and Grier made to leap forward as well, but at a sharp whistle from the older Etaine, they froze, quivering and growling, the hair on the backs of their necks standing up like little spikes.

She raised an ebony eyebrow. "Seems like an easy choice, doesn't it?" she said casually. "Big, scary creature. Traditional enemy of the Sidhe hounds, too. I guess it *must* be Maiden, huh?''

Etaine frowned. She looked from Brae, to Moifinn, to Creidne, then back to Brae again. The youngest of her three champions was almost shaking with impatience, the oldest was standing easily with a faint smile on her lips, but Creidne was watching the creature with a look of such dark disapproval that Etaine was suddenly reminded of her own mother and what usually came after such a look.

"Mother," she said firmly.

"You sure?"

Etaine glanced from one to the other. "Oh, yeah."

Without changing her expression or drawing her sword, Creidne walked forward until she stood ten paces from the snarling creature. It rushed forward, howling like a hundred banshees, but came to a disorganized halt as Creidne simply crossed her arms deliberately, managing to stare all three heads in the eye at once. Uncertainty crossed their faces almost at the same time. Creidne's expression turned to a flat, impatient scowl.

"Well?" she demanded.

The first head drew back while the second snapped at it and the third lurched forward.

Creidne's left foot began to tap very slowly against the ground.

"I'm *waiting*."

The second head joined the first while the third wove back and forth uncertainly.

"Don't *make* me come down there."

The creature fled.

With a disdainful sniff, Creidne crossed to where it had stood. As she reached for the small drop of blood left behind, a stone scratched against her hand and a tiny bead of her own blood seeped out to join the creature's lying in the grass. The two became a small red jewel just as Etaine had dreamed it would and Creidne picked it up and tossed it at the older Etaine as she rejoined the others.

"When you've raised as many as I have," she said in answer to Brae's mystified expression, "you come to learn what's empty bravado and what isn't."

They barely had time to absorb this before the second creature attacked.

It seemed to be made of reeds and mist and sea grasses all dancing and weaving in a current of air that only it could sense. Thin, almost childish voices filled the air and Etaine froze as its words reached out to wrap about her like strands of spiderwebbing; words of weakness and fear and failure and shame. The closer the creature came to her, the more paralyzed she became. She heard Brae speaking to her, shouting at her to choose, but her own voice had fled to join the creature's and she couldn't form the word until Moifinn caught her by the arm and jerked her about to face the other Etaine. She frowned. The other *older* Etaine—the Etaine that must have faced this combat and obviously survived—was watching the creature with a cynical sneer so familiar that it gave her just enough strength to speak one word:

"Crone."

With a feral grin, Moifinn leaped from the mound. Arms outstretched, she shouted the words of an ancient spell and, with a clap of displaced air, took the form of a huge, white crow. Great wings beat the air, harder and harder, battering at the creature with a cacophony of new voices that shouted of life and living, of growing and changing, and learning and winning, until it bowed under the onslaught, and finally fell to sink into the earth.

Once again, it left a single drop of blood behind, and once again Moifinn reached for it and a stone drew a second drop from her hand to mingle with the first and form a small red gem. Once again she presented it to the older Etaine, and once again, before they had a chance to collect their thoughts, the next creature streaked toward them from the trees.

A freezing-cold mist enveloped it like a shroud. Its eyes were huge and black, its clawed fingers, gnarled and twisted with age. At every step the grass beneath its feet withered and died and, as it raised itself up and screamed, the horses bolted and the dogs fled into the woods. Brae hurled herself from the mound only to slam against the invisible barrier once more and as she turned, snarling in rage, she saw Etaine collapse. Creidne caught her in her arms, cradling her head as she fell and Brae rounded on the other, demanding an explanation.

"You can't fight until she chooses you!" the older Etaine shouted over the creature's screaming.

"I'm the only one left! This is my challenge!"

"No, it's not. It's Etaine's! She has to choose!"

"She can't!"

"She has to!"

Brae dropped to her knees. Catching up Etaine's hand, she squeezed her fingers.

"C'mon, Etaine," she urged. "Just say the word, just say it."

Etaine's eyes rolled back in her head. "Wha . . ."

"You know the word I need!"

"Biscuits?"

"Very much the wrong word! Maiden, just say Maiden, Etaine!"

"Mai . . ."

Brae whirled about, but the older Etaine was shaking her head and she snapped at her in frustration. The creature lunged for the mound, its claws outstretched . . .

". . . den."

With a scream of fury, a great white dog with red ears hit the creature in mid-leap. The two of them crashed to the mound in a tangle of tangled limbs and flashing teeth. As it hit the ground, the creature suddenly became an eagle with razor-sharp talons and black, savage eyes. It slashed its beak across Brae's shield arm, opening up a great gash that splattered the ground with blood, and with a scream of rage and pain, Brae twisted in midair, tearing a huge mouthful of feathers from its back. Gripping one wing between her teeth, she tore it free and the creature spun about to become a huge gray rat. Its claws raked against her muzzle, then her face, as the pain snapped Brae back into human form and, with a howl, she caught it up in her teeth, and not even bothering to change back to hound form, broke its neck with a savage shake of her head. She flung its body to one side, but as it touched the ground, it rose up as a great white stag with blood red hooves. Thundering forward, it cracked Brae across the skull and she went flying, but was up again in a heartbeat, ducking under its belly to tear at a vulnerable hamstring. It hobbled away on three legs, then spun about in the form of a giant wild boar. As it raced at her, Brae dove toward the mound and caught up her sword, driving the iron blade into the creature's belly even as it caught her through the shoulder with one flashing tusk. Boar and warrior went tumbling off the other side of the mound to finally come to rest on the other side, bloody and still.

"The three gems of the Fianna."

The four women crouched on the mound glanced over as the last of the afternoon sun filtered weakly through the trees. Creidne was cleaning the worst of Brae's wounds while Moifinn was comforting Etaine who'd collapsed in hysterics, certain that Brae had been killed. But as Brae raised her head long enough to spit a gob of blood and matted boar's hair onto the ground, she calmed enough to turn a baleful glare on her older self.

"What?"

"The three gems," the older Etaine repeated.

"Are mine."

"Not yet. Your champions won the combats . . ."

"Barely . . ." Brae muttered.

"But to win the gems you have to tell me what the combats mean."

Etaine's face flushed a dangerous red. "Don't tell me this was all just another lesson . . ." she warned.

The older Etaine shrugged. "The three gems of the Fianna," she repeated once more, "are its three strengths used to fight and defeat its three weaknesses. The first . . ." she held up Creidne's gem, "is lack of discipline. Defeated by . . . ?" She gave Etaine a questioning glance.

Etaine snarled at her. "Strength of will, I suppose," she growled after a moment.

The older Etaine tossed her the first gem. "And strength of will is attained by what?"

Etaine gave an explosive breath. "Practice, like everyone's always telling me."

Her older self nodded. "The second weakness," she continued, "is lack of confidence—you wouldn't know anything about that, would you?"

Etaine ignored her.

"And it's defeated by what?"

"Killing your know-it-all older self? I'm kidding!" Etaine raised both hands. "C'mon, return to a sense of humor; I'm trying to. Strength of . . . let's see, heart?"

"Heart." The second gem was tossed after the first. Creidne rolled her eyes, but Moifinn just lit her pipe with an inscrutable expression.

"Attained by?"

"Experience. I'm not *that* obtuse, you know."

"We'll see. Third: lack of physical prowess. Defeated by . . ."

"Strength of . . . well, the body, I should think."

Beside her Brae gave an involuntary hiss as Creidne began to clean the nastiest of the wounds on her arm.

"Attained by . . . ?

Etaine frowned. "Well, decent amour would have been a good start," she observed dryly.

"I agree," Brae added.

The older Etaine just raised an eyebrow at her.

"Really big teeth?"

The cynical sneer returned to the other face.

"Well, I don't know!" Etaine shouted, finally losing her temper. "Practice, experience, valor, courage, eating enough red meat even!"

"Patience."

"What?"

"Patience," the older Etaine repeated. "The patience to work and train and struggle, experiencing successes and failures until you reach your goal." She tossed her younger self the final gem.

"I thought she was supposed to figure that out herself," Moifinn noted dryly.

The older Etaine just shrugged. "I got tired of waiting." Jumping from the mound, she vanished into the trees.

There was silence in the clearing until Brae coughed weakly.

"Anyone seen my dog?"

"I got tired of waiting?"

As the sounds of Etaine's party—laughter and singing generously mixed with shouts of alarm—issued from the Court of Learning's wide stone windows into the cool, moonlit garden beyond, Moifinn leaned back and lit her pipe with a disbelieving expression. Beside her, Creidne shrugged.

"Maid, Mother, and Crone. Some things change, some things remain the same."

"I suppose. I had hoped Etaine might gain some wisdom with her years, though."

"I imagine she will when she's older."

"Older? How old did you think she was?"

"Thirty, maybe?"

"I'd have thought closer to fifty."

"Likely we all saw differently."

"Hm. Brae?"

Brae glanced up from the ground where she was being frantically ministered to by a very contrite Balo and Grier.

"What?"

"How old did the other Etaine seem to you?"

Brae shrugged. "I dunno, her own age, I guess. I never really noticed. Why?"

"Never mind."

"Like I said," Creidne snorted, "Some things remain the same."

"I won, didn't I? What needs to change? And you have to admit it was a great fight." Brae craned her neck around carefully. "Still think I'm a half-trained puppy, Moifinn?"

"I suppose not so much," the older woman allowed. "I seem to have been reminded just how a true puppy behaves. But I hope you learned that you can't just leap into battle without thinking, especially into a battle that isn't yours."

"The worst battle turned out to *be* mine," Brae reminded her.

"Serves you right for staying in Maiden," Creidne chided.

"I suppose I should have gone over to Mother; then I could have just glared my enemy into submission."

"It's a skill that takes years to master. I doubt you have the patience to learn it."

"Hey, my gem *was* patience, remember? And besides, I don't see why I'm the one who had to learn anything," Brae retorted. "It wasn't *my* quest, after all."

"So you didn't learn anything?" Moifinn prodded. "Did you?"

"Perhaps that I'm too old to go wandering about on some girl-child's vision quest. But, then I already knew that. Creidne?"

"That I wouldn't be fourteen again for all the magic in Tir Na n'Og. But, as you said, I already knew that also."

"No wonder we didn't get to keep our gems," Brae grumbled. "And mine should have been a lot bigger than yours. I shed the most blood."

"Etaine's dream only made provision for one drop each. Perhaps you should have fought more carefully," Creidne answered.

"Tell that to the eagle-rat-stag-boar thing."

"Physical strength is the domain of the Maiden," Moifinn stated in a lecturing tone that made both Brae and Creidne roll their eyes. "Just as strength of will is the domain of the Mother and strength of heart that of the Crone."

"Which do you suppose Etaine will turn to?" Creidne asked.

Brae chuckled. "Is there a fourth choice?"

"She'll go to Mother," Moifinn stated firmly.

"No!" Brae raised her arms in a posture of mock horror, but Creidne nodded ruefully. "Yes, I imagine you're right," she agreed. "Anything else would be *foolish,* wouldn't it?"

Moifinn snickered. "And on that note . . ." Tapping her pipe clean on a flagstone, she rose with a gleeful expression. "I'm off to Etaine's party before the children drink all the beer and get *foolish.* Are you coming, Brae?"

She nodded. "I could drink. I hurt . . . everywhere, but I could drink. Creidne?"

The other woman shook her head. "Let the Maiden and the Crone have the revelry. I'm tired and I'm hungry. I want a bath, a hot cup of mead, and someone to rub my feet. And don't get too carried away. You owe me a brace of coneys."

"Etaine and I'll go out hunting for them first thing tomorrow morning," Brae promised. "If I can move by then."

"Oh, no, you won't," Moifinn retorted. "Etaine will be spending tomorrow learning verses from Aitheid and Tochmarca, and if you so much as *try* to lure her away, I'll have your otherworldly pelt for a lap blanket."

"It would be a pretty ragged blanket."

"I'm good with my needle."

"Ouch."

"Don't you forget it." Moifinn tucked her pipe into her belt. "But you never said what you learned, Brae," she noted. "You must have learned something."

Rising with a groan, Brae caught sight of a familiar figure standing in the doorway, arms crossed, expression an equal mixture of annoyance, worry, and exasperation. She grinned.

"I learned that you should always have sex *before* battle," she answered. "But then, as you said, I already knew that." Whistling to Balo, she made for the door. "And that you're never too injured for a biscuit. Beyond that, why worry about it?" She turned. "Tell Etaine I'll see her when she's done versing and we'll go for a run," she said, then tucking Matha's arm in hers, very carefully headed inside, Balo at her heels.

THE THINGS SHE HANDED DOWN
by Russell Davis

Russell Davis lives with his family in Arizona. He has published numerous short stories, and a handful of novels in various genres under a couple of different names. He divides his time between freelance editorial consulting, writing, and teaching.

SEVERAL DAYS BEFORE she dies, I am standing on the back patio of our house. The last of the day's sun is slanting down through the autumn trees, making the trunks look black in the shadows. I am sipping coffee and smoking a cigarette. I am outside because outside is where I don't have to face the truth. I am a writer, and I can imagine realities far different from my own.

She is inside; she is cooking dinner, or resting or reading or playing with my children. This is what I tell myself. These images are not true, but they are more comforting than those that assail me when I am inside. She is dying, I can see that—any fool can see that—but the acceptance of death is a slow process. I would rather bend my mind toward the lies I've been telling myself for weeks: she is getting better; it looks worse than it is . . . somehow, I can save her.

It is cold outside, and when I toss my still-smoldering cigarette to the ground, the butt hisses when it hits the wet grass. Even with the patio door closed, I can hear her voice, calling for me to come to her room. I pretend I am imagining things. I don't want to go inside yet—better to stay out here in the fading light with my lukewarm coffee and my memories intact—but another voice inside me demands that I answer her. This is the writer voice, the one that whispers in my head during moments of extreme tragedy: *This will be good for a story one day.*

Once, her voice had been a rich alto, capable of extraordinary range. I have heard her voice seduce, sing, or—when angered—strip the skin right from the bone. Now, her voice is tired and raw. A rope frayed to a few thin threads. When I don't answer her right away, she stops calling for me. I tell myself I will go in to her in a few minutes. When I am ready to see her, ready to see the truth of these moments.

My coffee is cold now, and the first stars are appearing like the white eyes of the dead in the darkening sky.

That's a nice little image, the writer voice says. *Let's hang on to that one.*

I laugh to myself, softly, afraid that my wife will hear me and think I'm losing it. There is no ready, there never will be. I could stand out here until . . . it's over . . . and I still won't be ready.

I toss the contents of my cup over the porch rail. As children, we believe in immortality. We believe we are safe, that our loved ones are safe. We don't know any better. In time, we come to understand that these feelings are illusions brought about by a lack of experience. Everyone dies sometime. But this cold knowledge is somehow never translated to our parents. They cannot die, won't ever die because . . . because in the darkest hours of our lives, when we are most frightened, we want nothing more than to call out, like lost children, for our mother or father.

If they can't answer, if they don't answer . . . if all our echoing screams are for naught . . . then to whom can we turn? The answer, of course, is nobody. Even the warm comfort of a much loved, cherished spouse is no replacement for the safety we feel wrapped in the arms of a parent.

These ramblings do no good. Inside, my mother is dying. She knows this. I can read it in her eyes like lines of text on a page. I know it. She can see my shuddering fear as though I am four again, and looking to her to make the nightmares go away. We both pretend nothing is wrong. She will get better. We lie to ourselves because to do otherwise may actually *invite* the inevitable. Knowing that death is coming doesn't mean we're in any rush to see it, let alone acknowledge it.

I light another cigarette, and my wife brings me more coffee. It steams in the air, and the writer voice says, *like the ghosts of children*. For a minute, we both stand there and stare out into the night. Then she says, "She's asking for you."

I nod. "I know. I'll be in in a minute or two."

"Take your time," she tells me, then turns and goes inside. The patio door slides on its tracks and closes. I try to think of a metaphor that doesn't involve trains for the sound it makes, but nothing comes to me.

Time, I think, that's the one thing we don't have. And what the hell would we change if we had more? What would it change?

Nothing, the writer voice says. *Not one single thing.*

We'd do things differently, I tell myself.

The writer voice laughs.

I don't want to go inside, but I know that I must. She will need help getting into the bathtub tonight. She has mentioned that she wants me to cut her hair. Once, it had been long—blond waves cresting down to her shoulders. Now it hangs limp and ragged and, strangely, burned. She fell asleep in the bathtub two nights ago and caught her hair on fire with a cigarette.

She wants me to cut it short, and I have agreed,

though a voice inside me—not the writer voice, but the tiny spark of child that still remains screams in protest. Her hair has always been long and beautiful.

And now it's like her, the writer voice says. *Dying like unwatered wheat.*

Shut up, I tell the voice. Save the comparisons for later, for after.

But that's what you're thinking, isn't it?

Yes, I admit to myself, I am thinking that. I am making mental comparisons of her in my mind. I am remembering this journey toward her death and thinking she is like the Fates. I have seen her as Clotho—the fair maiden who spun the thread of my existence into being. I remember her role as Lachesis—taking the thread of my life and determining its measure. And now she is Atropos—but rather than cutting my thread, she is snipping her own.

I sigh, hating the comparisons, hating the nature of my mind that forces these images forward for my perusal. I take a drag from my cigarette and toss it away, watching the embers trail behind it like sparks from a comet's tail.

Burning out? the writer voice asks.

I don't answer. I have to go inside.

Atropos is waiting.

"She's not answering my questions and she won't come out of her room. She hasn't really eaten anything in a couple of days. You've got to come home." My wife's voice is quiet, filled with sorrow, but not for herself, or for my mother—for me. "It's time."

"All right," I say. "I'll be there shortly. Keep the kids away from her until I get there. There's no point in scaring them."

"You're right," she says. "See you in a bit."

"Yeah," I say, and hang up. The writer voice is gibbering with excitement, *Go-Go-Go,* it chants. I make up enough work to do that it's another hour before I leave the office and go home. It is too short of a drive, five minutes perhaps.

My wife and children are in the living room. A fire burns in the fireplace and the only lamp that is on is a corner lamp that casts odd shadows on the ceiling. I stop in the threshold, trying to force myself to move forward. My wife meets me there, takes my hand.

"Is she still in her room?" I ask.

"Yes," she says. "She's not talking."

I nod. How can I blame her? If I were in her situation, would I want to talk, knowing that the words I might speak would be flawed? *You'll* never *shut up,* the writer voice assures me. "I'll go back there," I tell her. "Let's see what I can do."

My wife doesn't respond. She doesn't have to.

"Keep the kids busy," I say. "I don't want them to see this."

"I know," she says.

I walk through the house. The children remain in the living room and I briefly wonder what my wife has told them to keep them so sedate. It doesn't matter, I decide. What matters is going forward, step by step, through the house to her little room in the back. My wife has left the lights on.

Over and over, I repeat to myself that I must not show my mother I am scared. I must not allow her to see my fear because instinct will force her into a mode of comforting me, and she doesn't have the energy for that. Her door is open a crack, enough for me to look inside.

She is lying on the bed and for a moment, my eyes trick me. At first, I don't see her as she is *now;* I see her as she was *then.* A young woman, Clotho, just finding her strength. Memory comes . . .

"It's a wonderful thing to believe in God," Mother says. *"It also makes for a hell of a crutch."*

*"A crutch?" I ask. "Why is faith in God a crutch?"
I am nine, perhaps ten, and looking for answers.*

*"Because people tend to use it as an excuse for . . .
well, for damn near anything," she says. "God's will,
they will say, when someone dies. It's all part of the
plan, when something goes wrong. And so on. Think
of your own examples—no doubt, you've encountered
plenty." She takes a sip of her drink and a drag from
her cigarette, then adds, "If there is a plan, I haven't
been notified."*

*I nod in agreement. "But then why do so many peo-
ple believe?"*

*"There's nothing wrong with belief if it's not used as
a crutch. My advice: believe in yourself first and God
second. God helps those who help themselves . . ."*

Looking through the crack in her door, remembering, I realize that I got the message of this conversation wrong. What I heard is believe in yourself and
God when and if it's convenient—and it's usually not.
She is dying, the thread of her life unraveling before
my very eyes, and if I could find the strength or the
conviction, I would gladly take up the crutch of faith.
I would pray like a Baptist preacher on fire.

I slip into the room. "Mom?" I say. I don't want to
touch her. She is wearing a heavy nightdress of some
kind, but her frame is so small and wasted that I can
see her bone structure through the cloth. She looks . . .
fragile, and I am afraid I might hurt her. "Mom?" I
repeat, louder.

She doesn't answer. The rise and fall of her breath
is irregular, her mouth open as her body fights for one
more exchange . . . and another . . . and another. I
steel myself and check her pulse. It is thready, and I
wish for a stethoscope and a blood pressure monitor.
I wish I was a doctor and not a writer.

The writer voice says, *You've got to take her to the
hospital now. You* know *you do.*

I shake my head. She has said she doesn't want to go to the hospital, doesn't want to see a doctor. She *knows* she's dying and doesn't want to be poked and prodded.

You can't let her die here. The setting is all wrong.

Shut up! I snap at the voice. Just shut up.

The voice quiets and I comb my memory for medical knowledge that's applicable, but most of what I know is either related to severe trauma or severe trivia—neither of which will help when someone is suffering from . . .

Liver failure! the writer voice crows in my head. *Malnutrition! Haley and Haley's! A whole plethora of problems! Her whole fucking body is coming apart and you watched it and did nothing. She's been sick for a long time, drinking herself to a slow death, and you watched because that's what writers do. They watch . . . and they write. You'll write about this someday.*

I want to argue with myself, but . . . it's pointless. I did watch. What was I going to say? Who the hell was I to tell her to stop? I watched as her life swirled around the drain and the only thing we ever talked about was politics, Imus, and my kids. We *never* talked about us. And now, it is perhaps far too late for that.

She gave me life, taught me how to measure it, and measured me in the process—and now she is dying. The Fates were real and the last of them is sleeping in a daybed in my guestroom, disguised as my mother.

"Mom?" I say again, touching her shoulder and shaking her. Her whole body moves at the slightest touch. "Mom? You've got to wake up. Tell me what's going on."

Finally, she stirs. Her voice is slurred, weak. "What? What is it now?"

"Mom, you've got to wake up. We need to talk." I will be strong for her, compassionate but firm. "Let's go, Mom."

"I just want to sleep here," she says.

"No," I say. "Wake up, wake up right now. You . . . you need to get moving. There's work to be done."

And the word "work" brings another memory to me . . .

"What do you mean you don't want to go to work?"

"I just don't," I say. "There's a party over at Ron's tonight and I thought—"

"You thought?!" my mother says. Her voice is rising in volume and pitch. "That's exactly what you didn't do. You're not thinking at all."

"Because I want a fucking day off?"

"Because most of the world is filled with people who want a fucking day off!" she says. "Your success in life, how you measure up to others, is determined by your willingness to work. You want to party? Jesus, son, there's always another party. You don't take a day off because you want to—you take a day off because you have to! Successful people work."

"Yeah, but—"

"No! No 'but.' If you don't come into work today, don't bother coming back at all. You don't see me taking days off; I've got you to support. And what I don't need on staff is another person more interested in a party than they are in a paycheck."

She stomps out of the room, and I begin to change clothes—my black and whites for work . . .

How is it possible, I wonder, that this one woman has been so many things to me? She has been mother, father, friend, confidant, employer. How is it possible that all of that has led to this? Her lying here, dying, a withered crone of a woman whose thread of life is so short it is no doubt measured in hours, a few days at the most . . . and I have done nothing to stop it.

The word "work" has stirred her as well. "What work?" she says. "What do you need?"

"I need you to wake up, Mom," I say.

"Fine," she snaps, sitting up. "I'm awake. What do you want?"

"Mom, you haven't eaten in a long time. I *need* to take you to the hospital. Please. Do you want me to drive you or do you want me to call an ambulance? Can you walk out to the car or should I carry you?" I'm babbling and I know it.

She can't walk, the writer voice whispers. *You have to call an ambulance.*

She shakes her head and lies back down. "I don't care," she mumbles, trying to drift back into whatever state she'd been in when I'd woken her. "Just let me sleep."

"No, Mom," I say, shaking her shoulder again. "You need to stay up. You need to tell me what you want me to do." I'm looking for permission from a woman whose mind is all but gone.

It's what you're supposed to do, the writer voice tells me. *You ask permission—it makes for a better story.*

"Don't care," she says. "Do whatever you're going to do." She pauses, breathes, and I think she's drifted away again, but then she says, "You always have."

"Sir? Is that your mother they brought in a few minutes ago?"

"Yes, ma'am," I say. "Are you the attending on call?"

The doctor nods. She has a foreign accent that fits the precision of her words and gestures. "Yes, I am." She offers a hand and a last name I couldn't hope to pronounce, then tells me that she's already looked at my mother.

"So, what's the situation?" I ask.

The doctor shakes her head. "Not good," she says. "Obviously, she's in critical condition. We still have some tests to run, but I can tell you that most likely her liver is failing or has failed completely. There's probably other organs involved at this point as well."

I nod. "That's why she's so badly jaundiced, correct?"

"Yes," she says. "When the liver fails, jaundice is one of the signs. Also, the level of ammonia in her blood is astronomically high. We're giving her something for that now, trying to lower it."

"And?" I prompt, knowing the answer, but fated to ask anyway.

"And, to be honest, I don't think she'll last more than a few days. Most patients in this situation don't. The body just . . . gives up." The doctor stops, considering her next words with care. "How much does she drink?" she finally asks.

"More than she should," I admit. "But with some reason."

"It would have to be a very good reason to drink that much," she says.

"You've noticed the scarring on her legs and arms, her pelvic region?" I ask her. "Did you note the sores?"

"I was going to ask you about that," the doctor says. She takes a pen from her pocket and clicks it open. "Does she have any other illnesses?"

"Haley and Haley's," I tell her.

"What?" The pen stops suddenly.

"It's a variant skin disease," I tell her. "Very rare. The medical name is pemphigus." I explain that the disease is an autoimmune disorder. The pen writes notes as I talk.

"What's the treatment?" she asks.

"Damn little," I say. "The specialist told me it was like being dipped in a liquid fire that you can't put out. He said to give her whatever she wanted—except a gun."

"Gun?" the doctor asks, looking puzzled.

"So she couldn't kill herself," I say.

"That's . . . that's horrible!" the doctor says.

I shake my head, and point to the room where my mother is. "No," I tell the doctor. "That's horrible. I should've bought her the gun and the bullets a long time ago. One end is messy, but quick; this one is just messy."

The doctor shakes her head. This reasoning doesn't appear to work for her. "We'll do all we can. You can go in if you want." She turns away to go and order more tests.

The emergency room is quiet and I walk across the hall to the room where my mother is. On the other side of the door, I can hear the slow *beep—beep—beep* of the heart monitor. I don't want to go in, not yet, and I pause outside the door. The doctor's reaction was understandable, I think, but instead of giving her the gun, I let her keep the bottle.

Death is death, the writer voice says. *It's all in how you portray it.*

I ignore the voice. For the first time in my life, I'm beginning to truly loathe being a writer. I don't need a story or a metaphor in this circumstance. I just want to do this part of this thing right. For the first time ever, my mother and I have truly reversed our roles; I will be forced to make decisions for her—and how can I possibly have the wisdom to do that?

I open the door and step inside. She's fully awake and staring at me with those eyes that I have been pierced by my entire life. "Where have you been?" she says. Her voice is waspish and sharp.

"Out talking with the doctor," I say. "How are you feeling?"

"Horrible," she says. "Why did you bring me here?"

"I had to, Mom," I tell her. "You needed help that I . . . I couldn't provide."

She sighs and leans back on her pillows. "Oh, bull-shit," she whispers. "That's such bullshit."

My mother has moments of pure wisdom, and this is one of them. She's telling me that if I'd wanted to help her, I'd have given her the gun and the bullets. "I don't want this," she says. "I don't want to be here."

I sense that she's getting ready to drift again, her voice is growing softer. "I know, Mom," I tell her. "Let's just see what they say, okay?"

"Whatever," she mumbles. She drifts back into sleep and I'm puzzled by her shifts—awake and aware, drifting and confused. I don't fully understand.

Another doctor steps into the room. He makes al-most no sound, and Mother doesn't stir. "How's she doing?" he asks me.

"All right, I guess. What now?"

"I need to talk with her, assess her cognitive func-tion," he says. "Can you wake her up?"

"Sure," I say, thinking that if she doesn't want to get up, Jesus himself couldn't rouse her. "Mom, wake up," I say, touching her shoulder. "This doctor needs to talk to you."

Surprisingly, she stirs. "What doctor?" she asks.

She is lying on her side, facing the wall, and I must stifle the odd urge to laugh. "The one behind you," I say.

She struggles to roll over and does so. "What do you want?" she asks him.

"Just to ask you some questions, ma'am," he says. "Is that okay?"

Before he even starts, I begin to feel sorry for him. He's young and has no idea that he's about to walk into a threshing machine. "Whatever," my mom says. Her voice is casual and more aware than it's been in several days. I can see her preparing to do battle and inwardly I wince.

"Great," the young doctor says. "Do you know where you are?"

"In a hospital, obviously," my mother replies. "Where do *you* think we are?"

"Uh-huh, and what state are you in?"

"Old and confused," my mother admits. She smirks as the doctor jots rapid notes on his clipboard.

"That's good," the doctor says. "And what's your date of birth?"

"November twenty-fifth," she says.

"What year?"

"None of your damn business," she says with only the briefest of pauses. She doesn't know and doesn't want to admit that.

"Okay," he says. "And can you tell me what city we're in?"

This one catches her and she looks to me for help. As usual, I find that I cannot help her. If the doctors can't assess her true condition, how can they help her?

She shakes her head and doesn't answer.

"That's okay," he says. "Can you tell me who the President of the United States is?"

She's drifting again, but her eyes clear. She loves to watch the news, argue politics. She looks at me and says, quite clearly, "If this idiot doesn't know who the President of the United States is, I'm not answering any more of his questions." She rolls back over and closes her eyes.

The doctor shakes his head ruefully and gestures for me to follow him out of the room. I follow him, pleased at her answers. There were sparks of Clotho and even Lachesis, sharp and quick, mature enough not to want to be insulted. Perhaps it is a sign that this version of her, Atropos, hasn't won quite yet.

The doctor closes the door to her room behind me. "Is she always like that?"

"Like what?" I ask, playing the innocent.

"Ummm . . ."

I decide mercy may be in order. I've felt the sting of her tongue a few times myself. "That sharp?" I ask.

"Yes," he says.

"Sometimes," I say. "When she feels she's being talked down to."

"Oh," he says. "Well, anyway, you saw that she didn't know the answers . . ."

"I know, but who does?" I'm trying not to be glib or flip, but it's happening anyway.

"You know what I mean," he says.

I nod. "Why does she do that? Sort of awake and aware one minute, the next, she's not."

"It's the ammonia in her blood," he says, back on comfortable ground. "It causes brain damage. If we can't get the level down, she'll go into a coma. She may anyway. That's sort of what she's doing now, drifting in and out of that."

"So . . . now what?"

"Now we move her to the intensive care unit, and we wait and see. We'll make her as comfortable as possible. When was the last time she had a drink?"

"I don't know," I say, shrugging. I've seen her with a cocktail in her hands so many times that to distinguish times without one is impossible.

"We'll get her moved shortly," he says, beginning to turn away.

"Doctor," I say, stopping him. He turns back. "What are the odds right now?"

He shakes his head. "Poor," is all he says, and then he turns away again.

The thread is growing short indeed, the writer voice says. *But the ICU will be interesting, while it lasts.*

I can't help it. I agree with the voice.

I go back inside the room and I wait for them to come for her. She only wakes once or twice. At one point, when she seems aware, I ask her, "Are you scared?"

"A little," she says.

She has never admitted fear to me before. "It's okay," I tell her. "I'm not going anywhere and I won't let anything happen to you."

"You can't stop what's supposed to happen," she says, then drifts off again.

Atropos is winning.

At four o'clock in the morning, I am wandering the hospital in search of coffee and thinking about fate, or rather my own personal version of *the* Fates. The coma has begun and all I can do is wait and see. They have told me that they will do an ultrasound in the morning to assess her organs and see how much damage has occurred.

I find a pot of coffee, pour it into a Styrofoam cup, and head back toward the ICU. If fate is what will happen no matter what, I think, then what role do *the* Fates have? My thoughts are skittish, like young horses running, and I can't seem to stay focused.

How do our parents become so intertwined with our own destiny? I've been living most of my life trying to *please* my mother, to make her proud—I still am. I couldn't allow her to see my fears, how I desperately wanted to save her. Her life was made up of events that molded me; to be less than she would have expected in this time . . . I can't imagine doing that at all.

I find my way back to her room and the beeping of monitors. She stirs, slightly, in her sleep and groans. The nurses have told me this is normal; she is uncomfortable, perhaps, but not in any real pain. I watch her as I sip my coffee. I fear they are saying this to comfort me, that it is an easy lie told to desperate sons.

You'll have to write the eulogy, you know, the writer voice says. *And find a copy of that damn song, "Rhap-*

sody in Chartreuse" or whatever she wanted, for the
service. But the most important thing is writing a real
stunner of a eulogy.*

The voice is right again. I will have to write the
eulogy—but not now, not until she's . . . until it's over
and she's . . . dead. There, I've said it, if only to
myself. She's going to die, I'm going to write her eulogy, and then . . . well, then, life will go on.

But with brand new material! the writer voice all
but screams. *Think of the possibilities in this!*

Oh, shut up! I tell the voice. Just let it be for a
while.

She never let you be . . . the writer voice says.
Never once . . .

The writer voice is dangerous. It knows everything
about me. I know this from long experience, but it
has trapped me in another memory as easily as I might
reach out and shut off the monitors attached to my
mother's heart. And this memory is also about fate . . .

"Is this what you want to be all your life?" My
mother gestures around the restaurant. "A waiter? You
want to be stuck doing what I do forever?"

"Of course not!" I tell her. "I'm just not ready yet."

"Then get ready," she snaps. "You have to go to
college—especially if you want to write."

"I'm writing now," I tell her.

"No," she says. "You're playing at it now. You've
got talent, but you need the skills to back up what fate
gave you naturally. You've got to sharpen them against
minds that are more trained than yours."

"So, I'm not good enough? Is that what you're saying? If I don't go to college, I'll never make it as a
writer?"

"No, that's not what I'm saying. I'm saying that each
of us has something we do well—some better than others. I could have painted. You might be able to write."

"But you don't paint professionally."

"More's the pity," she says. *"If I'd had the choice, I would've painted. I didn't have the choice. You do. Go to college."*

"But—"

"It's time you did this. You've been fucking around for almost five years. If you're going to write, you're going to have to go. Destiny isn't something that happens to us, like an accident. Destiny is something that unfolds around us, something we grasp as it passes by. Grasp yours . . ."

In the quiet darkness of her room, I laugh softly to myself. I had gone to college, and the writing was better for it. Not as good as it would be someday, I suspected, but better by far than it had been. What I hadn't counted on was that it was an addiction, a disease not unlike hers that consumed the mind with its intensities.

"If only you'd known, Mom," I say to her sleeping form. "You'd have probably told me to stick with waiting tables."

Oh, bullshit! the writer voice screeches. *She knew you had talent and wanted you to develop it.*

What talent? I ask myself. The talent to write poems and tell stories. There's a contribution to society.

You tell your truths disguised as stories and poems. Sometimes, you entertain. In the end, what you write is your way of giving something to the world.

Oh, truth, is it? I say to the voice. I don't tell any truths. I can't even face my own.

Maybe that's why I'm here.

I try to block out the voice, block out everything. I try to focus on the monitor beeping away, the dim light of the approaching sunrise. I would have to call the office, let them know what was going on, and run over there to pick up manuscripts later today.

My mother's breath hitches in and out, stops, starts and continues. I wonder how long she can last like this, catatonic and not herself in any real way.

As long as she's supposed to, the writer voice says. *And not a minute more.*

Another doctor comes in just after six and orders her ultrasound. "I'll get back with you as soon as I have the results," he says, already moving on to his next patient.

I nod, though I'm not sure he even notices. When they come to take her, I decide to go home and change clothes, update my wife and children. I don't dare leave for long; time is running rapidly now, I think. She could slip away while I am gone and I'd already been irresponsible enough. I should have given her the gun and the bullets.

On the drive home, I think about what she has given me; what I hoped to one day give my children. I make a mental list of the things she's handed down: an overblown sense of personal responsibility, a work ethic that would make a farmer blush, and . . . the words. She'd never once hesitated to buy a book for me or encourage my dreams of being a writer. I'm sure there were times when she'd been considering a choice between a meal for herself and a book I wanted—and chosen the book.

And if our parents give us gifts, what do we give them?

Purpose, the writer voice answers. *What the hell would you do without your kids?*

Rest peacefully, I think as I pull into the driveway. Maybe what she's handed down to me, what I'd maybe give my own children, if I didn't screw it up, wasn't a work ethic or a sense of responsibility or even encouragement. Maybe the only things handed down were really a brief time, a moment and a place where love wasn't always conditional. Where fate, or *the* Fates couldn't touch you at all. Emotional safety.

Nice sentiment, the writer voice says. *Think you can sell it?*

I ignore the voice and go inside.

I have a strange sense of urgency now, and purpose. I have to be there when she dies. Maybe that, I think, is wisdom.

Hospital hours are long hours. When you're waiting for death, time has no real meaning. She lasts three days, and we spend them together. I talk with her a little, but about inconsequential things. I don't want to disturb her if she can hear me in whatever world her mind currently occupies. Her body slows down, one thread frays at a time, a tapestry unweaving itself. Her muscles stiffen as though she is preparing herself for the grave or the physical challenges of rigor mortis. She never wakes from the coma, never says another word.

The writer voice talks a lot, but I have tuned it out completely by the second day in the hospital. The more it speaks, the more guilt I feel. *She* gave the gift of writing to me.

On the final morning, I hold her hand, though I am not seeking to bring her comfort, but only to comfort myself. As her time runs down, I tell the nurses to leave and not come back unless I call for them. I watch her breathe—in, pause; out, pause. I can feel the end coming, rushing toward us like the inexorable movement of the Earth itself. I am powerless to stop it. For as long as she'd held my life in her hands, protected me, nurtured me, forced me to measure up to whatever exacting standards she believed in, in this moment, I cannot give her life back to her. And if I could, she would refuse.

In, pause; out, pause. Slower and slower. I want to

pray, but somehow, I don't think I have the strength of will. It is clear to me, looking on it, that she *wants* to die. She'd known it was coming and has faced her ending with all the bravery and fortitude one would expect from a lady of character, and one who has seen all the aspects of the Fates and found some form of comfort in each of them.

The strangest thing happens then. The sunrise comes through the window, shooting prisms onto the walls, and as the light moves across her face, I see again the young woman, Clotho, who brought me into this world. The sun moves, and I see Lachesis, the mature, confident woman who has held the thread of my life in her hands, measured it, and has—perhaps— not found me wanting. And then the autumn rain clouds cover the sun, and I see her final form, what she has become. Atropos. The cutter of thread and the ender of life.

I am watching her as the last breath leaves her body, and I suddenly know what I will write for her eulogy. I will write it tonight, and somehow find the strength to say what she has known was her fate all along.

She would tell me that all parents must be their children's Fates. I can hear her now, the three women I knew, three voices blending into one that is uniquely hers. "We create our children," she says. "We weave them as best we can into the tapestry of the world, and eventually, the thread is cut and we leave."

The price of wisdom, the writer voice says, *is death.*

I call my wife and tell her it's over. To come get me and bring me home. To bring our children so they can say good-bye. Soon enough, they arrive at the hospital, and I watch as my daughter, who looks like my mother, tries to comprehend that this good-bye is different from all the others she has ever said or ever will say.

That night, I start on the first draft of the eulogy. I

am allowing the writer voice access again, and I am trying to find a way to talk about expectations and the things she handed down.

I type the words and they flow onto the screen:

THE WORK OF MY MOTHER'S LIFE WAS ME.

SEEKING GOLD
by Jane Lindskold

Jane Lindskold is well-known for her Firekeeper saga, which began with *Through Wolf's Eyes* and has continued through four novels. Another recent novel is *The Buried Pyramid,* in which she takes a break from feral women and wolves to write an archaeological adventure fantasy set in 1870s Egypt. Lindskold has had published fourteen novels and over fifty short stories. She lives in New Mexico with her archaeologist husband, Jim Moore. See her Web site, www.janelindskold.com for more.

STANDING OUTSIDE the tent where her younger brother struggled for breath and life, Andrasta wondered if in her deepest heart she actually wanted the boy to die.

Andrasta's name meant "dawn rider" in the old language of the Gharebi. That name had been the last fair omen in her life, at least as Andrasta, looking back along that life from the vantage of her nine years out in the world, saw it.

She had been born during a storm of freezing rain in early spring, brought into the world in a slave hovel, on a pallet set by a smoking fire. Her mother had not been attended by women of her own clan, nor of her husband's, but by a filthy Ootoi slave woman. The first sounds Andrasta's ears had heard had been the yowling songs of the enslaved Ootoi, not the proud praise chants that would have been sung by her mother's Moon Sisters.

Yet Andrasta might have lived down this ill-omened beginning had it not been for the reason her parents had been in that slave camp on the night of her birth. Her father, Feneki, was the third son of Cescu, a powerful warlord, owner of ten thousand and more horses. Persuaded by Cescu's second son, the warlord Louks, Feneki had convinced his wife that fortune would be theirs were Telari to bear their first child among his father's herds, for this was the very season when the horses were dropping their foals.

A horse proud warlord such as Cescu might make a boast of his wealth and pride of family by giving the newborn child every foal dropped that birth night—a gift that might mount to hundreds of horses. And this Cescu might have done had Louks and Feneki succeeded in their plan, but the gods had intervened, frowning upon greed that would trade on a strong man's honor.

Spring, who oversaw many births, awakened the child early in her mother's womb. Then she called on her father Winter, to lead in the storm herds along the route over which Louks was taking them to Cescu's camp. Cloudy skies and stinging sleet drove the small caravan off course, until finally they must take refuge in the slave camp.

Worse yet for the brothers' ambitions, Cescu had not reached his years as a commander of warriors and owner of much wealth without being wise in the ways of intrigue. He saw into the heart of his sons' duplicity. Had Louks and Feneki succeeded in their arduous undertaking, Cescu might have rewarded their boldness nonetheless. Their failure met only with his contempt—and Andrasta bore the weight of that contempt.

Cescu did not disown her, but he granted Andrasta none of the treasures that were usual at the birth of a son's first child. As her years unfolded, Andrasta was called far less frequently than the other grandchildren to ride pillion on the warlord's saddle and hear his stories. Her achievements with horses and with bow met silence rather than gifts and praise. The rest of the clan took their lead from the chieftain, so Andrasta's reception was cold wherever she went.

Telari, Andrasta's mother, did what she could to counterbalance Cescu's influence, but her family was a lesser clan already bound in fealty to Cescu, so Telari did not dare protest her daughter's ostracism openly. All Telari could offer her daughter was her own knowledge and training. This was a fine gift, for Telari was both warrior and priestess, but the grudging respect Andrasta earned from the other clan members through her skills was not the same as being within the sunshine of the warlord's pleasure.

For his part, Feneki distanced himself from his first-born child, as if in doing so he might distance himself from his father's disdain. Feneki's delight when, three years after Andrasta's birth, Telari bore him a son was unfeigned. The rich gifts of horses and silver chased with gold that Cescu gave on this occasion were as much reward for Feneki's unflagging obedience to his father in the interval since Andrasta's birth as they were presents reflecting a grandfather's joy at a new scion to his clan.

Andrasta tried hard not to resent little Cu, as the boy was called—having been named Cescu in base flattery of his powerful grandfather—but she couldn't help herself. Even Telari, Andrasta's one champion, now had less time and energy for her daughter. The pregnancy had been hard, and Telari had often been ill in the six years since. Andrasta had heard it whispered that Telari had been cursed by the Ootoi who had been midwife at Andrasta's birth, but Telari denied this could be so. She felt her troubles lay elsewhere.

In private, Telari told Andrasta that she thought her woman's parts had been damaged, not by the unborn Andrasta, but by the hard riding Feneki and Louks had forced Telari to do on that night when the gods turned their backs. Telari had not been well since, and Cu had been born only after several miscarriages.

Andrasta didn't know what to think. Certainly Louks and Feneki bore no signs that the gods continued to disapprove of them. Where Feneki had sought to win Cescu's approval through perfect obedience, Louks had transformed himself into the boldest of warlords. Though now missing an ear and terribly scarred about face and arms from numerous battles, Louks was lauded as a hero whenever he came home from leading his chosen war riders.

Only on Andrasta and Telari did the gods' disfavor still seem to rest. The illness that had seized hold of young Cu, just when the boy was becoming the pride of his grandfather and the laughing heart of the clan, seemed the latest sign that the gods were not done tormenting them.

Thus it was that Andrasta stood outside the infirmary tent, hearing the muffled hum of the low-voiced talk within, wondering if her brother, her rival, would die, wondering, too, if there was no bright and joyful Cu to distract them would Feneki and Cescu finally have to accept Andrasta and grant the girl her due.

Telari's voice broke Andrasta from her reverie before the girl could resolve this matter.

"Daughter, to me."

Tying a scarf of finely woven cloth over mouth and nose as she had been taught, Andrasta lifted the tent flap and came as bidden. She gave her mother a deep bow, then offered matching ones to her mother's companions. Only then did she let her glance stray to the back of the tent where Cu lay on a cot. His breath came hard and the tight, purplish-blue spots that clustered on his exposed skin were livid as engorged ticks.

Andrasta looked away from her brother's suffering and at her mother. Telari's skin, usually golden-brown, was pale—not the ivory pale favored by city women, but sallow and yellow. Telari's dark-brown almond eyes were sunk above cheekbones that cut knife-sharp beneath tightly drawn skin. Her dark hair, which usually held the shine of a raven's wing, was lank.

"Mother?" Andrasta said. "You summoned me. How may I serve?"

It was the formal greeting, one favored by the strict customs followed by Cescu's clan. Had they been alone, Andrasta would have hugged her mother, but there were others present. One was a man—a healer. The other was a woman—a priestess and auger. Both were strangers to Andrasta, for the severity of Cu's illness was such that Cescu had ordered the most skilled he could command to attend upon his grandson and these had come without delay.

Telari did not waste words. "Your brother is dying. He has sunk into unwaking sleep, and a low fever burns what strength is left in him. When the fuel is gone, he will die."

"How long?" Andrasta asked, horrified. It was one thing to idly contemplate what a death might mean to her. It was another to see a once lively boy so still and know there was no hope.

The healer spoke, "It might be tomorrow; it might yet be weeks. Cu's life has stilled to where he needs very little to sustain him. We can slip some honey between his lips, a bit of water, but eventually that additional fuel will not be enough to sustain his inner fire."

Hearing this, Andrasta forgot tradition and custom and the haughty manners of the warrior caste. She hugged her mother close and felt bones beneath her flesh. Cu was not the only one wasting away, but no fever other than a mother's love burned in Telari.

"My daughter," Telari said, her voice soft, words coming slowly, "you may be able to save your brother."

"Me?" Andrasta asked.

The priestess, not Telari, gave reply.

"We have a legend," the old woman said in a cracked voice, "a very old legend, that may hold a germ of hope. It says that if a maiden will stand alone alongside the road, waiting through the dark watches of the night, and if she will ask a question of the first rider to come along on a white horse, then what the white horse's rider tells her will be a true solution to whatever problem is posed."

Andrasta's mind spun with questions. What road? Cescu's people, like all the Gharebi, were nomads. They had no roads such as city folk made. Who would ride a white horse? Everyone knew white horses had weak hooves. White foals usually ended up in the stew pot before they even learned to stand.

Andrasta asked neither of these questions, only rose from her mother's embrace and stood as tall as she could beside Telari, her hand resting on the seated woman's too thin shoulder.

"I am a maiden. Show me the road, and I will wait until a rider on a white horse comes, even if I wait every night for the rest of my life."

Andrasta felt Telari's relief in the slight slump of her mother's shoulders, but again it was the priestess who spoke.

"The road will be evident to you or so legend says. Walk away from this place where the feet of animals and people may dull your ability to see the road. You may take with you food and drink, and whatever weapons you prefer, but no companion."

"Not even a horse?" Andrasta asked, thinking the vigil would not be too bad if she could make it astride Flame's warm back.

"No horse nor dog nor even head lice if you would think of them as company. I will prepare you if you so desire."

Andrasta felt Telari's wish that she accept in a sudden intake of breath, a breath that said Telari had not hoped for even this much assistance.

"I thank you," Andrasta said. Bending to kiss her mother on her cheek, then crossing to look where Cu lay breathing so slowly, she made her bows and followed the priestess outside.

At twilight, scrubbed with hot water and cold, dressed in clean shirt, trousers, and high-laced boots, Andrasta went forth from her grandfather's camp. No one took much note of her, for not taking note of Andrasta had become a habit. Even more, with the illness of Cu, no one wanted to risk the contagion of the bad luck.

Andrasta wore no hat. Her hair—as black and shining as her mother's was now lackluster—was braided and clubbed at the back of her neck, a warrior's hairstyle, though Andrasta had never been to war. This was a high honor indeed, but as the priestess herself had dressed Andrasta's hair, no one dared protest.

As Andrasta trudged away from the camp, she missed Flame, her bay mare, more than she wanted to admit. It wasn't just that her booted feet hurt— for the Gharebi rarely walked when they could ride. Andrasta missed the mare's company, and the reassurance that Flame's very presence always granted.

Flame represented the one thing in her life that Andrasta had done unquestionably right. In the winter of their fifth year, all Gharebi children began their first serious test. This consisted of selecting an already pregnant mare from any or all of the herds that traveled with the clan. This selection was noted by the clan leader. When the mare foaled, the foal and its training was given to the child.

Most children were guided by their parents, but Feneki had already all but disowned his daughter. Telari was suffering from one of the many illnesses that followed Cu's birth. Thus, Andrasta must make do on her own.

Like any Gharebi child, Andrasta could ride before she could walk. She took to going at dawn among the gentled horses and selecting a mount. Gharebi horses were trained to kneel at command, so it was easy enough for Andrasta to get astride. Then, alone, and, she thought, unnoticed, she went out each day and inspected the mares.

She watched to see which stallion covered which mare, learned what she could about which mare had borne strong foals in the past, and made a mental list of her choices. Andrasta suspected that she would be given last choice and so did not think she would have a chance at any of the famous brood mares—even if she had wanted to risk her grandfather's censure by claiming such a valuable foal—but there were many others. When choosing day came, Andrasta had nearly her first choice.

No one mocked her, as Andrasta had feared they would, but she was aware of sidelong glances she could not interpret. No matter. Each day she continued to ride out, and her riding had more purpose now. She watched over her brood mare like the horse's own guardian spirit. She brought the mare treats, bundles of herbs that Telari had taught her were good for the blood or otherwise strengthening. Finding these, especially in winter, was not easy, but Andrasta was, if nothing else, persistent.

Andrasta wasn't present when her chosen mare foaled, for horses prefer to give birth at night, but she was there the next dawn. At first sight of the new foal, Andrasta knew that no one would find fault with her choice. The filly was perfectly shaped, without the boxy head so common in newborns. Her coat shown brilliant red-gold in the light of the rising sun, with dark points rising past the knees. The filly's bristly mane and tail were dark as well. Bay was considered the most propitious of all colors for a warrior's horse. It was the color that the hero Rangest's chestnut stallion had been burned when the hero rode him into the sun to steal fire for the Gharebi.

Now that she was older, Andrasta knew Flame was a clichéd name to have given the filly, but from the wisdom of her nine years she forgave herself. After all, she had been only five.

If Andrasta had thought Flame's excellence would win her Cescu's approval, she had been wrong. Flame did win Andrasta some measure of respect from her peers, and even from some of the lower ranking adults.

When the time came, Telari asked a young acolyte of the Moon to assist Andrasta with training Flame, and he did so willingly, saying loudly to all who listened that had never there been a better student.

Andrasta missed Flame deeply as she made her way over the sear midsummer grass, looking for a road where there could be no road. She missed the confidence the horse gave her, the friendly, unquestioning affection. She was lonely, but she didn't let self-pity make her less watchful. This near the great herds, big predators were scarce, but the littler ones, the ones which would gladly scavenge or hunt as opportunity presented, were plentiful. Now that summer grew hotter, and the hunting was no longer easy, the big predators would be returning as well.

Andrasta chose her path back over the way Cescu's people had already traveled, for the beaten trail was as close to a road as she could come. Soon the tents would be stowed and the people would follow the herds to fresh grazing. Andrasta wondered if Cu could survive being moved, and the thought quickened steps that had been lagging.

The girl walked steadily on, stopping only a few times to remove her boots and put ointment on blisters rubbed raw. The second time she saw how her slipping socks were contributing to the problem and bound them to the top of her boots with the laces from the neck of her shirt. After this, she did better, and felt well-pleased. If anyone would care, she'd pass on this trick, but doubtless it would be thought of use only to slaves and others who were forced to walk.

By twilight, Cescu's camp was much reduced in view. By full dark the flickering lights of the many campfires were stars on the ground conversing with those cooler lights in the spreading blackness of the heavens.

How am I to keep to a road in the dark? Andrasta asked herself. Thus far she had guided herself by walking along the wagon ruts, but they made for uneven footing. After stumbling many times and falling twice, she knew she could not keep to them.

But the legend did not say I needed to walk along the road, she reminded herself, *only that I must question the first rider on a white horse to come along the road. I suppose I could just stand here and wait.*

But even a summer night is chilly when one stands still, so Andrasta continued walking—rather, limping— along. Her slung bow was heavy over her shoulder, and her quiver bumped against her back. She felt very glad she had not taken a sword with her, but had settled for a long hunting knife. She had little training with a sword, but the knife was as familiar to her as her fingers and might prove at least somewhat useful—though she had no idea how.

Eventually, the moon began to rise, her face almost full, her light washing out the nearer stars. It was by that light that Andrasta saw the road.

It was white, shining, and, like a rainbow, both solid

enough to seem touchable and shiveringly insubstantial.

Andrasta rubbed her eyes and looked again. The road was still there, but whether it ran along the ground, through the sky, or between earth and sky, Andrasta could not be sure. What she was certain of was that this must be the road she was to wait along.

She did so, tucking in her shirt where the tail had come out of her trousers, finger-combing her hair into some semblance of order. She straightened her shoulders, holding them back, and her head high and proud.

The exhaustion of many hours spent walking argued that nothing in the priestess' directions said that Andrasta had to remain standing, but the girl knew that were she to sit, even for a moment, she would fall asleep. As it was, the blisters on her feet seemed almost friendly, the stinging pain of each one nagging her to wakefulness.

Andrasta stood. After a long time she heard the sound of horse hooves walking along packed earth. She looked both ways along the road, and from her right saw a rider on what initially she took for a white horse. A second glance gave lie to this first impression. The horse was a dapple gray, pale, yes, but not white. The rider was a young woman, almost a girl, clad in green. Her mein was grave but kind.

Andrasta longed to ask the dapple's rider if she had passed someone on a white horse, but something made her stay her tongue. She had been told to ask her question to a rider on a white horse. Something warned her it might be counterproductive, even dangerous, to speak to any other.

The rider on the gray went by, acknowledging Andrasta with an inclination of her head. For a long time after the sound of her hooves had faded from hearing, Andrasta continued her vigil. Just when she was won-

dering if she might need yet watch another night, there
came the sound of trotting hooves on the packed dirt,
accompanied by the jingle of a harness.

Into Andrasta's view, moving briskly along the white
way, came a beautifully caparisoned chestnut stallion.
The stallion's trapping were such as the most powerful
warlords put upon their favorite mounts when making
a show. There were not only saddle and bridle all
shining with gold, but embroidered wrappings for the
mane and tail, and an elaborate headdress that made
the horse seem to have a stag's antlers.

The rider was Gharebi in appearance, clad, as was
the horse, for show in armor made entirely of gold.
He carried weapons, but these, too, were too elaborate
to be meant for real use. Now, though—having seen
this rider and the one on the dapple gray who came
before—Andrasta had her doubts as to whether there
was anything of what she would call reality about the
riders who used this road.

As before, even when the gaze of the rider rested
upon her, Andrasta held her tongue. She had been
told to speak with a rider on a white horse. For such
she would wait.

Again a long wait, and this time came a rider on a
bay so like Andrasta's own Flame that she wanted to
cry aloud in pleasure. This rider's gait was a canter,
and his gaze barely brushed her, but she was certain
that in him she saw the hero Rangest, he who had
stolen fire from the sun.

Andrasta longed to run to him, for Rangest was
among her own greatest heroes. She had long dreamed
of performing deeds as daring and marvelously clever
as his own. But she remembered that she was to speak
to a rider on a white horse. Though her heart broke
within her, she let Rangest go by without the smallest word.

Andrasta's heart had not yet stopped aching at this

lost chance when her ears caught the sound of galloping hooves. Raising her head, she saw the unmistakable flash of white upon whiteness. Within a brilliance
that made her eyes hurt, she saw a white stallion surg-
ing down the road like a flash of lighting.

Andrasta was drawing her breath to speak when she
realized that, at the speed at which his horse bore him,
the rider would be to and past her before she could
do anything but shriek. She saw her choices in an
instant: shout, fail, or . . .

Even as she shaped the idea in her mind, Andrasta
was in motion. She flung herself into the road, waving
her arms and flagging down the galloping horse. Dust
that stung like salt filled her nose and eyes, but Andrasta did not blink or wipe away the tears that
streamed down her cheeks. She waved her arms and
jumped, knowing she would be trampled, wondering
whether her body would be found or whether it would
remain a red smear on this shining road.

The white horse screamed in rage, but as it seemed
more fleet than any horse Andrasta had ever known,
it also seemed more dexterous. It answered to its rider's hand on the reins, pulling up short, its muscular
chest touching Andrasta's upheld hands.

Andrasta spared no moment for marvel, but stepped
out from under the horse's curving neck, onto the road
where she could see the rider more clearly. He was
what and all she had feared as she had watched his
kindred ride by—Father Winter—the same who had
sent the storm which had driven Louks and Feneki
from their goal, the same who had made certain that
Andrasta forever carried the shame of being born in
a slave's hovel.

Father Winter was like a Gharebi in appearance,
and yet not. He had the broad, flat features prized
among them, the high cheekbones, and the slanting
eyes. His hair was white as the hoarfrost that shim-

mers to life on the morning grass. His drooping mustaches were white as well, but whether icicles grew from them or they were in truth icicles, Andrasta could not tell. The eyes that peered down at her from slitted sockets were so pale a gray as to be almost without color. Their expression distilled every droplet of the disdain that Andrasta had seen in her grandfather Cescu's gaze.

Yet Andrasta held her head high and met those pale eyes squarely, even as she had been told was polite between warrior and warrior. She felt the cold that washed from Father Winter, but did not permit herself to shiver.

When the rider did not speak, Andrasta realized she must.

"I thank you for stopping, Father Winter."

"What do you want of me, maid?"

"The answer to a question."

"Only one question?"

Andrasta started to ask, "Am I permitted more than one?" but perhaps the spirit of her hero Rangest had touched her in passing, for she saw the trick in time.

"My question is this, Father Winter. My brother Cescu, son of Telari and Feneki, is dying of illness. What must be done to cure him?"

Father Winter did not acknowledge Andrasta's cleverness at sidestepping his trap, but the girl was accustomed to having her achievements unacknowledged, and so this stung only a little. Without preamble, Father Winter answered her question plainly and clearly.

"Three griffin feathers are needed for the cure. One must be burned beneath Cu's nostrils. One must be ground into powder and the powder fed to him. The third shall be a quill in which griffin blood must be carried. That blood must be mingled with the boy's own. Then not only will young Cescu be healed, but he will rise to become a hero to rival his grandfather in attaching honor to their shared name."

Andrasta stared up at Father Winter. Confusion spun in her thoughts. Griffin feathers? Blood from a griffin? How could these be found? This cure was impossible, a cruel joke of crueler gods. Everyone told stories of griffins, but had anyone ever seen one?

Father Winter was shaking his horse's bridle, signaling the horse on, but he paused when a second question slipped from Andrasta's lips.

"How long does Cu have?"

"Two days," came the cold reply. "Now run and tell your mother what you have learned, child. You've done all she has asked."

The words held the icy breath of contempt, but Andrasta refused to let that sting show. Instead she bowed politely as Father Winter rode away. Then she stood alongside the white road, trying to remember everything she had heard about griffins.

"They live beside rivers that run with gold," she said aloud, "and guard the gold. They have the lower parts of lions, but the upper of giant eagles. They are fierce, but not cunning or wise. Their favorite food is horseflesh, but they will settle for any hot meat."

Andrasta paused and straightened her bow over her shoulder, still speaking aloud for the courage her own voice brought her.

"Two days. Two days and Cu is gone. Two days and . . ." Andrasta shook her head, banishing the evil thoughts that came to her. "Two days is not enough time for me to run home, for debate and decision. The search must begin now, but how and where?"

A slight ringing of harness leathers came to her ears, and Andrasta turned, expecting to see Father Winter returned. Instead, there stood her hero, Rangest.

"Rivers run from mountains," he said. "From there,

too, comes ore. Were I to look for rivers running with gold, I would look for mountains."

Andrasta stared at Rangest in wonder. He was every bit as handsome as she had imagined, but far finer than his handsomeness was that his eyes looked upon her with kindness.

"There are no mountains near here," Andrasta said, and saw the corner of Rangest's mouth quirk in the smallest of smiles. "But neither was there a road, and yet there is a road. Perhaps there is a reason that— great hunters though they are—none of my uncles or their cousins have brought home a griffin pelt to adorn their tents."

"Even so," Rangest replied, "the way to mountains that cannot be will be long—especially for one who must make the journey in two days. I cannot carry you there, but I can tell you this. Consider whistling, but if you do, take care lest you break your heart."

Andrasta gave Rangest a bow so deep that her head nearly brushed the glowing white of the road. When she rose, he was riding away. The fire his smile had lit in her heart remained even as his tall form receded, and Andrasta felt braver and finer than she could ever before remember—except, perhaps, on that dawn when she first saw Flame and knew her choice had been good.

"Flame!" she said, suddenly understanding at least part of Rangest's parting riddle. She had trained Flame to come to her if she gave a certain whistle, and she felt sure that if she were to whistle now, Flame would come.

Andrasta raised her fingers to her lips, then paused. *Their favorite food is horseflesh,* she remembered, then placed fingers to lips and shaped the shrill whistle nevertheless. Battles were not won without risk, and Rangest had all but told Andrasta that she could not hope to reach the mountains on foot. Therefore she

needed Flame. It would be up to Andrasta to defend
the mare when the time came.

By the time the sun rose, the white road had vanished and Andrasta was surveying the revealed landscape from her vantage astride Flame. What she saw
struck her as instantly odd. If she looked back the way
she had come, she could see the smoke curls and dust
that announced where Cescu's clan camped. If she
looked in the opposite direction, mountains raised
their bulk, rough and craggy against the pale blue of
the early morning sky. Her choice was clear. The way
home was open to her, but so was the way to the
griffins.

Andrasta had carried dried fruit and meat with her,
filled her canteen with fresh water, but the vagaries
of the wind carried the scent of roasting lamb from
the camp and made her stomach growl. In one direction was home and hot breakfast, the latter garnished
with a tale that would surely astonish all who heard
it. In the other direction were monsters and mountains, both quite probably supernatural. Andrasta
knew what her choice must be, but as she turned
Flame's head toward the distant blue-gray peaks, she
felt the tug of home.

All through the morning Andrasta rode through tall
grasses untouched by her grandfather's herds. Sometimes she gave Flame her head, other times forced the
mare to walk and conserve her strength, napping as
she rode. By midday, they were traveling over rising
ground. The mountains were definitely nearer, but
Andrasta had discovered an uncomfortable anomaly.
If she looked back over her shoulder, Cescu's camp
remained as close as it had been that morning. Home
was so very close, and the temptation to retreat
never diminished.

Finally, Andrasta disciplined herself to look ahead,

never back. It helped, but only a little. She kept imagining wolf packs and great cats stalking through the tall grass. She made herself trust Flame's sharper senses, and refused the urge to twist around and scout—and the even stronger urge to run home.

"Your mother will be worried," said voices in Andrasta's head, *"and doesn't Telari have enough to worry about?" "You are behaving as foolishly as Feneki, taking on more than is your due." "You are dooming Cu, for how can a mere girl-child win against griffins?" "Is it fair to push Flame into such danger?"*

But though Andrasta must listen to the voice of her worries, she could refuse to heed them, and so she rode on, her only company her good mare and her fears.

By midafternoon, Andrasta and Flame were close enough to the mountains that individual crags were easily seen—as could the winged figures that swooped between them. At first Andrasta had taken them for eagles, but soon she could tell the build was all wrong, the body longer behind than any eagle's could be, the whole trailed by a long and lashing tail.

Evening found Andrasta and Flame on a long, winding trail that ended at the edge of a mountain meadow. The meadow was bordered on one side by a lively, chattering stream that ran, as legend had promised, over bright nuggets of gold. There were trees in the meadow, broad-leafed and offering welcome cover from the griffins that soared high overhead.

Andrasta watered Flame, then picketed the mare where there was both grazing and ample cover. Foraging allowed the girl to augment her own dry supplies with some fat, sweet plums. Andrasta considered fishing, but having already decided that a fire would not be wise, and not yet hungry enough to relish the thought of eating raw fish, she settled for the smaller luxury of soaking her dry meat before chewing on it.

Andrasta had been awake all the night before, and though she had dozed some while Flame carried her toward the mountains, she had been too edgy to really rest. With twilight the griffins had retired to their high aeries, and Andrasta resolved to also sleep. One day had gone by, but she had another before Father Winter had said Cu would be doomed. Already a plan, uncomfortable in its implications, was shaping in her mind.

Nothing troubled Andrasta and Flame that night—perhaps the griffins made these meadows unwelcome to other predators, perhaps some kindly eye watched their rest. Andrasta rose with her namesake dawn. After making her ablutions and shifting Flame's picket to where the mare could find fresh grass, she considered her admittedly limited options.

She could climb and attempt to locate precisely where the griffins had their aeries. If griffins were like most creatures, in the summer the young would still nest with their parents. Nothing in Father Winter's instructions had said the blood needed for Cu's cure must come from an adult griffin. There might be shed feathers about the nest that Andrasta could gather.

But what if Andrasta could not reach a griffin's nest? There was no reason winged creatures would build their nests where a ground-bound animal could reach them—and every reason they would not. And how long would such a search take her? Too long, most probably, for Andrasta was a plains child, and her bruised and blistered feet were not trained for climbing.

She considered another plan.

Scouting the meadow had revealed signs that deer, mountain sheep, and rabbits all had come to this place to graze. If Andrasta and Flame remained quietly under cover, the wild creatures would likely return to their routine. This had been one reason Andrasta had not lit a fire the night before. Wild things were sensitive to threat, but Andrasta had seen no sign of humans in this meadow or indeed since she came to the foothills of the mountains. It was quite possible that the wild denizens were innocent of humankind, and so to them Andrasta's scent would be a curiosity, nothing more.

This plan was perhaps the wisest, but Andrasta could not forget that time was running out for Cu even as the sun extended her warming rays. If the wild creatures chose to remain shy and cautious, if the griffins were not in the mood for venison or mutton, then time would run out and despite Andrasta's well-meant efforts, Cu would die.

That left one plan, one which turned Andrasta's belly sour even on contemplation, one she had known she must use perhaps from the moment Rangest had spoken to her along the white road.

Hands trembling despite her resolve, Andrasta went and untied Flame's picket rope. The mare nuzzled her face and hands, looking for another sweet plum or some other treat. Andrasta fought down a surge of tears, but a few escaped nonetheless. Flame lipped them from her face, liking the salty taste.

"We're going to war, my friend," Andrasta said softly. "This is no better, no worse. I will watch carefully, but you must obey me or even the slightest hope we will come through this is lost."

Flame seemed to understand, or at least she heeded the serious note in Andrasta's voice. The mare followed without even pulling at the succulent grass as Andrasta led her to the center of the meadow, out away from the shelter of the trees.

"Kneel!" Andrasta commanded. "Lie flat!"

The Gharebi's warhorses all learned these commands: the one permitting quick mounting, the other providing an archer shelter over which she might shoot. Flame obeyed with an alacrity that told Andrasta that the mare expected a treat. She slipped Flame a bit of dry apple, then gave her final commands.

"Still!" she said. "Stay."

Then feeling like the worst kind of traitor, Andrasta left her mare lying among the grass, bait to draw a griffin from the sky. Taking partial shelter beneath the trees, Andrasta strung her bow and stilled to watchful immobility—stilled her limbs, but not her thoughts. These nagged at her as before, but now they had added another possibility.

"You saw the streams. Truly they run with gold. Make a bundle of those nuggets and no one will care if Cu lives or dies. You will be sung of around a thousand fires as the warrior who won home gold from the mountains of the gods. Flame will be safe. You will be a hero."

In her mind's eye, Andrasta could see how it would be, how she would carry the nuggets in a bag made from her shirt, how she would set the bundle in front of her grandfather and the treasure would spill forth, brilliant as sunlight against the dark furs that carpeted Cescu's tent.

Andrasta fought the temptation, keeping her gaze on the blue sky above until her eyes ached. Still the image seemed more real than did the blue firmament or the grass that tickled her arms and made her want to scratch—more real, even, than the mare that lay obedient, brown eye rolling in confusion toward her mistress, wondering when this training exercise would end.

When Andrasta first saw the glint of griffin feathers against the sky, her imagination saw it only as gold glittering amid the waters of a pond. Flame's apprehensive nicker pulled the girl to the present. Andrasta hissed commands she knew Flame must struggle against every instinct to obey.

"Still! Stay!"

Moving slowly so as not to catch the griffin's eagle eye, Andrasta tightened her bowstring, then set shaft to string. She pulled back, feeling confidence in the controlled power, yet very aware that she must make this first shot count. The griffin was curious, seeing an apparently dead or ill horse where the afternoon before there had been none. Did the griffin remember seeing them climb the slopes to the mountain meadow, or was this a complete anomaly—a god-given meal?

Andrasta's arm was trembling from maintaining the pull on her bowstring when at last the griffin began its descent. The bulk of its lion parts meant that it could not dive as a hawk or eagle would have done, but must come in more slowly. Even so, it came dreadfully fast.

Andrasta focused, willing herself to wait until the griffin was in range of her arrow, waiting until she had a clear line on its exposed underbelly. She did not know if a griffin kept its heart where a lion did, but that seemed her best chance.

She loosed her arrow just as Flame's nerve broke and the mare rolled, scrabbled her hooves into the turf, and fled. The arrow hit home, but missed the heart shot as the griffin changed course to go for its suddenly moving meal. Andrasta had another shaft to string more rapidly than she would have believed possible. This one caught the griffin in the hindquarters.

Screaming in terror, Flame bolted across the meadow, but the griffin did not follow. It had reared onto its back legs to claw at the arrow in its under-breast, but the wound from Andrasta's second arrow caused one leg to give. Now the griffin lay bleeding, its dark red blood puddling amid the grass that Flame's weight had crushed flat. Feathers were scattered on the grass, pale gold against the green.

Andrasta ran forward, bracing another arrow to her bowstring. The griffin was both beautiful and terrible—and she saw that though it was in pain, its injuries might not be mortal. Her bow was a girl's bow, not a man's and the monster's chest muscle was thick and heavy—as it must be, she would have realized if she had thought, to allow the creature to fly. The griffin had plucked the first arrow out, and even as Andrasta watched it wrenched free the arrow in its the hindquarters.

Now the griffin stood, balanced awkwardly on its three strong legs, wings testing the air, ready to flee or to fight, eagle eye studying the strung bow with what seemed intelligent understanding as to the source of its hurt.

Suddenly, Andrasta could not kill the creature, not even to win Cu's life. The look in the griffin's eyes showed fear, not fury. Instead of shooting, she waved her bow as she might have a stick at a dog, shouting as loudly as she could.

"Go! Get! I mean it! Go, or I'll loose this arrow, just see if I won't!"

The griffin leaped in fear at the sound of Andrasta's voice, and that leap carried it into the air. Laboring hard, the broad wings bore it upward, blood from its open wounds dappling the girl like rain. Once the griffin was away, Andrasta did not watch. Her gaze had fastened on something that looked remarkably like hope.

The griffin had shed feathers and fur both in its twisting to remove the arrows, and had bled freely over the meadow. Among the plants that Flame had crushed flat was a broad-leafed weed of some sort, and blood puddled in that fragile chalice.

Andrasta dropped her bow and ran forward, picking up the nearest plume as she did. It was a wing pinion, possessed of a broad quill. She cut off the tip with her knife and carefully poured the blood from the leaf into the hollow area within. She held this, wondering how she would plug it, settling for a bit of rolled grass, and a dab of damp clay from the bank of the stream.

By the time Andrasta had secured this prize and gathered two more plumes, Flame, her head hung low in shame for having failed, had come dragging up. Andrasta raised that hanging head and kissed the mare.

"You've been braver than any horse has reason to be, my heart's own Flame. It's easier to fight or flee than it is to hold steady and bear what comes. It's the lesson my mother has been teaching me all my life, had I but the wit to see."

Andrasta longed to take some trophy for herself—perhaps a bit of griffin's fur to spin into a bracelet—but she had gained wisdom enough to know the sound of a new temptation. Taking nothing more than the three feathers and fresh water to fill her canteen, she mounted Flame and rode from the valley.

"I hope you heal, griffin," she said to sky. "I meant you harm, but I am come to regret it."

A now familiar voice startled her. Turning, Andrasta found Rangest riding on his own fine bay along the trail at her side.

"Griffins give each other injuries more severe than that in their mating flights. The griffin will recover. You?"

Andrasta smiled shyly. "I am uninjured, as if a god watched over me."

"Watched," Rangest said, "nothing more. Your deed is your own, of your own doing."

"But not yet done," Andrasta replied. "I have a long ride home yet."

"Home has always been close," Rangest said, "but ride fast nonetheless. Your mother is worried—and your grandfather, too, though his tongue is too frozen with pride to admit so."

Rangest was gone before Andrasta could find the words to thank him, and when Flame stepped from the mountain path, the mare walked amid the astonished people of Cescu's clan.

As Andrasta rode through the camp toward the infirmary tent, she heard around her exclamations of wonder and shock, for all noted she was dappled with fresh blood. In explanation, Andrasta held high the three golden feathers. She knew that from this day forth none would deny her a place of honor in the clan, but she did not brag on her adventure.

Young maid she might still be, but now she had a woman's wisdom as well.

OPENING HER DOOR
by Alexander B. Potter

Alexander B. Potter resides in the wilds of Vermont, editing anthologies and writing a variety of fiction and nonfiction. His short stories have appeared in a number of anthologies including the award-winning *Bending the Landscape: Horror* volume. He edited *Assassin Fantastic* and *Sirius: The Dog Star* for DAW Books, and a third anthology *Women of War*, is forthcoming from DAW.

HE SLIPPED OUT the side door into the cool night air and concentrated on pretending no one could see him. Part of him still believed that if he couldn't see anyone else, he must, by definition, be invisible. Invisibility offered comfort and was to be sought and cherished. He'd made a study of being invisible most of his life. He doubted anyone would wander the streets of his neighborhood past midnight, but caution lived in his head.

The moon shadows cloaked, but didn't hide him completely. Too much moon. Ironic, given the full moon provided the occasion he sought. He picked up his pace even as he counseled himself not to run. Running drew attention. The faster his legs moved, the more he spoke in his head. *Slow down, careful. Careful.* The grass left cool trails of wetness on his bare feet. His toes dug into the earth with each hurried step. His destination came nearer with every breath. In moments he stood before the small neighborhood temple.

He felt for the door's groove to fit his hand inside. Fingers curling, he squeezed, pressed. The door slid back with a low grinding. He made a mental note to bring his tools over tomorrow afternoon. Make the door slide smoothly again. He'd been doing small maintenance around the temple for years. No one noticed or thought it odd, as far as he could tell, and it gave him good reason to be around the temple. For now, he just stepped out of the moon's glare and into the darkness beyond the door, closing it behind him with another rough rasp.

Walking through the silent temple, he didn't even pause to light a lamp or a wall taper, picking his way by memory and routine. How many nights? How many nights praying for wisdom, asking for guidance. A bare width of his own thin hand from the altar, he stopped. Tonight . . . tonight he would accept that guidance, whatever form it took. Dropping to his knees in one straight fall, he felt the crack of solid stone under his bruised knee joints, cool, almost cold. No preliminaries tonight. The full moon called and She stirred in the very air. Sitting back on his heels, he opened his hands palm-up on his thighs.

Closing his eyes, he reached for and found the quiet place in his head. His knees hurt and the cold floor chilled him. He wrapped his attention around the quiet place only to have it slip off like the drops of water condensation down the sides of the chalice after he filled it. Reach, grab, hold . . . and slide.

Unquiet crept up on him from all the usual daily places, but he kept pushing it away and reaching again. And again. Reach, grab, wrap, hold . . . hold hold . . . and slide.

He knew why it was so hard tonight, why everything was so close to the surface of his mind. Worry. Fear. Anxiety made his palms itch and his fingers curl inward. Time was pressing. He turned seventeen in one week's time. The Call, the pressure, kept growing louder in his head, all through him. He knew now that he couldn't ignore it . . . if he'd ever been able to, which he doubted.

At seventeen, young men and women declared their choice of apprenticeship from among the choices they'd studied in the previous two years. At seventeen, young *women* dedicated themselves to the Goddess, declared their service, if that was their path.

He knew if he wanted to reach the elusive, quiet stillness within, he needed to get past the blinding thrum of "time is running out, time is running out," but the strength of fear could not be underestimated. It pushed back at him, lapping up against his mind in waves.

He couldn't do this. Accepting the inevitable offered no more answers than pushing it away.

It wasn't right. Not the way things were done. Worse, it could be an insult to all that he worshiped.

He'd misunderstood. The feeling, the pressure, the certainty . . . all a mistake.

They'd laugh for days, if they only knew. Every single one of them. The entire village. The entire city.

He gave the thoughts an angry shove. Self-defeating. Never mind that it all rang with the authority of truth, especially that last, and oh, he could just *hear* them now.

"You want to what? Don't be absurd. Out of the question."

"Has it escaped your notice that you're a boy*? I mean I can understand how it might have."*

"What on earth makes you think She would have you?"

"Serve in Her temples? I always knew you were a strange one, but now you've gone and truly lost your senses."

Grinding his teeth, he tried to kick all the fears, all the voices, all the lies, out of his head. Finally he took a deep breath and carefully detailed a mental door,

heavy and wooden. He swung it open and invited all
the voices to walk through, then slammed it behind
them with enough force to rattle his own teeth. Sucking in air through his nose in desperation, he released
it through his mouth and reached again, keeping his
mind blank of everything but the door he'd imagined,
adding creative locks to it at random.

"Blessed Trinity, it's the only answer. Please, please
guide me on the path." He forced his voice to slow
and measured his words. Begging wasn't right, no matter how dire his circumstances. "Blessed Trinity, *you*
are the answer. I thank you for your guidance on the
path." He sank into the cadence, clicking locks shut
in time with the words, and in the rhythm he found
the stillness in his mind. "Blessed Trinity, you are the
answer. I thank you for your guidance on the path."
True calm welled up from his center, and with it, the
certainty. *It doesn't matter what they think. It only matters what I know.* "Blessed Trinity, you are the answer.
I thank you for your guidance on—"

Between one word and the next a firm hand stroked
his hair, and warmth crawled through his legs where
they rested on the stone floor. "You know, sweetie, if
you would stop doing this in the middle of the night,
you wouldn't get so cold." The amused alto touched
him as tangibly as the fingers that now tilted his chin.
His eyes flew open and he looked up in awe.

And surprise.

All things considered, he'd expected the Maiden.

The woman seated on the altar in front of him,
ensconced in a warm amber glow, was most definitely
not the Maiden.

Lounging comfortably on the low wooden surface,
She embodied full womanhood in Her prime. Even
seated, Her length of crossed legs spoke to a height
above his own, shoulders broad and arms strong.
Heavy red silks draped over full curves, capturing the

flickering light and tossing it up to catch in the straight fall of blonde hair. Startled, he realized the glow didn't emanate from Her being, but came from the candles he hadn't lit, now burning steadily.

"My Lady," he breathed, "I am honored by your presence." *Finally, finally,* a voice in his head chanted, with something like fear and relief combined. *Confirmation.* He'd known, part of him had always known, that if he came forward with sincerity, with true acceptance, She would acknowledge the Call. Despite his . . . liability. The Call inside, too strong to ignore, bringing him to his knees before Her, no matter the consequences.

"As I am honored by your dedication," She smiled down at him, then glanced sideways as a black rat scampered up onto the altar and straight up Her arm. She let it settle onto Her shoulder then turned back to him. "You don't have to make this so hard on yourself. There's nothing wrong with answering the Call on a sunny afternoon."

"The moon," he managed quickly, while his inner voice called him a liar. The cover of even a full moon night kept away more prying eyes. "I thought—"

"Ah, yes." Her smile widened, her eyes knowing. "You are a thinker. I like that. So, you've decided, then? The day of your seventeenth year approaches. Time to decide for certain."

"There is no decision," he answered simply. "I know. I have heard the Call for as long as I can remember."

"And you have *decided* to listen?" She murmured with careful emphasis, one finger stroking the rat's head where it nestled on Her shoulder.

He ducked his head, shamed heat in his cheeks. "Yes. I no longer question what I hear. I am sorry, My Lady, that I did not understand sooner." The words weren't quite right, as part of him had understood all his life. He remembered sitting before this very altar when he could barely reach to light the candles, with the certainty sitting inside his head like a tiny growing shoot of ivy. So much surrounded it, so much sought to choke it out, but a circle of earth completely untouchable seemed to surround the little green life force, and no matter how many times it was stepped on, it sprang up again. He had *known*, for as long as he could remember knowing anything at all, exactly what the Call was, exactly what he heard echoing deep within his chest. He remembered walking through his day-to-day life as a child with the three aspects close enough to touch every time he shut his eyes, feeling Them in every step he took. Remembered seeing each aspect of the Trinity occasionally even with his eyes open.

And yet, true understanding came slowly. As a child, he only knew what he felt. The older he grew, the more at odds what he felt became with what he was told, and he learned quickly not to talk about it in order to avoid the odd looks, the uncomfortable pauses, the outright hostility. Then came the conscious effort not to hear. Not to feel.

He stared at the stone beneath his knees. Would he be found unacceptable, because of his long denial of Her? Would She hear his weak words as an excuse? *I am sorry I did not understand sooner.* His eyes itched and stung.

Her hand cupped his face again, and strong fingers lifted his chin. "There is no shame in confusion. You are unusual. There are not many who walk your path. How could you know? You had no one to help you understand."

Staring into the loving acceptance in Her face, he felt a sob catch in his throat. "I had you," he whispered brokenly. "I had you."

Kneeling down off the altar, She gathered him into

Her arms and pulled him close. "Ah, but I can be a lonely comfort and don't think I don't know it. You do not disappoint me. Don't delude yourself that you do."

The warmth of Her embrace brought the emotion crashing over him in an unexpected wave, and he collapsed against Her chest. The sudden release of tears shocked him. Too much tension, too much anxiety, too much fear and worry built up over how many years of internal struggle? Too many. Her understanding words absolved his greatest concern and the relief shook him all through. The ache inside dissolved in bits and pieces, melting away like a lump of ice-hard snow in the salt of his tears.

When he calmed, She let him sit back and dried his face with a fold of red silk. The rat still perched on Her shoulder chittered at him. "Better?" She asked with the same gentle smile.

"Better," he hiccuped with a watery smile in return. "You're not—" He stopped himself, still fearing giving offense.

"—what you expected?" She grinned, the knowing look back in her eyes. "Oddly enough, I hear that quite a bit. But let me guess. In your case, you were expecting the Maiden?"

He shrugged and rubbed at his nose with his sleeve. "I came in ready to swear my celibacy," he clarified.

"Well, if that would make you happy, you're welcome to do so. But I'm more of a mind to see folks dealing with those frustrations." She winked at his startled look and tousled his hair, lifting herself gracefully back onto the altar.

"I thought, given my . . . circumstances, that if my service had any chance of being accepted, it would likely be with the Maiden." He paused and took a deep breath. "D–does it? Have any chance of being accepted, I mean?"

Getting comfortable again, She looked down at the floor as a round skunk trundled up to Her foot and started snuffling. Reaching down, She scooped it up and settled it on Her lap. At his startled recoil, She shrugged, mindful of the rat. "You're the one who came out here in the middle of the night. You're getting the nocturnals." She scratched the skunk's head. "Your service was accepted a long time ago. The Declarations of Service at seventeen are mostly a formality. Anyone truly Called knows it long before. All We needed was your acceptance of your Call."

"Even though I'm–" his mind stuttered, ". . . male?"

The compassion and admiration in Her face told him She heard the mental stutter and understood. Again, the waves rose and emotion swirled, his eyes prickling. But She was speaking and the maelstrom retreated before his concentration.

"You're not the first, and you won't be the last. You're just . . . rare. Special. Few are those in male form Called to the Goddess. Rarer still because there are those who are Called who simply cannot or will not answer." She smiled and reached out for his hand. He watched their fingers interlock. "We needed to know that this is the Call you truly hear, the path you truly choose."

This time his voice came strong and easy. "To me, there is no choice to the matter."

"I understand," She nodded, voice soft. "I could wish there was, for your sake, but then I would not have you in my Service, and I would count that a sore loss."

His throat tightened at the pride in Her expression. "I finally understand what I've always known. I choose to acknowledge and hear the Call. I choose to declare my service."

"It is not an easy path, but you already know that. Better than anyone, I would imagine. What of your sisters? How will they take the announcement, do you think?''

He found himself shifting off his knees, settling cross-legged on the floor, hand still linked to Hers. Something felt settled, inside of him. Looking back, he would realize he'd passed the first gate, but at no time in the future, no matter how many times he reviewed and studied the exchange, would he ever be able to pinpoint the exact moment the transition came. All he knew at the time was that the pressing anxiety left and a comfort spread through him. "I honestly don't know," he confessed. "I think at least some of them will be all right, even if they don't understand. But I just don't know." He trailed off. "I planned, if accepted, to offer to leave if it would be easier for them. Serve in a temple elsewhere, where people don't know me, or them."

"We are everywhere," She nodded. "It is a fair option, but one I believe you should share with them before deciding. And the rest of the town?"

The shrug was irritable this time. "I don't know. I don't care."

Her hand squeezed his fingers. "Caring is one of your greatest strengths. Don't let go of it. Your capacity for care is the primary reason I am before you, not the Maiden, not the Crone. You could serve any of us well, but my aspect is most suited to your nature. Continue to care. Just remember to care for yourself as you care for others."

He sat staring up at Her and a slow smile spread over his face. "This is truly happening. It's begun, hasn't it?"

Releasing his hand, She placed Her own on his head. Staring him directly in the eye, She spoke, Her voice ringing like bells. "You are mine, Arin Michael. Go forth and show my claim to the world." Her voice dropped back into conversational cadence as She ruffled his hair again. "But start with your sisters, won't you? And be prepared. Be gentle with yourself. You're likely the only one who will be. And now, go get some sleep."

He rose on shaky legs with Her hand on his elbow. She stood, too, cradling the skunk in Her other arm. *I was right about the height,* he thought, dazed, staring up at Her. "You are—" He stopped, unable to put it into words. "I am yours," he finally said.

She smiled and patted his head. "Yes, dear. I know. Now go to bed. Trust me, you've got a big day tomorrow."

He backed up a few paces, then bowed. Rising, he turned and left, feeling Her proud smile warm on his back the entire way.

He peered around the partially open door to Catarina's office at the courthouse, then eased inside. His sister's dark head stayed bent over her work, so he cleared his throat.

"Arin! Come over and sit, I didn't hear you arrive."

He came all the way into the room, closing the door behind him. He dropped into a chair, wondering if maybe another time wouldn't be better. He drew a deep breath and shook himself sternly. No better times were *left*. He turned seventeen next week. He had to start, and start here.

He had an order all worked out, planned carefully between the time he'd come back inside from the temple the night before and when he finally fell asleep. Catarina first, then Kerynne. On to Harleigh and Genniver, and Laraine last.

He had an idea Laraine might be hardest, perhaps because they were closest in age or because they'd always had a rough relationship, up until she had children and he'd taken so completely and unequivocally to her brood. Their relationship was certainly the most complicated. But Catarina and Kerynne were his best hopes for working out his wording, explaining the unexplainable. He wanted to start here, with Catarina, the eldest, the other bookend to the family. The one who understood. The one he always came to for advice and support.

"You know my birthday is next week."

"Of course. Have you made your decision? You've been so noncommittal. Laraine says she's quite positive she can get you in at the jewelers with her, but somehow I don't know that gem polishing holds your interest." She flashed him a smile. "I know you've spent time with Kerynne at the Healing Guild. And what with Harleigh's position, you could step into the Guard without any trouble. Of course, my offer stands to—"

"I've decided," he cut in quickly, and felt his stomach curl as her smile widened. "I want to pledge myself to the Goddess," he managed in one full rush. Then, somewhat slower but no less shaky, "Next week I'll declare my service."

Her smile froze. "You want—" she stopped. The smile wilted at the corners. "But you . . . can't. You're a man."

"Men serve the Goddess, too."

"Well, yes of course, in the general sense. But they don't pledge themselves to service. You're speaking of temple service. Like a Priestess. Priest*ess*," she stressed.

"There have been men who've served in the temples. Just not very many of us."

"Who told you that?"

He met her gaze directly, clenching his hands to keep them from trembling. "The Matron."

Catarina went white about the lips but otherwise didn't react. Finally, she spoke again. "You hear—" She didn't finish.

"I've been Called," he acknowledged softly. "My

Call was accepted last night. I've known for years, but it's taken me some time to understand."

She gave a short, jerky nod. "Nothing like cutting it a little close," she said with a strangled laugh. "Well. This is different." He watched her face, but her expression remained smooth and unreadable. Only her eyes betrayed the activity racing behind the façade. He knew she was considering and understanding all the ramifications. "It makes a kind of sense, actually. We always knew you were different. Special."

He felt hope catch and take root in his chest. Her calmness encouraged him, though he supposed it could be just shock. He held his breath as she stood and circled her desk, then leaned against it.

"You're sure?" she asked, gently. "You're *very* sure?"

"It's difficult to explain exactly *how* sure. I just *know,* on a visceral level."

She searched his eyes for long moments, then something in her face relaxed. She nodded again. "And this will make *you* happy?"

With those words, he knew. Relatively speaking, everything would be fine.

He pushed through the door to his room and flopped down on the bed. And so it went. Five explanatory conversations and an amazing number of "well, that makes sense" responses. Had *everyone* known? Why had he bothered struggling with it for so long?

He stared at the darkening ceiling, too exhausted to get up and light a lamp. Guessed, maybe. Suspected, more likely. Not *known*. At the very most, knew something was . . . off.

All told, the day progressed better than expected. He'd hoped, he'd prayed, he'd thought they would all do well because they were strong, smart, tough, beautifully-spirited women who cared as deeply as he did. Any one of them could have been Called, and not for the first time he wondered, why him? From a religious perspective he knew the answer—they were destined for other ends. Serving the Trinity was his path, for reasons beyond knowing. Most of him trusted those beautiful spirits to be able to listen, and hear, and love him even if unable to understand. Most of him. Lingering fears had clouded his eyes.

But from the Healer's Guild to the Guard House, from Genniver's house to the jewelers, and back to the courthouse, generally calm responses abounded and no one overreacted. Well, Laraine did comment "I think you're completely insane," but, honestly, that was better than he'd expected. She worried for her own children who looked to him with such shining, susceptible eyes. He'd smiled gently and spoke the clearest truth, knowing it to the depths of his bones. "No one answers a Call that is not there."

And of course it had been Genniver with the "You're not going to start chopping bits off, are you?" Leave it to her to put the unspoken right out there on the table as bluntly as possible. He'd been rather pleased with his own retort— "Not tomorrow, no, if that's what you're wondering." He knew he hadn't truly answered her, and was surprised she didn't push it. They'd laughed together and that, too, was all right.

Kerynne and Harleigh, as expected, had accepted with calm nods, careful words. Harleigh always had been more worldly, either through her service in the Guard or simply by her nature; she knew "difference." Kerynne . . . well, much like Catarina, Kerynne just understood things.

They were all so similar and yet so different. Completely individual women in so many ways, strung together by an invisible, indestructible cord of feeling and blood. The same tightly braided entity that lived in him, coiled strong and wild in his center.

Never so strong as when he heard five different

voices repeat five different versions of "Why would you leave? Can't you serve at the Central Temple here?" What of husbands' reactions? "What of them? This is us. This is family." What of the children? "They love you so much, they would be crushed if you left. We would rather have you here."

Never so wild as when he watched five pairs of wide eyes spark with an identical flare of possessive, protective fire when he mentioned that some in the village might not be inclined to support his declaration of service. "Let anyone try to stand in your way." Five tiny women in various vocations, only one professional military, with hackles bristling in full defense.

For him. Over a fight they barely understood themselves.

Yes. Let anyone try. Women protecting their own gave a new definition to ferocious.

The doors to the Central Temple of the Goddess stood wide open, letting in the sun from the courtyard. He strode past two Maiden acolytes in white, returning their nods of greeting. A Priestess in red stood talking quietly with a second Priestess, an elder in black. Both turned as he approached and he recognized them as Meriel and Ruth at the same moment he became suddenly aware that the two acolytes were now following him.

The anxiety he'd thought banished sprang up again, and his stomach knotted. The Priestesses looked at him with inquiring expressions as he reached them. Both exuded a quiet power that calmed him. He'd spent his life surrounded by capable, powerful women and the familiarity felt like a welcome.

Still, what he had to say, to ask, would be unusual to say the least.

Coming to a stop, he consciously stilled his twitching fingers and lifted his chin. "I–I'm here to . . . I came today—" All the carefully rehearsed words he'd gone over with Catarina disappeared. He swallowed hard. Ruth watched him with the sharp gaze of a crow. He focused on Meriel, the red robes helping him to picture the Matron as she'd sat before him two nights past. *All We needed was your acceptance of your Call.* He opened his mouth and stopped thinking. "I am Called. I choose to accept the Call."

Meriel clapped her hand to her mouth and turned to the laughing elder. "Did I tell you?" Ruth caroled. The two young acolytes rushed off, talking excitedly.

As Meriel turned back to face him, he saw the grin between her fingers. "We've been expecting you."

"You—" He paused and realized the only answer. "She told you?"

Ruth reached out and caught his hand. "She told us all to expect Her new *male* acolyte today. The entire Temple had the same dream. We've been debating . . . well, that doesn't matter now. Personally, I think She didn't want any of us keeling over with heart failure. Now remind me of your name, son?"

"Arin."

"Of course, of course. Got a passel of sisters, don't you?"

"Five older sisters."

"Hmm." Her eyes twinkled. "Good preparation, I suppose. A pity you won't be marrying. Coming from that kind of training, you'd make someone a wonderful husband."

"Ruth," Meriel interjected. "I think we agreed I should be having a conversation with Arin."

"Of course, of course. Don't know why you're worrying, though. She wouldn't have sent the dream if She hadn't been sure." Ruth released his hand and pinched his cheek. "Go with Meriel, boy. She needs to make sure you know what you're letting yourself in for." She winked and turned her attention to herding a small crowd of acolytes who had appeared from nowhere, shifting from foot to foot and whispering behind hands. When they saw him looking, a number of them waved before allowing themselves to be ushered away.

Meriel gestured and he walked beside her to a door at the rear of the Temple, leading into the offices. "This is different," Meriel said with a smile. "As I'm sure you're aware, not something that happens every day. You've created quite a stir."

"Not my intention, my lady." He sat in the chair she guided him to and gave her a helpless look as she settled in the one beside him.

She nodded. "And yet, you know it will?" she asked kindly.

He ducked his head. "I don't like making a stir. If there was any way I could do this without . . . well. I would prefer it, certainly."

"The Call is that persuasive."

A statement, not a question, but he answered anyway. "More so, *pervasive*. It's a force, inside of me. I've lived with this pull my entire life, I—"

As if realizing his agitation, she sat forward and cut him off with a touch on his arm. "You understand there is no question. She has accepted your Declaration. The Temple's acceptance of your service is a given."

Catarina's assurance rang in his ears. He'd wanted to believe her, but he hadn't been sure. Meriel's confirmation eased the tightness in his ribs. "No one will mind? I mean none of the Temple women?"

Meriel grinned. "I didn't say that. There are certainly those who serve who have some questions, not to mention some doubts. There are those who would prefer this not come up, and who were fervently hoping the dream was some esoteric riddle. Priestesses are no more infallible than anyone else, and don't let anyone tell you differently." She tilted her head and studied him. "But there are also those of us who understand that this happens occasionally. Men," she paused, tilted her head in the other direction and rephrased, "ones such as you being called to serve are unusual but not unheard of; those who can hear and accept rarer still."

He startled at the phrase. "That's exactly what She said."

"The Goddess encompasses all things. The Matron seeks balance, and we only find balance in the acceptance of all parts of ourselves. Each person who struggles with your presence as an acolyte of the Temple must face and accept the piece of him or herself that gives them pause, as you have accepted the strength of the Call and this part of yourself."

Balance. The word struck a chord and reverberated through him. He could practically feel the vibrations in his fingertips. *Balance.* For the first time ever he thought he could truly feel it, at a soul-deep level. He nodded, thinking of all the years he turned away from that balance, and how easy it was to fight against without even realizing. Which meant, on a community-wide level? "Stir is going to be putting it mildly, isn't it?"

Meriel laughed. "I wish I could tell you different. The Temple population will be fine in time. We aren't the only people, however. As Ruth alluded, it's my duty as the Matron representative to assure you understand the full extent of your commitment in declaring service to the Goddess."

"My life becomes Hers." *It already is.*

"Yes. And you're aware that, as a *male* acolyte, there would be limitations on some of your abilities, some of your duties and tasks for the Temple?"

He paused, catching both the careful phrasing and the meaningful look that accompanied it. He smiled, another weight of question and anxiety lifting off his shoulders. "I understand completely."

She sat back, satisfaction apparent in her decisive nod. "Welcome to the Temple of the Goddess, Arin."

He rang the bell cord at the door of the Guild and let himself in. The Healers and their support staff were used to him visiting Kerynne. Those present nodded to him and moved on with their tasks. He made his way to Kerynne's desk and grinned at her expectant look. "Went very well," he reported happily.

"Good." With a matter-of-fact nod, she stood and gathered her coat and bag. She followed him outside, bidding her fellows good evening. They struck out for her house on the usual path they took on the nights he came to dinner with her and her sons. "Look what I've found," she said casually, rooting in the bag she carried.

He glanced over at her as a flash of red caught his eye, then stopped short on the path. A brilliant red robe unfolded from her hands. She stopped as well and held it up to him.

"Maybe just a little bit big, but what do you think? I thought it was very lucky to find one so near your size, considering you're taller than most Priestesses."

He caught up a handful of the deep, rich fabric and stared. "It's . . . where? Where did you get it?"

"I was looking for work breeches for the boys at the second-hand clothing shop. I saw this. I knew you wouldn't be able to afford to have any robes made for a while yet, and . . . well, I know it's not the exact thing, a little out of date, but they don't care what style, do they? They'll just want you to wear red like the other Matron acolytes. Especially in the beginning. I mean you'll need something for the Declaration ceremony and—"

He released the material warming in his hand and

stopped her nervous chatter with a hand on her arm. With glittering eyes he accepted the robe and folded it over his arm. "Thank you," he said softly. "It's perfect. Thank you."

Dipping her head she smiled and nodded, then started walking again. "By the way, it's pork tonight, and we've got some of those odd potatoes, you know the ones—"

Clutching the robe to his side, he followed her on down the path.

He stood before the door leading into the central room of the Temple of the Goddess, one hand pressed against the carved wood. He could hear voices lifted in song out in the main chamber. He smoothed the sleeve of the red robe. Beside him, two other acolytes-to-be stood and waited as well, trading nervous smiles with him every few minutes.

The singing trailed off, signaling their cue. Opening the door, they trooped out single file, and he waited his turn before the altar. As the rope belt of induction was braided around Lilah's waist, he let his eyes circle the room. Most faces smiled honest pleasure, or at least polite blankness. He didn't pause on any one person, simply marked where his sisters grouped, and focused his attention back on the proceedings.

Lilah came back to stand beside him, and he moved forward to take her place. Meriel stood before him speaking the words of welcome and affirmation. The ceremony washed over him as he spoke in turn, moving in a carefully choreographed pattern as if he'd been doing so all his life. The thought occurred to him that in fact he *had* been moving through his life in a carefully choreographed pattern, and he looked forward to finally dancing free.

To each question he stated his response, feeling the words rise up to fair jump off his tongue, until Meriel intoned, "And how do you come to know the Goddess?"

He opened his mouth to speak the ceremonial response, that the Goddess is immanent, and to be aware of the world is to know the Goddess. His eyes lit upon the line of his sisters, chins lifted proudly, eyes steady, his nieces and nephews standing clustered about them. As his gaze touched that of each sister in turn, he felt the same swell of emotion the Matron called forth in him. The line of Her jaw, the shine of Her eyes, the strength in Her shoulders, the curve of Her cheek . . . suddenly in each well-loved face he saw Her, the echo of Her, the promise of Her.

When the words formed, he spoke them as clearly as he was able considering the thickness in his throat.

"I have five older sisters. I have always known the Goddess."

THE UNICORN HUNT
by Michelle West

Michelle West is the author of several novels, including *The Sacred Hunter* duology and *The Broken Crown*, both published by DAW Books. She reviews books for the online column *First Contacts*, and less frequently for *The Magazine of Fantasy & Science Fiction*. Other short fiction by her has appeared in dozens of anthologies, including *Black Cats and Broken Mirrors*, *Alien Abductions*, *Little Red Riding Hood in the Big Bad City*, and *Faerie Tales*.

HUNTING THE UNICORN in the big city isn't exactly a simple proposition. Unicorns being what they are, sleek bastards, they're steeped in old lore, as if lore were magic.

Some of the lore is true, mind you; there's always a bit of truth in any old legend, if you know how to sift through the words. Words often get in the way. Maggie's my sometime partner, when it comes to things that exist outside of whatever passes for normal. She's got half a family—which is to say, herself and the kids—and a full-time job, besides. But she's got a bit of a temper and a memory that just won't quit. She takes the whole business personally.

Me? I never did.

I was raised by my grandmother, a tough old woman with a mouth like a soldier's and a pretty strong right hand, to boot. She had some standards, expected good grades, and carried a weary disdain about life that pretty much seeped into everything I ever tried to do. It wasn't so much that she laughed at me—although

I might have mentioned she was a touch harsh—as that she saw through me.

It was hard to dream much, in my grandmother's house. And make no mistake, it was her damn house. Small, squat building, red brick painted in a drab gray, porch up the backside of the house and round the side to the front. Garden for days, and in a city house, that says something. She didn't much believe in grass; it was a waste of water and sun, in her opinion. No, she grew useful things. Herbs, spices, fruits, vegetables. No flowers for her either, although I sort of liked them when I was younger. Flowers in her garden always withered and died, and I learned not to plant 'em.

You get odd communities in the city. My grandmother was at the center of ours. When she wasn't drinking, she was often on that porch, and she had words of wisdom for any poor sucker who happened to stop within earshot of her chair. She had a cane that she used like a gavel—she sure as hell didn't need it for walking—and a voice that could make thunder seem sort of pleasant.

But I learned to love her. It was an uphill battle for the early years of my childhood, and much of the affection I feel for her is hindsight and odd memory. She told me things I hated, when I was young, and watching them prove true was both a liberation and a bitter reminder that that old woman *knew* things.

She didn't believe in magic.

Which isn't to say that she didn't believe in Unicorns or Elvis sightings. She thought astrology was idiotic, thought crystals were stupid, and could spend whole days deriding the healing powers of just about any newfangled fad. She had God's ear, in a way— she believed in God—but whatever he had to say to her, she didn't share.

But I was talking about Unicorns.

Because Maggie got it into her head that she had

to have one. Time of year. Time of month—I don't know. Maggie's like her own mystery, as different from my gran as night from day; part of the same continuum, if you look close enough, but really, how many people do?

"Mags," I told her, "this is stupid."

Maggie, hefting her six-month-old onto the perch of her left hip, gave me The Look. Shanna, her oldest, is four, and because Shanna is both capable of listening and repeating what she hears, Maggie's gotten a little less verbose when she's in a mood. Doesn't matter. The Look pretty much says it all.

So when she turned it on me, I shut up for a bit. Not for long; living with Gran, I learned how to talk. If I hadn't, I'd've probably been a mute—that woman could *talk*. "Look, you've got Connell and Shanna to think about now."

"I'm thinking about them," she said, in that cast-iron voice of hers. "It's not for me."

Now, Maggie's no idiot. "Look, you *know* the stuff about healing powers and unicorn horns is just shit. Besides, they look healthy enough to me."

Connell obliged by spitting up on her left shoulder. It's not one of his most charming activities, but we're both used to it by now. Maggie, determined, didn't even bother to reach for something to clean herself off. And Connell, being the age he is, can swallow or spit with equal comfort. I glared at him, but he just thought it was funny. He usually does.

Baby laughter is a type of disease; it rots the brain. I spent a few minutes descending into that language that isn't really language at all, and after liberating my finger and my glasses—both of which he'd grabbed—I turned back to Maggie.

"You're not getting enough sleep."

She looked like she was fit to spit herself. "It's not sleep I need," she snapped.

* * *

Creation is an act of defiance. Whose, it's hard to say. Unwanted pregnancies happen all the time, and if you've the mind, you can end 'em. But Maggie's a special case. I've known it for a while. My grandmother told me, before she passed away.

Maggie moved in two houses down the street, and let her grass go to seed the first summer, which is high on the list of mortal sins as far as my gran was concerned. But there are worse sins—barely—and she sent me along to check things out.

Turns out Maggie, being single, was in that constant state of exhaustion that also comes with being newly parental, and, as she put it, either the grass went or she did. Given that Maggie has eyes to die for (and a temper to die by), I thought it was a fair trade, and after introducing myself, I trudged on back to Gran's place. And then trudged back to Maggie's with a lawnmower. I'm not that fond of gardening, in case I hadn't made that clear, but there are forces of nature you just don't ignore, and Gran had decided that this particular woman needed some help.

After I added a new layer of burn to the upper side of my arms and face, I asked my gran why she was so interested in Maggie. And the old woman gave me The Look—oddly enough, it's pretty much the same as Maggie's—and then launched into a bunch of stuff that made me wish I hadn't asked.

"Mark my words," she said, after saying a whole lot of them, "Maggie is special. She's the mother."

"*The* mother?"

"The mother."

Given that we live in a neighborhood which is more or less overrun with kids of all ages, colors, and volumes, this struck me as a tad woo-woo, even for Gran.

"Gran," I said, sitting down on the porch steps so

she could comfortably tower over me, "what's so special about this mother?"

"She," Gran answered, with a sigh that indicated she didn't think much of my intellectual faculties, "doesn't have much choice."

"What's that supposed to mean?"

Gran shook her gray head, and her face wrinkled as she pursed her lips. "You think about it," she told me. "You're not always going to be this carefree. You have to *know* things."

That one caught me short. "Gran?"

"That's right," she said, pushing herself up out of her chair. "I won't be here forever, and when I'm gone, no one's going to do your thinking for you."

I remember thinking, at the time, that that would be a bit of a relief.

Asking Gran a question always involves a certain amount of humiliation, because to her, they all seem stupid. It's like she reads answers that are written across your forehead, only you're illiterate, even when she gives you the mirror. She'd spent the day working in the herb garden, and smelled of crushed bay leaves and smoke. But that aside, she was on her throne, and waiting with less patience than she usually did.

I used to think the pipe she smoked was an affectation, a way of making her seem even more weird than she already was. I was younger then. Not even my memory can encompass that fact that she must have been younger as well; she never seemed to change. Even her clothing seemed to weather the passing of fad and style.

"All right, Gran," I told her, taking my seat on the stair, "I've been thinking."

"And?"

"I'm stupid."

She snorted, smoke coming out of her nostrils as if she were a wizened dragon. The ritual of emptying her pipe stilled her voice for a few minutes, which was its own kind of mercy. I don't smoke pipes, but I have a fondness for them anyway, probably because of her.

"I've talked to Maggie," I told her. I didn't tell her how *much* I'd been talking to Maggie; it wasn't her business.

But her eyes narrowed. "So what."

"She's not that fond of men at the moment, but it seems like she has a reason."

Gran snorted. "That's it?"

I shrugged. "She's got two kids."

"A boy and a girl."

"Pretty much."

"And a cat."

I'm not a cat person. "And a cat."

"Good. And?"

"A messy house. A better lawn. A job she hates just a little bit less than she'd hate welfare."

Gran inhaled. Exhaled. Frowned. "You're right," she said, spitting to the side. "You're stupid."

"I said that, didn't I?"

"Doesn't mean I can't."

My turn to shrug. "So what about her makes her *the* mother?"

"She didn't tell you?"

"I didn't exactly ask."

"But she didn't tell you?"

"No."

Tobacco ashes flew as she gestured. It was a pretty rude gesture for an old lady, and I dodged a few stray embers. "And you couldn't tell."

"Obviously."

She grabbed her cane, and I thought she might hit me with it. But she didn't. "Then maybe she doesn't know," she said. Using it, for a moment, to stand. It was the first time in my life I thought she looked old, and I didn't like it. "She's the mother," she said quietly, "because she was born to be the mother. It's a responsibility," she added, with a trace of sarcasm. "And a duty."

"Well, she's certainly had the kids."

"She *had* to. You ask her who the fathers were?"

"I got the impression she wasn't going to say."

"She can't."

"What?"

"She doesn't know." Not exactly the sort of thing you'd expect from your grandmother—at least not in that tone of voice. Tired voice, not judgmental. "She might think she does. She'd be wrong. If she'd never touched a man, she'd still have had those kids."

"She did say something about birth control. No, I'm not going to repeat it."

"She's angry about the kids?"

I shrugged. "She's angry about being alone with them, if I had to guess."

"Don't guess. I makes you sound—"

"Stupid. Yeah, I know." I chose the next words with care. She was still gripping the cane. "How did you know?"

"That's probably the first smart question you've asked all day."

Given that the rest of them had to do with lawn care, a thing she generally despised, this wasn't hard. "Does that mean you'll give me an answer?"

"I'm thinking about it."

I waited her out. Have I mentioned she loved to talk?

"I'm the crone," she said at last.

"And that makes me the maiden?" I couldn't keep the bitter sarcasm out of my voice.

"You?" Neither could she.

Having retreated back into the realm of idiocy, I waited, cheeks burning some. "I guess that's a no."

"Big damn no. You think I've taught you how to tend a garden all these years for nothing?"

No, because you're a sadist. Smart me, I didn't say it out loud. She rapped my knuckles anyway.

"I'm getting old," she continued.

I didn't point out that she'd *always* been old.

"And I'm getting tired." She sat down again. "And the damn pipe keeps going out."

"Gran—"

"There was another mother," she said at last. "And the maiden, which is definitively *not* you, so get that thought out of your head."

It wasn't in my head any more. "Another mother?"

"The mother," she told me quietly.

"What happened to her?" Because it was pretty clear that something had.

"She died."

Thanks, Gran. Guessed that. "When?"

"When I was younger."

"You weren't the crone then?"

"Damn well was."

"What *happened?*"

She shrugged. "War," she said at last, her eyes gone to blue. "She lost her son."

"Lost him?"

"He died."

"And she couldn't have another one?"

"No."

I frowned. "The kids are special, too?"

"The children are the mother's. They define her. She always has two."

"How did he die?"

"I told you. Pay attention. There was a war. He was in it. He didn't come back."

"And she died?"

Gran nodded quietly.

"Her daughter?"

And shrugged. "Her daughter buried her mother."

"That's it?"

"That's it."

"Then what—"

"It's been a long time," Gran continued. "Since there *was* another mother." She got up again. "Better that I talk to her, since you're so useless."

"Gran, Maggie's—"

She rapped the porch with the cane tip. "You going to get out of my way, or am I going to have to go through you?"

I got out of her way, and trailed after her like a shadow. I *liked* Maggie. I didn't want to subject her to my grandmother without offering a little cowardly moral support.

Gran snorted at the grass. Emptied her pipe on it and shoved said pipe into her apron pocket. Then she marched up the walk, which was short, and knocked on the door with her cane. It opened. No one was behind it. I hate it when Gran does that. Then again, I hate it when she does anything that defies rational explanation.

She walked into the small vestibule. It was littered with the debris of two children; coats, boots, shoes, a smattering of disheveled and empty clothing, a dirty stroller. "Margaret?" She shouted, standing in the center of the mess as if she owned it.

Maggie came out of the kitchen, frowning. Connell was on her hip. She saw me, and the frown sort of froze.

"This is my Gran," I told her.

And lifted. "I've heard a lot about you," she said, extending a hand. Her left hand; her right hand was full of baby, and she had nowhere to put him down. Maggs is pretty practical.

Gran took it in that iron grip of hers, but instead of shaking it, she turned it up to the light, as if to inspect it. The frown that Maggie had surrendered, Gran picked up. "This won't do," the old woman said, in as stern a voice as she used on the racoon who had the temerity to inspect her garden.

"What?"

"What's this ring?"

"Detritus."

"Good. Take it off."

Maggie shot me an "is she sane?" look. I shrugged.

"It's a wedding ring," Maggie told Gran.

"I *know* what it is. Why on earth are you wearing it?"

Maggie shrugged. I knew the shrug. It was nine-tenths bitterness and one-tenth pain, and I personally preferred the former.

"You aren't the wife," Gran said, in her most imperious voice. "You're the mother."

"Funny, that's what my ex said."

Gran ignored her. "This is the boy?" She asked. I started to say something smart, and thought better of it. At his age, it was hard to tell.

"This is my son, yes."

"And the girl?"

The "is she sane" look grew a level in intensity. "My daughter is in the backyard digging her way to China."

Gran nodded, as if the answer made sense. Given that she'd raised me, it probably did.

"Well, he looks healthy enough." She pushed past Maggie, and Maggie looked at me. I shrugged. Gran made her way to the sliding doors of the kitchen and took a look out. "So does she."

"Thanks. I think."

"Give me the ring." Gran said.

"Yes, she's sane." I added. "Mostly." I held out my arms for Connell, and Maggie slowly handed him to me. He was pretty substantial, and he was squirming, but he wasn't angry. Yet. Hands empty, she looked at my gran, and then looked past her to me. She took off the wedding ring slowly, twisting it around her finger as she did.

Her expression made it clear that she was humoring the old lady for my sake, and I'd owe her. Given that I took care of her lawn, I figured we were even. Stupid me.

Gran took the ring and held it up to the kitchen light. Snorted, moved toward the sliding glass doors, and held it out to sunlight instead. She swore a lot. Closed her fingers around the ring, as if exposing it to light at all were a sin.

"What's wrong with the ring?" I asked.

She opened her fist.

And I saw it up close, for the first time. It looked different than it had when it had been a flash of gold on Maggie's finger. It was bumpy, but gleaming, more ivory than golden, and its pattern was a twisted braid.

"Not a braid," the old woman said, pursing her lips coolly. "A spiral."

"A . . . spiral?"

"This was fashioned," she continued coldly, "from a Unicorn horn."

Maggie stared at us both as if we were insane. But she didn't immediately reach out and grab Connell, so insanity of our kind wasn't immediately dangerous.

"It's a binding," Gran continued quietly. "And part of a binding spell. I'll take it to study, if you don't mind." It was like a request, but without the request part. She marched out of the kitchen, ring once again enclosed in her leathered fist.

When she'd also slammed the front door behind her, I looked at Mags. "Sorry," I said.

"That's lame," she replied. But she rubbed her finger thoughtfully, looking at the white band of skin that had lain beneath the ring for years. "She's a strange old woman," she added.

"Tell me about it."

After the loss of the ring, things changed with Maggie. I didn't notice it all that much at first, which gave Gran several opportunities to wax eloquent about my intelligence. But shedding the ring, she seemed to shed some of her helpless, bitter anger. She wasn't as constantly tired. She even helped with the yardwork, although it took much longer with her help than without it, because Connell could crawl into everything, and Shanna insisted on helping, too.

Connell discovered that dirt melted when you put it in your mouth. He wasn't impressed. Maggie picked him up with affectionate disdain, helped him clean out his mouth, and put him down again; he was already off on another spree of discovery.

She became happier, I think. Stronger.

And then, one day, when winter had come and everything was that white brown that snow in a city is, she invited my grandmother over. I came as well.

We sat down in the kitchen—all meetings of import were to be held there—around a pot of dark tea. Too bitter for me, it seemed perfect for Gran. Maggie herself hardly touched it.

She said, "I know I'm biased," which was usually the signal for some commentary about her children, "but sometimes it seems to me that my children are the most important thing in the world."

"It seems that way to all mothers," I said. "About their own children."

But Gran simply nodded. Quietly, even.

"Was that ring *really* made from a Unicorn's horn?"

"What do you think?"

She shrugged. "I think that once I was willing to let it go, I was happier. But there are a lot of men—and women—who could make money telling me that."

Gran nodded. "Too much money, if you ask me." Which, of course, no one had. Before she could get rolling, Maggie continued. She chose all her words carefully, and she didn't usually trouble herself that way.

"I feel," she continued softly, "as if, by protecting them and raising them, I'm somehow . . . preserving the future."

Again, not uncommon. But something about Mags was, so I didn't point it out.

"That I'm somehow helping other mothers, other sons, other daughters."

Gran nodded broadly, and even smiled.

"Which makes no sense to me," Maggie continued, dousing the smile before it had really started to take hold, "because it isn't as if other mothers aren't doing the same. Protecting the future." Smart girl, Mags. "And it isn't," she added, with just a hint of bitterness, "as if other children aren't dying as we sit here drinking tea."

"We aren't the arbiters of death," Gran said quietly.

"What in the hell are we?"

"You're the mother," Gran replied. "I'm the crone."

"And the crone is?"

"Knowledge. Experience. Wisdom, which usually follows. Not always," she added, sparing a casual glare for me.

"You said I was the mother."

"You are."

"For how long?"

"Good girl!"

Gran can be embarrassing at times.

"Who was the mother before me?"

The old woman's eyes darkened. "You're the first one in a long time."

"Why?"

She spit to the side. "If I had to guess," she said, with just a trace of fury, "I'd say those damn Unicorns have been up to no good. Again."

"You mean there were other mothers?"

"Like you, but not as strong. I should have known," she added. There is *nothing* worse than Gran when she's feeling guilty.

"What happened to the last one?"

"She failed."

"How?"

"Her son died."

Maggie closed her eyes.

"Wasn't her fault," Gran added. "But it doesn't matter. Her son died, and she died as well. Left a daughter. It should have passed on, then."

"It's like a public office?"

Gran shrugged. "Sort of. It should have passed on. Maybe it did. I'm not as sharp as I used to be."

"But you're older. Isn't wisdom—"

"Shut up." She lifted her cup, drained it, and thunked it back down on the table top. "Even the old get tired. Especially the old." She hesitated for just a moment.

I didn't like the sound of the silence.

"I'm better at hiding than I used to be," she finally said. "And I never answered your question."

"Hiding? From what?"

"You'll find out, girl. And that's a different question. You're the mother until your children are old enough to have children of their own."

"And then . . . my daughter?"

"Probably not. It doesn't pass down bloodlines. But when they are, you'll be free."

Maggie said, "You've never had children, have you?"

And gran's voice was surprisingly bitter. "Oh, I've had 'em," she answered. "Outlived them all."

Maggie reached out and placed a hand over Gran's in something that was too visceral to be called sympathy. "When is it over, for you?"

"I get to choose," the old woman replied.

"And I don't."

"No. I often thought the mother got the rawest deal. No choice at all about having the children, only a choice about how they're raised. Raise 'em well," she added, "and the world changes."

Maggie looked openly sceptical. "The world?"

"There's a lot of difference between 1946 and 1966," the old woman replied softly. "And trust me, you wouldn't have liked living in either year."

"You're going to be with me for a while?"

"While you learn the ropes," Gran replied. "But don't be an idiot. Learn quickly." She got up and headed toward the front door.

Maggie's voice followed her. "If there's a mother, and a crone," she said, the growing distance forcing her to speak loudly and quickly, "what about a maiden?"

Gran's snort carried all the way back to the kitchen.

"She's a strange woman," Maggie said at last. "How old is she?"

I shrugged. "I asked her once."

"What'd she say?"

"She almost made me wash my mouth out with soap. It wasn't considered a *polite* question."

Mags laughed. I love it when she laughs.

"She'll probably answer that one later. She likes to parcel out information."

"Why?"

"Because she's sadistic."

*   *   *

Winter passed. Darkness made way for longer days and the snow melted.

Maggie started to garden, which scared me. Not only did she start, but she took to it with a passion that was only slightly scarier than the ferocity with which she watched out for her children.

Things *grew* when she touched them. Me? I'm no black thumb, but green isn't my color either; it takes work. I envied Maggie, the way I envy someone with a natural singing voice. I would have put my foot down when she started collecting stray cats, but hey, it wasn't my house. And the kids seemed to like the cats—Connell even managed to survive pulling out a whisker or two from one of them.

But it wasn't until the height of summer that Gran chose to answer the question about the maiden. She invited herself over to Maggie's. Apparently, all conversations of import were to be held at Maggie's. I think this is because Gran didn't particularly care to have children destroying the knickknacks in her house. Either that or because Gran's cats weren't as tolerant as Maggie's.

Tea was like ritual, although without the fuss. The pot sat in the center of the table; Connell toddled his way around the chair, and Shanna drew pictures while laying flat out against ceramic tile. Unfortunately, some of those pictures tended to bleed off the page, so the floor was a bit more colorful than it had been when the previous owner had laid down said ceramic tiles.

"So," Gran said quietly. "You've started gardening."

Maggie's smile was calm and warm.

"And cat collecting. I'd advise you to take up a fondness for rabbits instead."

"Why?"

"Less of 'em. They're still work," she added. But she shrugged. "The kids are growing."

Maggie smiled fondly. She still looked like the same woman I'd first met—but not when she smiled. "I wanted to thank you both. But I also wanted to ask a question."

Gran snorted. She had her pipe in her hand, but she didn't light it. Mags would have thrown her out of the front door and watched to see how many times she bounced; she respected age and wisdom, but smoking around her children was a definite no-go. Gran seemed to expect this, and as she was in Mags' house, she obeyed the unspoken rules.

"You're the crone. I understand what you do."

"What?"

"You preserve wisdom," Maggie replied. "Collective wisdom. Maybe bitter wisdom."

"It's all bitter."

"Maybe. But necessary."

That got a "good girl" out of the old lady.

"I'm the mother, and I understand—I think—what that means."

"Better harvests," Gran said.

Maggie raised a brow.

"It's true."

"Well," she said, looking doubtfully out at her garden, "we'll see." She picked up her cup, staring at the cooling tea. "What does the maiden do? Preserve our innocence?"

Gran snorted. "You've been reading those trashy novels again." It was a bit of a bone of contention between them.

Maggie chose to let the matter drop; she really *was* curious.

"Look," Gran said, with open disgust, "just how *innocent* do you think you were when you were a maiden?"

"Well," Maggie said, defensive in spite of her best intentions, "I wasn't *the* maiden now, was I?"

Gran laughed. "Good answer! No, you weren't. But

I'm going to tell you that you're confusing innocence with inexperience."

"That's her way of saying stupidity," I added.

"Got that." She looked over at her daughter, who had finished her odd drawing and had started in on another piece of paper. Shanna was humming a song I tried very hard not to recognize. Because Gran didn't hold with television much either.

"You think that the maiden is supposed to preserve stupidity?"

"*I* didn't use the word."

Gran snorted again. "Innocence implies guilt."

"Stupidity implies—"

"Not guilt," Gran snapped, before Maggie could get started. Watching the two of them, I could almost see a familial connection between them, and you know what? I almost got up and slunk out of the room. "Innocence is a Unicorn word. It's a defacement. It's a linguistic injustice, an act of defilement."

"Unicorns speak?"

Gran's laugh was dark and ugly. And unsettling. "You wore that ring for how many years, and you have to ask?"

Maggie's turn to get dark. "It didn't exactly whisper into my ear."

I *really* wanted to be anywhere else.

"It *did*. You just weren't listening. You want it back? I'll give it to you. You'll probably hear a lot more now."

Maggie's brows rose. "You didn't destroy it?"

Gran hesitated for just a second, and a shudder seemed to pass through her. "No."

"Why?"

"I'm no warrior," she replied.

"The maiden is a warrior?"

Gran was quiet for a long time. "At her best," she said at last, "she can be."

"And at her worst?"

"Lost."

"Was there a maiden, back when there was a mother?"

Gran said nothing at all for a long time. Silent Gran? Always made me nervous.

- "Look, what *is* the maiden about?"

"Sex," Gran replied primly.

Maggie stared at her as if she'd started speaking in tongues.

One week later, round two.

"So, the maiden is about *sex?*"

"That's what I said."

"If she's about sex, she can hardly *be* a maiden."

Gran shook her head. "That's Unicorn talk," she said firmly.

"Will you *quit* that?"

"I could call it something else, but you probably don't want Shanna to repeat it at school."

Maggie hadn't asked for the ring back, and failed to mention it. Gran failed to offer. This was an armistice.

"The maiden has always been the most vulnerable of the three," Gran continued. "The hardest to find. The hardest to keep."

"Why?"

"Because."

"It's the sex."

"Something like that."

Maggie turned to me. "Your grandmother is driving me crazy." Unfair, trying to drag me into the discussion. "It's because of the sex, right? There aren't a lot of young women who don't. Have sex."

"It's because of the sex, but not in the way you think. You're thinking like a Unicorn," she added. So much for armistice.

"Look, what *are* Unicorns? I've seen a lot of pretty

pictures, and I've read a lot of pretty books. I've done more Internet research on that than I have on almost anything, and my saccharine levels are *never* going to be the same. For something malignant, they seem to occupy a lot of young girls' minds."

"Not the practical ones," Gran snapped.

"Fine. Not the practical ones. Are we looking for a practical girl?"

Gran seemed to wither. "No," she said at last. "We're not. That's why it's so hard. To find her. To save her."

"She dies?"

"Not the way you or I do. But her gift is the easiest to lose. It gets passed on, but sometimes it's just the blink of an eye."

"Unicorns are usually associated with purity."

"What the hell is purity?" Gran snapped. "A bottled water slogan?"

Round three.

"Okay. If the maiden *isn't* defined by *not* having sex, and she isn't defined by purity—which," Mags added, holding a squirming Connell while trying to get him to eat, "I'll agree is pretty nebulous, I have two questions."

"You've got a lot of questions. How, precisely, are you intending to pay for the answers?"

Maggie glared. It was a pretty glare. "By being the mother," she snapped.

Gran nodded, as if this was the only answer she expected. "What are your questions?"

"One: there are three. Maiden. Mother. Crone."

Gran nodded.

"You've been waiting for me."

Nodded again, but more wary this time.

"But we're only two. The third one must be important."

"She's important."

"But you weren't waiting for her."

Snorting, the old woman said, "I wasn't *exactly* waiting for you either. I just knew you when I saw you."

"Fine. And the maiden?"

"You're not going to let go of this, are you?"

"No."

"Fine. Be like that. What's the other question."

"You haven't answered the first one yet."

"Never promised answers."

"She is *really* driving me crazy."

"Hah. You're getting there on your own."

"What is her role? Why is she important?"

"It's the sex," Gran said quietly. "And not the sex. It's not the act; it's the possibility inherent in the act."

Maggie looked pointedly down at Connell.

"The maiden never has children."

"Why?"

"Because children are the mother's. Try to pay attention."

"So she gets to have—"

Gran held up a hand. "She's important, because she's dreaming," she said quietly. "Dreams are fragile, and endless; they're also a tad self-centered. Have to be. Heroes dream. She's dreaming, and she can walk in any direction she wants. She has a freedom that neither you nor I have."

"You envy her?"

"You don't?"

"I've seen what happens to dreams," was the bitter reply. "Young girl dreams. You're right. I was stupid."

Gran's smile was bitter. Old. "I didn't say you were stupid," she said. She had, but I didn't point this out. "Or if I did, I didn't mean it." She sighed, and caressed the bowl of her pipe. "Sex is union," she said quietly. "When it's done right. Union of body. A glimpse of dream. It transfigures us."

"Sex is about babies."

"Wasn't always."

"Is now."

"Hah. You want my answer?"

Maggie shut up.

"Having sex doesn't destroy the maiden. Abstinence doesn't define her—*unless she lets it*. The maiden has freedom. But she doesn't see it yet. Maybe she will. More likely, she'll lose it; shackle it; accept what others tell her. By the time she wakes up, she's given over dreams to reality. She's become something solid, but she's not—"

"The maiden."

"Not anymore, no."

Maggie was thoughtful. "This is why you haven't looked for her."

"She's not entirely necessary," was the reluctant reply, "and she's much abused. Always. It's hard. To keep her. And it's damn painful to lose her," she added.

"How can you say she's not entirely necessary?"

"Sometimes dreams have edges. Sometimes they just cause pain."

"A world without dreaming—"

"There will *never* be a world without dreaming," Gran replied.

"Joan of Arc was a maiden?"

"Maybe. And look what happened."

"Buffy?"

"Buffy?"

"Television character," I told Gran. I started to explain, and she lifted a hand. "Maybe. First two seasons at any rate." Which *really* surprised me, given that Gran doesn't hold with television. "But she's *not* real. If she existed, she would be."

"So all we have to do is find—"

"We don't have to find anything." Gran stood up. End of conversation.

Question two was never asked.

Maggie's hands were on her hips. Unfortunately, no children were. This was her battle posture, and I didn't much like it. "Your grandmother drives me nuts."

"She has that effect on people."

"I thought wisdom was supposed to be soothing."

"Judge for yourself."

Maggie snorted. "We need to go on a Unicorn hunt," she said at last.

Which more or less brings us full circle. "Why?"

"Because."

More argument, which I've already mentioned, followed by grim silence, which I may have failed to add.

"The ring," she said at last. "I would have held on to that ring forever. And it would have cost me my life. No, I'm not saying it would kill me—but look at me now. Look at me then. I'm *alive* now. I live in the present." She walked over to her computer and flipped up the lid. I suppose it won't come as a surprise to say Gran doesn't hold with computers much either, so I'm not real familiar with how they work.

"So you want revenge?"

Maggie was silent. For a minute. "I think this is the first time I've ever understood why your grandmother calls you stupid," she said, in a flat voice.

"Ouch."

"Live with it." Maggie shouted a warning to Shanna, who seemed intent on turning two teetering chairs into a makeshift ladder. "I know the maiden is out there," she said at last.

"Pardon?"

"I *know* she's out there. I think she's close."

"How?"

"Because I feel younger than I have in years," she replied softly. "And I feel—right now—that I can do *anything*."

"You're the mother," I told her.

"Even the mother has to dream. Maybe especially the mother." She looked fondly at the head of her younger child. "Look at this." The computer was now flickering.

"Unicorn hunt."

"It's all garbage," she added. "I'm sure your gran was right about that." Big concession. "But there's got to be a grain of truth in this somewhere. What if," she added, as her fingers added prints to the screen, directly across the face of a painted woman with a delicate, horned head in her lap, "it's true?"

"What's true?"

"Not that Unicorns are drawn to virgins," she said, "but that they're drawn to *maidens*."

"Which is usually the same thing."

"In Unicorn speak."

"Don't you start that, too."

Maggie didn't seem to hear me. "If we go out on a Unicorn hunt," she continued, "we're bound to find the maiden."

"Okay. But."

"But?"

"What the hell does a Unicorn want with the maiden, anyway?"

"My guess? To kill her," she said softly.

"That's phallic."

"Idiot."

"And all that rot about Unicorn horns and healing?"

"I don't know. Maybe there's something in that. We can always find out." She paused. "But I'm guessing that Unicorns don't actually *look* like this either."

"They'd be pretty damn hard to miss."

* * *

So Maggie and I went over to Gran's house. Gran was waiting for us on her porch. Which is to say, she was sitting on it, her arms crossed, her expression pure vinegar.

"You know why we're here," Maggie said, without preamble.

"I might."

"We need your help."

Gran pushed herself out of her chair. "I don't have a lot of help to offer," she said at last. "You're going in search of the maiden."

"We're going in search of Unicorns," Maggie replied firmly. "And we're not certain that we'll be able to even *see* them."

"You might. She won't."

"I think you can see them well enough, if a glint of ring could tell you so much. We need to be able to *see* them."

"You won't like it," Gran said, as if that would make a difference.

"Doesn't matter. We'll live; we all do what we have to." She paused, and then added, "I'd like it if you kept an eye on the kids while we're out."

"That's your job."

"Yes. And I'd guess yours would be to find the maiden, which you *aren't* doing."

Gran relented so quickly it was pretty clear she'd already made her decision. "I'll go to your place," she said. "They won't be as safe here."

The tone of her voice made me wonder if I'd misjudged her reasons for keeping them out of her house in the first place. And I liked the older reasons better.

She gave us glasses. Sort of. Nothing you could wear on your face, though. She gave us some sort of sticky, foul-smelling ointment as well. "You might need it," she said. "But if you don't, don't waste it. Costs a fortune to make."

"Is that blood?"

Gran shrugged. The last thing she gave us—round fine, long strands of something that looked like hair—was Maggie's old ring.

Maggie looked at it, but she didn't touch it. "You carry it," she told me. I was looking at Gran.

"She's right. You carry it. It'll point you in the right direction."

"We can trust it?"

"To find a Unicorn? Yes. You can't use it against one, though. Don't even try. And if it talks? Don't listen."

"As if."

"There are a couple of other things I should have probably told you both. Maggie'll get a clue, once you've started. You might have trouble."

Great. "What?"

"You'll be walking old roads, if there's a Unicorn to be found."

"You're not talking about old city roads."

"Good girl."

"They're safe?"

"Not bloody likely."

"What does not safe mean?"

"You'll find out." She handed me the last item. It was a long dagger, slender and shiny. And not really legal, on account of the way it disappeared in the hand. "Concealed weapons," I told her doubtfully.

"You take it, or you're not going."

"What am I supposed to do with it?"

"You'll figure it out. Oh, and one more thing."

"What?"

"You wait until the full moon. You hear me?"

"Yes, Gran."

*   *   *

Maggie was different, that night. Different in pretty much every way I could think of. Clothing was different. Hair was pulled right back off her face, and her skin seemed almost silver, like moonlight incarnate. Her eyes were clear and dark, and she didn't look afraid. Of anything.

The cars made their constant background purr, punctuated by honking. Gran cursed them roundly as she joined us in front of Maggie's house. "I'll stay until you get back," she told us firmly.

"You'd better," Maggie replied. But her tone of voice was strange as well.

Gran seemed smaller, thinner, than she usually did. "It's your time," she told Maggie, "not mine. But you're right—the maiden is out there. I can see her in your face."

Maggie didn't seem to hear. I took a good, hard look at Gran. "Don't light that," I told her, because she was fumbling with her pipe.

"I know, I know."

So, with a ring for a compass, and one that swayed every time there was the faintest hint of breeze, we began to walk down the street. Maggie decided—for reasons that aren't even clear to me now—that we had to walk in the *middle* of the damn road.

"You've got kids to think of," I told her. "What the hell is wrong with the sidewalk?"

She didn't answer. Then again, if I'd asked Gran that question, she'd have clipped me with her cane.

Instead, she walked. She didn't apparently look at the ring to see which direction we should be walking *in*, but she had me for that, and I was thankful for streetlights.

"Do you think your husband was a Unicorn? I mean, your ex?"

"No."

"But the ring—"

"No."

"But you think a Unicorn gave him the ring."

"Yes, I do."

Light dawned, in the figurative sense. "Because then you wouldn't know."

She nodded.

"And if you didn't know—"

"I couldn't find them."

"Why didn't they try that on Gran?"

"I don't think your gran can do this," she said softly. "She's too far away from the maiden. And she *has* to be."

"Why?"

"Because of what she is. She can see the maiden in my face," she added softly. "But I would guess that *if* we manage to find the Unicorn, and *if* the Unicorn is with the maiden, the maiden will see her in my face as well."

I thought about that for a long time. "My gran does like you," I said.

"I know. She drives me crazy, but I like her, too." She gave me an odd look then. I didn't understand it. "She's tired." Maggie banked left. "But she's waited a long time, and I'm really grateful to her. She's the hardiest of the three of us," she added.

Looking at Maggie, I wasn't so sure.

I fingered the invisible knife, thought some more, and then asked Maggie, tentatively, if she wanted it.

Maggie's brows rose. "Me?"

"That would be no."

"Definite no."

"Why?"

"I'm the mother," she said quietly. "I don't think I could use it."

"Then I'll use it for you."

Maggie said nothing. After a while, I joined her in nothing, and we walked into the darkness.

When the darkness changed, I can't be certain. But the streetlights vanished, and the moonlight grew more distinct. I could see stars, cold and clear, without the haze of light and pollution as a veil. Trees passed us by; they were tall, weeping willows, and beneath them, water pooled in still, clear mirrors. Everything about this road was beautiful. But you don't live long with Gran if you're an obvious sucker for beauty.

I followed Maggie. Maggie glanced occasionally at the ring, tilting her head with a vague look of disgust as she listened to it. I didn't hear anything. But it was clear that in this place, she could. I almost envied her the ability.

"We should have gone on the new moon," she said. Something about her voice made my hair stand on end. But she didn't dwell on the "should have," and I was just as happy not to.

We made our way down a sloping hill, crushing flowers as we did; there wasn't any way to walk this place without leaving a mark. Maggie didn't seem to care, and because she didn't, I didn't. I never did like flowers much anyway.

And I discovered, that night, that Unicorns run in packs. This goes against conventional wisdom, but then again, everything does. We stopped for a minute while we watched these creatures cavorting in the shadows. The shadows cast by one huge tree that seemed to go up forever. I thought that it must go down forever as well, but then again, Gran leaves the weeding to me, and I've learned to take roots personally.

I expected them to be beautiful. And they were. Breathtakingly beautiful, in the sense that I stopped

breathing while watching them. Their white coats were
gleaming, and they looked like some sort of cross between a deer and a horse. But their horns glittered,
and it became clear after only a few minutes that they
weren't exactly involved in a dance of joy.

They were fighting.

I don't think they noticed us at all. I really, really
wanted to be unnoticed. But Maggie had other plans,
and she didn't actually take the time to impart any of
them to me. Instead, she ran the rest of the way down
the hill, as if her feet were on fire.

As if, I thought suddenly, her children were in danger. This is the danger of putting the full moon, the
old roads, and the mother together. I wouldn't have
guessed it, but then again, Gran never called me the
brightest star in the sky.

When she almost crashed into them, I was just a
few feet behind her. Running down the damn slope
had been effortless for her—but for me it was a constant battle not to wind up sliding down on my face.
The ground here was treacherous; it whispered.

And the Unicorns? They screamed. In outrage. In
fury. They reared up, muscles rippling on their hind
legs, horns no longer turned in casual cruelty against
each other, as they faced this unexpected intruder.

Maggie hardly seemed to notice.

But I knew that dying here was pretty much death.
It didn't matter if we weren't in the city; it didn't
matter if we weren't in reality. Had Gran told me
that? I couldn't remember. I'd try later.

Gran's knife in hand, I leaped in after Maggie, moving faster than I'd ever moved in my life. A horn hit
the blade, and the blade was no longer invisible.

I expected the impact to knock the weapon out of
my hand; it's not as if I use weapons, much. But that
didn't happen. Instead? The horn *gave*. The knife
passed through it. The Unicorn's scream of rage gave

way to a scream of what sounded—I swear—like mortified pain.

They had hooves, cloven hooves, and those should have been their weapon of choice. Would have done a damn sight more damage. But they didn't seem to clue in, and I wasn't about to tell them what to do.

I thought Maggie would; she's like my gran that way. But even if we'd started out hunting Unicorns, they weren't on her radar at the moment. And I couldn't see what was, but I could guess.

I would have been half right.

The Unicorns drew back when I approached; the knife was literally glowing, and a faint trace of black ran down its edge. I thought it was blood, but the wrong color. It probably was. Unicorn horns are tricky.

But they didn't approach us again, and no one was stupid enough to try the horn against the knife. I shadowed Maggie—literally. I knew that if I was too far away, they'd fall on her like jackals. Like really beautiful, really delicate, jackals.

She made her way to the tree they had been circling around, and I discovered a second thing about Unicorns. They can look an awful lot like men.

Or a man.

White-haired, but youthful, tall, slender, garbed in something that would probably pass any fashion test an enterprising high schooler would set—except for that horn. Middle of the forehead. Dead center. Glistening as it drank moonlight.

Maggie was mad. Not angry, which I'm used to.

Mad mother? Not a good thing. I tried to call out to her. No, I *did*. But she was beyond listening.

And in a second, I was beyond trying. Her eyes were better than mine. If she was seeing with her eyes at all.

Because beyond the man, was a girl. Bruised eyes.

Bruised lips. Skin the white that skin goes when fear has overtaken almost everything else. A lot of skin; exposed and framed by shredded fabric. Might have been a shirt, once. Or the top of a dress.

Schoolgirl, I thought. Maybe. She seemed *so young* to me as I looked at her, I couldn't think straight. I had never been that young. Gran said I was born old.

Should've been a hint.

But Gran could have *told* me that Unicorns are rapists.

We split up the minute the Unicorn turned. His eyes were a startling shade of blue, clear and bright in the night sky. He looked beyond us, for just a moment; saw what must have been there—the gathering of his pack.

His hands fell away from the girl as he shoved her, hard, against tree bark. Her hands gripped the tree as she tried to meld with it. Her eyes were dark, normal eyes. Her hair was dark and disheveled.

He looked at Maggie.

He looked at me.

He looked at Maggie.

He looked at me.

I held the dagger. I don't think I have ever wanted to kill *anything* so badly in my life. He laughed. He could sense it.

But Maggie moved not toward him, but toward the girl. He wasn't her concern. No, I thought, he was mine. Mother creates life. Crone sees its end.

I'll stay until you get back.

I lunged with the dagger as he lunged with his horn. He narrowly avoided losing it, and I side-stepped. I'm not much of a fighter, but I was fast enough; it's kind of hard to really get into a tussle when your pants have dropped past your butt.

I wondered if this was what naked *men* actually

looked like. Which was my stupid thought for the evening, and it almost cost me my arm.

The shadows were dancing at my back. The others were waiting. But they were a bit of a cowardly lot, when it came down to that; they knew what the knife could do, and they were willing to wait and see.

I could have despised them more if I tried really hard. But mostly I was trying to stay alive.

Losing battle. What had my gran said? She wasn't a warrior. I wasn't raised to be one either. His horn grazed my thigh, and the threads of my jeans unraveled at its touch, as if they were all trying to avoid the contact. I bled a bit.

He hit me again, and I bled more.

He wasn't laughing, but his eyes were glittering with rage. I had denied him something, and he intended to make me pay.

I would have died there.

I would have died had it not been for Maggie. At least I thought it was Maggie who came for me, Maggie who touched my shoulder, my wrist, my dagger arm.

But when Maggie took the dagger from my slowing hands, I knew I'd been wrong. Because Maggie was the mother, and she couldn't wield this knife.

The Unicorn's blue eyes widened, and he lost his form—which is to say, he reverted. It was certainly easier to look at him. Harder to look at the girl he'd had pinned to the tree a few wounds back.

She wasn't wearing much. But she didn't need to. She was utterly, completely beautiful in the stark night, and her expression was one that will haunt my nightmares for years.

She didn't speak a word.

Not a word of accusation. Not a word that spoke of betrayal. Nothing at all that made her seem like a wronged victim, or like any victim.

Crone see life's end?

Not like *this*. She used the knife as if she'd been born with it in her hands. And he bled a lot; she wasn't kind. Or quick. Or even merciful.

But he was very much alone, in the end. Packs are like that.

Later, I joined Maggie. Or Maggie joined us. The girl was holding the knife and her breasts rose and fell as lungs gave in to exertion, which was very distracting. Maggie had taken a sweater from her shoulders, leaving herself with a thin, black T-shirt. She put the sweater around the girl's shoulders in silence. Like a mother. Her hands were shaking.

They looked at each other, and then the girl looked down at the knife almost quizzically.

"It's yours," I told her.

"You're giving this to me?"

"No," I replied. "It was always yours."

She looked at it, and I handed her its sheath. She looked at that two. Her hands were shaking. "Did I kill him?"

I nodded.

"Good." And then her eyes started to film over. "You know, he said he loved me?"

I nodded quietly.

"And I believed him."

Before I could stop myself, I told her—in as gentle a voice as I could, "You had to."

"No, I didn't."

But she did. Because she was the maiden. I could see it in her clearly. Could see it; was horribly, selfishly glad that I would never be the maiden. I wasn't certain that she would stay that way either.

"He was a Unicorn," I told her, after a pause.

"He was an asshole," she said, spitting. Like a cat.

"That, too."

She gave me an odd look. "How did you know?"

"What?"

"That he was a Unicorn?"

"The horn was a dead giveaway."

"He wanted me because I was special." She was. I could see that.

"Yes," I told her, and I put an arm around her shoulder. "But he wanted to destroy what was special about you. Don't let him. Don't forget how to believe."

Maggie cleared her throat. "Your mother is probably worried about you," she said. In a mother's tone of voice. "And my kids are waiting for me. Why don't you come back to my place? You can phone her from there."

"I told her I was staying at a friend's house tonight," the girl said. She hesitated, and then added, "I'm Simone."

"I'm Irene," I told her, extending a hand. "And you can stay at Maggie's."

Maggie nodded quietly. She held out a hand, and the girl took it without hesitation. Good sign.

We made our way back to Maggie's house, but stopped at the foot of her walk. She looked at me, her eyes bright with moonlight. Simone was talking; she had started to talk when we had started to walk, and she hadn't stopped. She wasn't crying. She wasn't—at least to my eye—afraid. Rescue has its purpose.

"I think you should go in first," Maggie told me quietly.

I knew. I knew then.

"I'll be up; I think Simone and I have a lot to talk about." She hesitated, and then added, "We'll be waiting for you if you need company."

I nodded stiffly and made my way up the walk. Opened the door, which Gran hadn't bothered to lock.

Very, very little can get past Gran when she's on the lookout.

She was in the kitchen, beside a pot of tea. She looked up as I entered, and the breath seemed to go out of her in a huff. As if she'd been holding it since we left.

"We found her," I told my gran. "In time, I think."

"She's an idiot?"

I frowned, and Gran gave me a crooked smile. "You understand."

I nodded.

"Why it's hard to be the maiden."

And nodded again. "But Gran, I understand other things, too."

"Oh? That would be a change."

"I understand why it's hard to be the crone. To watch. To know and to have to sit back on your hands."

"Good." She rose, pipe in hand. "I'll be getting home, then."

"I'll go with you."

"I don't need company."

"I do."

She snorted. "You have company. Maiden and mother. I never thought—" She bit her lip. "I stopped hoping."

"You kept watch," I told her. "You remembered the old lore. You kept it for us." I offered her a hand, and she took it; her hand was shaking. Old, old hand.

"You'll be good at this," she said, as she rose. "But you take care of my garden, hear?"

"I'll take care of the garden," I told her. It was really hard. "And the house. And the lore."

"No television in my house."

"Yes, Gran."

"And none of that trashy garbage Maggie reads either."

"Yes, Gran."

"And don't think too much."

I laughed. I walked her out of the house, and past Maggie, who stopped her and gave her a ferocious hug. No words, just a hug.

Gran snorted, and lit her pipe; Maggie, unaccompanied by her children, took it in stride.

And me? I waited. I bit my lip and I waited.

I walked Gran home. I took her up to the porch. I let her get comfortable in her chair. I even sat on the steps, because I wouldn't be sitting on them again anytime soon.

I don't know when she died. I know that she was talking; that she was telling me all the things that she thought I'd forget. That she *also* knew that I wouldn't be forgetting them now.

Because I was the crone.

And she was finished. She could be tired. She could rest. She said as much, and then drifted off into silence, the way she sometimes did when she was satisfied with the state of her garden.

The silence lingered, grew louder, grew, at last, final.

And when it had gone on for long enough, I closed her eyes, took her pipe, and emptied it. I kissed her forehead. I would have asked her to hug me, but public displays of affection had always made her uncomfortable. I hugged her only afterward, because it wouldn't matter to her.

Then I made my way back to Maggie's house, carrying Gran's cane. The light was still on, and two thirds of my self were waiting for me to join them.

LOGAN-HOCKING
COUNTY DISTRICT LIBRARY
230 E. MAIN STREET
LOGAN, OHIO 43138

Tanya Huff

The Finest in Fantasy

SING THE FOUR QUARTERS	0-88677-628-7
FIFTH QUARTER	0-88677-651-1
NO QUARTER	0-88677-698-8
THE QUARTERED SEA	0-88677-839-5

The Keeper's Chronicles

SUMMON THE KEEPER	0-88677-784-4
THE SECOND SUMMONING	0-88677-975-8
LONG HOT SUMMONING	0-7564-0136-4

Omnibus Editions:

WIZARD OF THE GROVE   0-88677-819-0
(Child of the Grove & The Last Wizard)
OF DARKNESS, LIGHT & FIRE   0-7564-0038-4
(Gate of Darkness, Circle of Light & The Fire's Stone)

To Order Call: 1-800-788-6262